THE
POST

THE
POST

KEVIN A. MUÑOZ

DIVERSION
BOOKS

Diversion Books
A Division of Diversion Publishing Corp.
443 Park Avenue South, Suite 1004
New York, New York 10016
www.DiversionBooks.com

For more information, email info@diversionbooks.com

First Diversion Books edition January 2019.
Paperback ISBN: 978-1-63576-401-7
eBook ISBN: 978-1-63576-400-0

LSIDB/1901

For Mom and Dad

PART ONE

CLOSED DOORS AND HIGH WALLS

DAY ONE, 6:00 A.M.

E very morning, it's the same. The roosters start first, then the clucking of all the hens, and by the time I'm out of bed and half-dressed, most of the neighborhood is outside and picking up where they left off the evening before. Ten years on and I still haven't quite gotten used to the sound of chickens in the morning. But these are good sounds: reminders that the world is right again, and that all the gears are oiled, and that for all the catastrophic disruptions we've seen, we continue.

I open the curtains in my sitting room and go in search of the last of yesterday's bread, which I left somewhere among the books and papers that are still strewn across the carpet. When I can't sleep, I read. And when I read, I eat. It's a habit I picked up after the collapse. I wasn't much of a reader before, but after, with most of the electricity gone and nothing but dead signal on the radios, there was little else to do. By the time I got the idea to go to the DeKalb County Public Library, most of the good books had been liberated, so I had to be happy with obscure works on technical subjects. But no matter: when I can't sleep, I read. I have learned a lot in ten years, and some of it has even been valuable to me in my new line of work.

The bread has gone dry, which I expected, but I bite through it anyway. If I want anything fresh, I'll have to be down at the station by the time Regina Weeks's daughter brings her daily delivery. After I find a shirt clean enough to wear, I dip a ladle into the water barrel where my townhome's refrigerator once stood. There is a knock on the door as I'm closing the cover.

Deputy Adelaide Luther is leaning against the door jamb when I answer, looking no less haggard than she does on most mornings. She doesn't wake easily, and she likes to tell me that without a shower in the morning she's useless for the first three hours of the day. Of course, we don't get many showers anymore. I marvel that someone who was young enough to be going through puberty during the collapse can look so unkempt. Most people her age have handled the changes far better than my generation.

She pushes her dirty blonde hair away from her eyes as I open the door wide. "The sweep team wants us at the tunnel blockade," she says. "I've already sent for Pritchard and Kloves. We have visitors. The regular kind."

I go back into the bedroom and gather the rest of my clothes, which are all a few days overdue for a washing. I strap on my wristwatch and wind it a few times. After shrugging on my old Coast Guard Reefer coat, my only concession to any kind of uniform, I belt my knife and my SIG P229 service pistol. I have rarely had to draw my sidearm. It's mostly for show, and a reminder of an old life that looked very different.

Grumbling, I shut the door behind me. Unlike my deputy, I am very much a morning person. But I still need my breakfast, and it's looking like I won't get anything to eat for a while. I look longingly past Luther, down to the corn and bean fields growing in the reclaimed Freedom Park just beyond my house. I live on the northern side of the Little Five, with only the fields beyond. A quick walk from my townhome's front door will get me to the Carter Center barricade wall, which holds back whatever still roams Ralph McGill Boulevard and the midtown heart of the city. I've heard rumors that a group has reclaimed the hotels, which would make sense, but I've been hearing those rumors for years, and every time we send out scouts to confirm it, they come back with the same story of shriekers and hollow-heads.

In a way, that's to our advantage, and it's one of the reasons the people of the Little Five have chosen to stay. Grady Hospital and the hotels have been infested since the collapse, making the Little Five something of an island in a sea of monsters. We rarely get unexpected visitors: it takes guts to walk through that gauntlet. The only safe approach is through the tunnel that goes under the railroad tracks on the south side of our perimeter.

Luther and I walk through the center of the Little Five, along Moreland Avenue, into the morning bustle that has been a part of the rhythm of the "new" Atlanta for a decade. Most of the city was abandoned during the collapse, left to the horrors of the infected after the last of the world's foundations crumbled, and for a time the remaining Atlantans made forays into other parts of the city to collect food and weapons and whatever else was needed to rebuild society. But now, ten years on, we stay where we finally laid our burdens down.

This is my home. I was not born here—not within eight hundred miles of here—but I can think of no better place to spend the second half of my life. The people of the Little Five are good people, and they took me on as their chief of police. They knew I'd been in the Coast Guard for six years before the collapse when they asked me. I haven't seen ocean in a decade, and even before that my job experience wasn't what one would call local law enforcement, but the powers that be in this place saw an opportunity when I arrived at their makeshift fences with my daughter in tow.

With three officers under my command, I keep the place safe and under control most of the time. Petty theft and domestic disturbance take up the bulk of my attention these days, though from time to time we get miscreants looking to steal food and equipment. They rarely make it past our perimeter fence.

The Little Five takes its name from the five-point intersection at the heart of the neighborhood, and it is here that most of the day's activity occurs. With the old shops having been converted to housing and the upper floor apartments packed full with families, business happens outside, on the sidewalks and in the plaza, well into late fall. We tried a few years back to reclaim the nearby Edgewood shopping center—more for housing than for shop space—but we found it to be inconvenient. The spaces were simply too large.

Children are playing in the street, some inscrutable concoction involving an old soccer ball and stacked truck tires that might charitably be called a game. I envy them, sometimes. They don't have to worry about cars, or strangers in vans, or any of the perils I knew or was told about when I was young. But most of the time I remain aware of how constrained their lives will be. There are only a couple dozen of them here, maybe half of Little Five's under-eighteen population, and they will never know the thrill of meeting schools full of kids their age or stealing their parents' car keys on a hot summer night.

But I suppose they don't care and won't miss what they never had in the first place. The handful of children under the age of ten have never lived in any other world. Even the older ones hardly remember their lives before.

And all around them, the Little Five's shop stalls are crowded with the business of barter and exchange. The busiest of these is always Regina's. The community's most prolific baker, she has become something of an institution here, and she operates her large stall while her sixteen-year-old daughter handles deliveries. Although Luther is impatient to get to the tunnel wall, I linger a moment at Regina's stall, since I know I won't be getting any of her bread until I'm back at the station.

The aroma is familiar and comforting. Perhaps that's because it doesn't remind me of anything from before the collapse: I never experienced freshly baked bread until settling here. I imagine it smells like the inside of a western homestead or a winter-bound New England farmhouse from two centuries ago. And a lot like a home should smell.

Regina is a tall woman, maybe ten years older than I am—fifty or so—with close cropped white hair and a strong Georgia drawl that belies her pre-collapse radicalism. The story goes that she was raised by anti-war domestic terrorists who once narrowly escaped arrest for firebombing a police station in Eugene, Oregon. Regina herself is nothing but gracious to me.

"I hear we have people coming up from Twenty," she says in a whisper. She means Interstate 20, which connects with Moreland Avenue about a mile south of the tunnel and serves as a safer corridor for people passing through the city on their way west or east—to Alabama or the sea.

"Word travels fast," says Luther, who is pacing impatiently behind me. "Faster than we do, anyway."

"You get on then, Chief," says the baker. "I'll make sure you have something warm when you get back." She winks at me, part of an old joke between us. What she's insinuating is not a serious proposal: Regina's husband, the mayor, would be a little put out.

The old parking lot on the northbound side of the main street has been converted into a biodiesel farm, operated by a young couple who were at Georgia Tech before the collapse. When the world's oil began to go sour, at the beginning of the end, the green power lobby surged to the front pages and began recruiting the best and brightest from around the country. Ernesto Vargas and Belinda Braithwaite were among them. Along with Micah Abraham's solar panel crew, which provides most of our electricity, they have kept the power on and some of the vehicles running for a few years now.

Braithwaite is the true eccentric among the three green barons—the rest of the "power company," as they like to call themselves. Her hair flies around her head like a curly, bedraggled halo, and she wanders the streets at night barefoot and muttering under her breath. But she's not crazy, as far as I can tell: she talks to herself to solve problems, and she's told me more than once that she's an insomniac. She also likes to ask questions, and as Luther and I pass by the farm on the way to the tunnel, she is already on the sidewalk ready to interrogate me.

"So it's true? People beyond the wall? On foot?" She shoves her thick glasses back up the bridge of her nose.

"That's what I'm told."

"Ask them if they have any copper wire. We're running low, and I'd really like to have spare wire in case Leuko has trouble again." Leuko is a white Volvo station wagon. "Oh, and glow plugs. That's what we really need. But they probably don't have those. No one bothers to keep them around if they don't know what they are."

"I'll ask, but I don't think they came bearing car parts." I walk more briskly, following Luther, until it occurs to Braithwaite that I'm in a hurry, and she wanders back onto her property, still asking questions but no longer directing them at me.

The tunnel is just beyond the biodiesel farm, and the tunnel wall is one third of the way through on both northbound and southbound sides. We built the wall closer to our side of the tunnel so that we would have some measure of control if any shriekers found their way here and decided to call their friends. Most days, we only get one or two hollow-heads, and if they come too close, they're easily dispatched with arrows. There is always one rifleman from the sweep team on the wall as well, but they spend most of their days playing solitaire.

Mayor Aloysius Weeks is waiting for us with my other two officers, Pritchard and Kloves. Pritchard has about twenty years on me, but he's a good shot. I brought him on mainly to satisfy the previous mayor's paranoia about an invasion of the infected. Pritch has done a good job keeping the peace since then, so I haven't seen any reason to let him go. And Augustus Kloves was my idea: a big, powerful black man with an intimidating voice, he styles himself as my enforcer whenever someone winds up too drunk to go home quietly at three in the morning. I like to tell myself that in his pre-collapse life he had a paradoxically benign occupation, like a certified public accountant, but it doesn't matter. The end of the world changes a person. I've never seen an exception to that rule.

Mayor Weeks is Regina's husband, but if I didn't already know that, I would never have guessed it. Where Regina is friendly and forthcoming, Weeks is closed off, reticent. He never says anything with ten words that he could say with none. I find this to be an admirable quality in a politician. There is a much lower risk of hearing a lie. Perhaps it comes from his time as a professor, before the collapse. He told me once that he used to teach a subject called "Southeast Asian religions." One of his books is near the bottom of a stack I haven't read yet.

The mayor shakes my hand as I approach the tunnel door. "A young girl, maybe fourteen, and a man. Thirties. With a shotgun."

So that's why I was called out here. With a few quick gestures I position Pritch and Kloves on the upper platform and Luther at the reinforced door at ground level. Pritch and Kloves make themselves visible and draw their weapons. Once they're in position, I spin the combination lock to the door and pull off the chain. I step through, and for the first time in what feels like ages, I am outside the Little Five.

I keep my own weapon holstered and my arms relaxed at my sides. Luther closes the door and locks it behind me. Before I approach the strangers, I scan past them at the light beyond the tunnel, checking for signs of hangers-on. Of course, if the strangers had made enough noise to be noticed by a group of hollow-heads, they wouldn't have gotten as far as the tunnel wall. Clearly, they were careful. If there are any roaming hordes nearby, they're here by chance alone.

"Good morning," I say, keeping my body language as nonthreatening as possible.

The young woman is pregnant. That's easy enough to see; she's at least seven months along. Her clothes are torn and dirty. Her shoes are missing shoelaces and held together with old duct tape. She hasn't washed in days, at least. She looks hungry, perhaps confused.

The man is not much better, but he at least seems to have his wits. Weeks was right: he's in his late twenties or early thirties. He holds his shotgun like a hunter, with the stock under his shoulder and his hand under the barrel. He carries it like it's loaded, though, and when he answers my greeting he swings the barrel a few inches in my direction. "Good morning," he replies, looking up at the upper platform where Pritch and Kloves are watching. His accent suggests he's from South Carolina. "We don't mean any harm. We weren't sure there was anyone still living here. But we could use some food and shelter, and the girl could use a place to rest."

Back in the early days, we let in anyone who found us and counted ourselves lucky that we had one more person who could help us rebuild. From time to time that turned out to be a bad idea, but on balance, it worked for us. I, myself, was one of the first people let through what was a much smaller wall at the time. Even Mayor Weeks didn't arrive until a few years after we'd built the perimeter fence.

The fact that the man has a shotgun doesn't suggest anything other than that he has a head on his shoulders. Outside of the protected neighborhoods, Atlanta and presumably the rest of Georgia—and maybe the whole continent—are unsafe for travelers on foot. Hollow-heads haven't been as much of a problem recently in this area, but I don't know how far these two have traveled. So I choose to give them the benefit of the doubt. "If you're willing to let us secure that weapon until you leave, I'll consider letting you through the wall."

It sounds reasonable enough, but most men in his position wouldn't take me at my word. He doesn't know anything about us. If we take away his only protection, that will leave him vulnerable to whatever we might want to do with him—or to the girl with him. I expect him to try to bargain with me, to find a way to keep his weapon and still be permitted inside. But he offers no resistance to my demand, setting his shotgun on the ground and pushing it out of reach with the toe of his badly worn boot.

I glance back at my men on the wall. They have the same curious expression that I must be wearing: they're as familiar as I am with how this dance is supposed to go.

"Do you have a doctor?" the stranger asks.

I rest the palm of my hand on my holstered pistol and look over the young woman a second time. She looks far too young to be carrying a child—but I've seen younger. The combination of a collapsed population and no functioning condom factories makes for a lot of teen mothers these days. We don't exactly encourage pregnancy, but we can't quite bring ourselves to show righteous indignation when it happens. We need the babies more than we need the morality.

But none of that is what worries me. Doctors mean illness, and that could mean fever. And fever drags along with it the potential for something worse. At last count, the Little Five boasted a population of six hundred—and four people whom we call doctors. I wish we had twice as many. They are indispensable to us.

The man must realize that I'm giving his companion more scrutiny, as he says, "The last doc she saw said she has—" and now he says the word carefully, to be sure not to make a mistake—"preeclampsia."

The air goes thin in my lungs. Had someone else been standing here in my position, the man might have needed to say more, to

11

plead more. But I know the word. I lost my wife two years before the collapse and nearly lost my unborn daughter because of what preeclampsia can become. The thought of this young woman suffering from seizures and stroke is enough to goad me into action.

"Luther," I shout, "open the door."

The chain rattles against the metal, and the door swings open with a low creak. I usher the strangers in, and as the woman passes me, I think I can hear her whisper, "Thank you."

I am about to follow them back into the Little Five when I spot another figure moving on the far side of the tunnel.

"Is anyone else with you?" I hiss at the man. He says no, and I draw my weapon. I aim in the direction of the newest visitor, knowing that my officers will understand the gesture. It doesn't take long before Pritchard grabs binoculars and identifies what I'm seeing.

"Looks like a hollow-head, Chief," he says in his usual raspy, homespun tone.

My skin crawls under my coat. If handled calmly, a lone hollow-head is not a real threat. But we don't handle them calmly, even after all this time. They look like human beings, but they behave like animals, and on some unfortunate occasions one or more of us will recognize a friend or loved one who was lost to us long ago.

We try to think of them as being already dead. I'm sure I'm not alone in feeling a complex combination of relief and remorse every time I have to shoot one. They may be empty shells, but they were once like us, and they are most certainly still alive. In the depths of our gallows humor, we sometimes wish they were truly "the living dead." Then, at least, we could put them down without feeling like monsters.

Instead, they are hollow-heads. The pandemic that ended the world made its mark by consuming chunks of its victims' brains. The parts that control the higher functions are little more than slop sloshing around inside the cranium. Personality is gone. Memory is gone. Gone, too, are all the cares of the world and all vestiges of civilization.

There is no cure. There was never going to be any cure. When the hollow-heads first appeared, the good oil was all but gone, and we were already out of time.

Braithwaite and one or two of the other mathematically inclined eggheads in the Little Five once did what they called a "back of the envelope" calculation and figured that ninety percent of the world's population succumbed to the disease. The entire world's survivors, then, were less than twice the population of pre-collapse America. Less than the population of India. Of the ten million people who lived in Georgia before, fewer than a million survived. How many are still alive today is impossible to know.

The hollow-heads are survivors, too. But they survive in a different world from ours, and they don't do back of the envelope calculations, or remember that there once was an India, or an America, or a Georgia.

They travel in packs, most of the time, but have just enough brainpower to send off scouts in pairs and threes to search for food—wild dogs, cats, deer, the occasional goat, and people. They also seem to be able to tell the difference between the run-of-the-mill hollow-head and the shriekers, and use shriekers as scouts when they can. Most hollow-heads don't make noise: they remain uncannily silent, even when they're agitated. A few, though—maybe one in twenty—still know how to scream. And because they don't care about their voices, and don't have the usual social anxieties about looking foolish in public, when they scream, they *scream*. Louder than anyone I've ever heard.

We make sure to put shriekers down quickly, remorse and self-doubt be damned.

The hollow-head at the far end of the tunnel looks to be alone. It's female, wearing rags that were once proper clothes, with blood-caked bare feet. For whatever reason, the infection is a jealous god,

13

and hollow-heads don't get sick like the rest of us. They don't get tetanus, they don't die of gangrene, they don't suffer from any of the ailments that come from being bruised, scratched, stabbed, or cut. They can bleed out like anyone, and if they get gut-shot they will eventually die of starvation or blood loss, but I've been assured by people who claim to know that hollow-heads don't even die from having their own shit seep into the blood stream. Frostbite still affects them, even if their limbs won't rot, and some of our scouts have seen them chewing off their own dead arms. But even that is only helpful to people living in the north. Here in old Georgia, where the coldest day is like a Pennsylvania spring morning, it's not enough.

This hollow-head is intact, all of its parts in the right places, which makes it more dangerous than the average. Still, I'm the one with the pistol. I wait and watch to see if it realizes I'm here, but all it does is shamble from one side of the tunnel to the other, munching on something hanging from its mouth. A rat, maybe. Because hollow-heads operate entirely on instinct, I can't rely on this one feeling full and deciding not to bother with me. If it sees prey, it will attack, full stomach or no, and if it's a shrieker, it will alert its pack.

Shooting a gun attracts hollow-heads only about half the time. Maybe the sound isn't natural enough, or it reminds their hollowed-out brains of thunder. No one knows. They certainly chase after voices, loud footsteps, biodiesel engines, and just about anything else. Even so, I don't want to waste a bullet at this distance, with this light. I inch forward, keeping as quiet as I can, trying to stay out of its field of vision. It reaches the northbound side of the tunnel and stops to rub against the concrete like a dog scratching an itch.

A few steps closer and I will be confident I can get a good shot to the chest. But that's not enough: I need to shoot the head. If she's a shrieker and I leave her with one good lung, she can still cry out in the few moments she has before she dies.

A perverse part of me wants to holster the pistol and use my knife, but I'm not that stupid. Being bitten by a hollow-head is almost always a death sentence. Sepsis sets in, the fever comes, and then you get six hours of feeling better than you ever have before, as every bad bug in your system is eradicated by the resurgent infection. But from there the descent is quick as your brain melts away in your skull. I've seen it happen more than a few times, and the worst part, without question, is being aware of your own devolution. It's like suffering from an aggressive dementia that destroys you between breaths.

The hollow-head stops pressing against the wall and turns, its glassy eyes finding me at last. Its shambling motions give way to the instincts of a predator in sight of large prey, and it propels itself toward me, arms reaching, blood-caked hands grasping for me. It shows blackened teeth and opens its mouth to scream, but I lodge a bullet in its throat. The body collapses immediately, a gurgling sound pouring out of its neck along with the blood.

My gun arm feels heavy, as if the moral ambiguities had weight. One would think that after ten years this would get easier. And maybe it has. Just not enough. I don't recognize the one I've killed, but it—she—used to belong somewhere. Her face once made her mother smile. I take a deep breath and remind myself not to think about such things.

I holster my weapon and return to the wall, fetching the stranger's shotgun along the way. Luther chains and locks the door behind me, and my other officers come down from the upper deck. Before I turn my attention back to the visitors, I tell the guards on duty to watch for more hollow-head scouts and to clear the body from the road.

The pregnant girl is seated on the curb. The man hovers nearby while the mayor tries to coax some words out of his companion. But she says nothing. When I approach, the man steps in front of her and reaches out a hand. I don't offer mine in return, but he is undeterred. "Thank you," he says with apparent sincerity. "I promise, we won't be any trouble to you."

"I'll have to judge that for myself," I say, trying not to sound too skeptical. "I'll have some questions for you, to figure out what your story is and to make sure you're not running a con of some kind."

Mayor Weeks turns to the man. "We will make sure you have clean clothes, food, and a bed for the night," he says. "But," he adds with a nod toward me, "Chief Edison will need to be satisfied. We can take your friend to our doctor now, if you'll go with the chief to the station and answer those questions."

Before I take the stranger to the police station, I crouch in front of the girl and look her over with as little intrusion as possible. She didn't speak to the mayor, but maybe she'll speak to me. "My name is Sam," I say. "How do you feel?"

Her eyes flicker toward me, but beyond that she betrays no response. She looks healthy, but that is meaningless. Preeclampsia doesn't show its signs externally. Her demeanor is from some other trauma or the exhaustion of walking in disintegrated shoes—or both.

"Okay," I say after a moment. "We're going to take care of you. You're going to be fine."

I tell Luther to take the girl to our makeshift hospital, then gesture for her companion to follow me.

The police station was formerly a mini-precinct of the Atlanta Police Department, conveniently located near the five-point intersection. Regina Weeks's daughter, Phoebe, is at the station when we arrive, unloading our daily delivery of bread onto a table in the lobby. Although she is four years older than my own daughter would be, I am reminded of what I've lost whenever I see her. She seems to have Jeannie's eyes and chin and a laugh that pulls on my memories like marionette strings. Sometimes the good memories are worse than the bad ones. I remember the last time my daughter laughed and all the minutes between that moment and her last.

"Good morning," Phoebe says with a bright smile. Her red-haired ponytail bounces. "I wasn't sure when you'd be back. Do you want me to take everything to the dry cupboard?"

"Yes, thanks," I say, unlocking the inner door to let her through. I bring our guest to my office and motion for him to take a seat across from my desk. The man's eyes roam back toward the door. I call out to Phoebe, asking her to bring in some of the bread for our guest. "You must be hungry," I tell him, and he confirms it with a nod.

"You'll find that most of the people here are friendly," I begin. "And part of my job is to make sure they can be that way and still be safe. If I don't like the answers you give me, or you give me any reason to think you'll be a danger to us, I won't hesitate to send you back out beyond the wall."

He nods again. "I understand. I know what it means to protect your boundaries. I know what's at stake. You won't regret helping us."

"Let's start with your names."

Phoebe enters with a small sack of her mother's bread. Phoebe is a smart young woman, but trusting, and always looking to please people. Asking her to bring the food here gives me a chance to see how the stranger will react to her.

"My name is Owen," he answers, and when Phoebe approaches him with the food he takes it with a quick "thank you." His eyes follow her for only a moment as she moves toward me; he focuses most of his attention on tearing pieces out of the bread and chewing rapidly. "The girl's name is Abigail."

"What about you, Chief Edison?" Phoebe asks me just above a whisper. She holds out the sack, and I take a piece of the warm bread, inhaling the aroma. The smell reminds me that I'm a small part of something important, something that keeps our world turning. We get most of our wheat flour from semiannual trade with one of the rural collectives south of Atlanta; they get biodiesel in exchange.

I thank Phoebe for the food, and she leaves, closing the door behind her. Her face showed eager interest in the stranger, but she has always been good about staying out of the way of important business. She must have learned that from her stepfather.

The way this man Owen referred to the young woman tells me a lot about their relationship. "So you aren't related to her," I say. "And it's not your child she's carrying. But you do know her. She's not just someone you picked up on the way."

Owen's lack of surprise at my conclusion is also telling. "We've been coming south on 400 and 85 for—oh, God, it must be a week now, at least. You know, I used to be—well, it doesn't matter. We came from Dahlonega."

Dahlonega is seventy miles away, a two day walk from the Little Five under good conditions. Getting through Alpharetta, Roswell, and then most of the metro Atlanta area couldn't have been easy. They would only have come this far south, into this more treacherous environment, if they had no other option.

When Owen doesn't continue, I prod him a little more. "Why did you leave? Was it overrun?"

"No, nothing like that," he says, finishing off his meal. "I had this idea that we could get down to Macon, where my folks lived. They were still there last I heard, some seven years ago. Abigail could have her baby there and stay a while, and then go where she needed to go after that. But it was bad enough getting here. We almost got caught a few times, and we've been having trouble finding food."

"Most of the shops were stripped bare years ago," I say, filling in the blanks. Owen and Abigail weren't well prepared for the journey. "It was just the two of you?"

"Just us."

"Why?" I ask.

"I—" he starts, looking to the windows. "We had to leave. It's not a good place up there, anymore. Maybe it never was."

"That doesn't really answer my question. From all you're telling me, you could be just two people who ran away from home. But you're not a kid, and if she's not your girlfriend and that's not your baby, why are you with her?"

Owen doesn't answer, so I press on. "Unless it affects us here, I don't really care why you left. But I need to know if there are people who are going to come looking for you. And I need to know if you're the sort of man who creates trouble and then leaves before he gets caught."

"No," he says before I can take a breath. "I swear, it wasn't anything like that. And no one is going to come after us." Owen pauses to look directly at me. "Abigail is a friend. I promised her that she would be safe. Her baby would be safe. If you need me to go, I will. I can go on to Macon like I planned. But please don't kick her out. She needs—she just needs one good thing."

It's hard to reject a plea like that in this world. Even so, I wish I had old world police resources at my fingertips. I might not have been able to check Owen's story, such as it is, but I would have had access to warrants and BOLOs. In the old world I'd have a telephone; I could call the girl's parents and be reasonably sure they were still alive. But even lacking all that, I still have my instincts. They tell me that Owen is not a pedophile, unless he is very good at hiding it or has a very specific type: he didn't take a second look at Phoebe when she delivered the food. And he isn't trying to justify taking the girl away from her home by giving me some long, convoluted story intended to obfuscate the truth. I'd expect that from someone with secrets to hide.

"What about her family? They won't come looking for her?"

"I don't know where they are. She hasn't told me anything about her parents. For all I know—"

I interrupt him with a raised hand. "They're not back in Dahlonega?"

"What? There? No. Of course not. For all I know, they're dead. She hasn't seen them in years." I let Owen stew in the silence that

19

follows, until he explains, "Abigail came to us about five years ago. A caravan of refugees, I was told at the time."

But he doesn't go any further. "Look," he says at last, "it's not my place to tell you most of this. You should ask her. She's not a bad kid. It's just hard for her to trust anyone else. She'll talk to you when she feels safe."

Owen's expression clouds, and I don't think I'll get much more information out of him now. Perhaps in a day or two he will be less reticent, or I will learn the whole of the truth from his friend. Pushing too hard right now will only agitate him and give him reason to do something stupid that we might regret, like trying to get back out through the tunnel wall. "We have a few empty apartments that we're using for storage," I say. "I'll see if we can't get some of that moved out, some furniture put in, to give you and Abigail a place to stay. But for now, the best I can offer is the cell here at the station. Which isn't as bad as it sounds, really. I'll try to make it comfortable."

"I understand." Owen rises when I do and shakes my hand. "I promise we won't be any trouble. Thank you. Is it all right if I see Abigail?"

◆

There has not been a real, board certified doctor in the Little Five for almost eight years—not since Ronnie Colbart was bitten on the leg by a hollow-head and succumbed two days later. We have two former nursing students and a vet technician, as well as a woman who was two years into a premed degree at Emory before the collapse. There isn't much that a doctor could do for us that this staff of four cannot, anyway. Antibiotics and antivirals are no longer effective to control the diseases that matter, and they've never done anything against the barbarian at the gate.

A few years ago, Marilyn Trainor, the former premed student, figured out that everyone—whole and hollow-head alike—has already been infected. At the start the disease was passed by simple touch or through the air. Most of the original victims died; a few became hollow-heads. This overpowered what little remained of the world's infrastructure. Those of us who didn't get sick assumed we'd never contracted the disease. It turns out, though, that we're just as infected as the dead were.

Marilyn speculated that the hollow-head disease is a virus that encapsulates in resistant hosts, remaining dormant until it is reawakened by high fevers from some other source. This is why hollow-head bites are so dangerous, even though they don't transmit the virus itself. And it is why we must be obsessively wary of pneumonia and influenza. Sepsis from hollow-head bites almost always leads to full-blown infection. Pneumonia has a "mortality" rate of around seventy percent, and we lost almost thirty people in the first three years from standard cases of winter flu. One of them was my daughter.

Our hospital, if it can be called that, is a converted restaurant on the northbound side of Moreland, across from the old BP gas station where Vargas and Braithwaite store their biodiesel. The staff of four live in apartments above and around the hospital, making house calls and coming up with whatever rudimentary medical concoctions they can put together with their limited resources.

Marilyn and one of the nurses, William Echevarria, are with Abigail when I arrive with Owen. Adelaide Luther is seated by the door, watching them. The girl is lying on her side on a long table, drinking watered-down tomato juice through a straw. Her clothes have been changed, the old ones left in a pile by the door. The shoes have all but fallen apart. The girl's bare feet are dirty and blistered from the road. The effort it must have taken for her to keep one foot in front of the other all the way from Dahlonega is astounding.

Echevarria is inspecting the girl's scalp with a magnet-powered flashlight. Every once in a while, he gives it a few good shakes to keep the light on. The hospital is one of the only places where solar- and bicycle-generated power stays on twenty-four hours a day. A few floor lamps add to the morning glow through the restaurant windows, but that isn't enough light to do a proper inspection for ticks and lice.

Marilyn comes to us at the door, her long black dreadlocks swaying against her back. They draw me in, as they always have, like the tendrils of a dream from which I never want to wake. "Good morning, Chief," she says, making it sound like she never knew me. "And you must be Owen." She takes Owen's arm and ushers him farther into the room with enough confidence that he doesn't object when she sits him down a table away from Abigail.

The pregnant young woman lifts her head when she sees him. "Owen?" she says, her voice soft and high.

"I told you the chief would bring him 'round," Trainor says. "But right now we have to give him a checkup like we gave you. William?"

Echevarria moves to the other table, talking to Owen while Marilyn brings me closer to the front window. She says, "The girl is in good health, and I think the baby is fine. Best guess, she's about eight months along. I'm concerned about the preeclampsia, though. There's not too much we can do about it, to be honest, except watch and wait."

Luther says, "She hasn't said anything about where they came from or why they were out on the road. I'd say she's in shock, except the doc doesn't agree."

"It's not shock," Marilyn says. "Shock implies a recent thing. Something that just happened. This behavior is more long term."

She hesitates to continue, but I need information. "What aren't you telling me, doctor?"

"It's complicated. Let's go outside." She ushers the two of us out onto the empty sidewalk, in front of the windows so that she can still keep an eye on Abigail.

"There's a question of privacy," she continues. "So I'm sorry, Adelaide, that I didn't tell you about it, but—"

"It's fine," Luther says, though her tone suggests otherwise.

"It's important," I say. "You said she's in good health. So if she's not sick—"

"She has scars," Marilyn says, quickly enough, I reason, to keep herself from changing her mind. "On her back and legs. The marks suggest multiple, probably repeated whippings." As she continues, her tone becomes increasingly clinical. "There is evidence of past sexual trauma. Burn marks, and what I believe may be vaginal scarring, suggestive of forced penetration. I don't have experience with those wounds, so I'm not certain."

I look through the glass at the girl sipping on her tomato juice, her eyes wide and fixed on us. Inside my head I hear the echoes of her screaming, crying out, sobbing for relief or rescue. Her current quiet, the bulge of her belly that makes her look more fragile than she is, only makes the contrast worse. The echoes, louder. The child within her perpetuates the violation, whether or not she has chosen on her own to keep it. I have not felt this mixture of anger and impotence in a long time.

"Do you think it was Owen?" Luther asks.

"No," I say. "I interviewed him. My sense is he brought her down here to rescue her from her situation." I can't even bring myself to name it.

When Luther glances at me skeptically, Marilyn says, "Men who beat women aren't keen on letting doctors examine them. And survivors resist examination, for fear of being blamed for revealing the secret. You saw the way she responded to him when he got here. He's probably the only thing keeping her going right now."

"She's going to need more than medicine," I say.

"I know," Marilyn says. "She's going to need people who understand. Maybe not all of it. But more than most of us. Owen got her out, but he can't get her through."

I once found strength in the knowledge that one day I would live beyond the reach of my tormentor, that my bruises and broken ribs would heal and be no more. But I believe these other violations will last longer. And they press against my heart in more demanding ways. They remind me that to save myself I had to leave my mother behind. My mother, who suffered more than I.

Maybe I can do for Abigail what I couldn't do for her.

"She's going to be okay," Marilyn says with a softness intended for me. "As much as she can be. We'll take care of her. She's safe here."

I know this. And I am determined to make sure it's true. Owen says she just needs one good thing. But we can do more. One can't be enough. We need to offer her a place for a better life than the one that she fled, until her wounds heal in body and mind and only the scars remain.

But I can't stop any of it or erase it. I can't change her past. And Dahlonega is seventy miles away. It operates by its own laws and enforcement, if such things even exist there. I can help Abigail to be comfortable here, but I will not be able to force her abusers to account for their crimes. I will not be able to give her what I have: the satisfaction of knowing, with absolute certainty, that she has outlasted them.

DAY FOUR, 9:00 A.M.

It's been three days since Owen and Abigail arrived in the Little Five, and at last there is an apartment ready for them. A handful of volunteers spent most of the morning moving boxes out of and furniture into a second-floor apartment above Cassidy's Bar in the center of town. Owen asked me why they were being given such prime real estate, and I pointed out that there's really no such thing in the Little Five. Besides, at night, it can get a bit loud downstairs.

Luther was concerned for a time about letting the young girl live in the same apartment as her much older guardian, considering they aren't related, but it's clear that she needs him nearby. I have seen the two of them out in the streets a few times in the last couple of days, and Owen's confidence is a stark contrast to the mouse-like behavior of his charge. She speaks very little, and never above a whisper, though I have seen her smile when she receives a kind word or some treat from one of the vendors.

Still, the relationship between the two strangers baffles me in some ways. It's not as if Owen has an outsized care for the girl, as far as I can tell. He keeps her at arm's length, without much more tenderness than two traveling companions might share, yet she clings to him like an older brother. And he doesn't seem to mind. So, who is Abigail to him? Why did he take her from that place? What made him care?

I haven't tried to speak to Abigail since the morning they arrived. She doesn't need my interference now. She needs a routine, a safe space to build up around her, before I can think of approaching her. To ask questions too soon, to demand that she remember the life she's left behind, would only be another assault, and it would gain her nothing. I am grateful to see that the girl is coming out of her shell just a little on her own. While the adults travel up and down the stairs to the apartment, she watches from the street with the mayor's stepdaughter, Phoebe, at her side. They are not the same age—Phoebe is a few years older—but they are becoming friends. Abigail's smile is lingering longer.

I should have expected it, of course. Phoebe has her parents' easy grace and likability. In another world, another time, she would have been more than a handful for Regina and Aloysius. Boys and cliques and all the trouble that a typical teenage girl can get into—but those days are gone, replaced with a throwback world where a person is thrust into adulthood much sooner.

I turn away at the sound of my name, called out by one of the sweep team members down by the wall.

"Scouts coming in," she adds, pointing out beyond our boundary. "Olsen and Lukacs."

I join her at the wall to welcome the two scouts back home. The men are both members of the sweep team, but they like to range more widely than the rest, and sometimes we don't see them for weeks. This time their excursion was brief: only eight days.

Olsen, a tall, thin man with black-rimmed glasses, is the first to the door. He is naturally dour, but the tension in his jaw is especially strong today. I only need to glance beyond him to know what happened. His scouting partner, Gabor Lukacs, has been bitten or scratched by a hollow-head or suffered some other injury that led to sepsis and fever.

Lukacs, staying back from the wall, shows me his left palm. In the afternoon light that shines through the door, a bite mark is clearly visible on the meat of his thumb. There are telltale signs of earlier swelling in his hand and forearm. Neither he nor Olsen need to tell me more. I have seen this before. We all have. Our losses exceed our successes, and we no longer have room for individual miseries. With time, each pain mixes indistinctly with all the others, and we tell ourselves we are hardened. Then fresh hurts remind us that the steel in our nerves is only fragile glass.

I send for a doctor and for Gabor's wife before turning back to the two scouts. "How long?" I ask.

Olsen says, "Yesterday morning. We got caught between two groups on our way back."

Lukacs calls across the divide between us, "The swelling went down three hours ago. The fever stopped right after. So we're looking at maybe four hours." His rational calm is not uncommon. If there is one good thing to come from all of this, it's that we pass on with much more dignity now.

"We left a cache of tools and supplies about ten miles south," Olsen adds. "I can go collect it—after. We wanted to hurry."

"Of course," I mutter, then beckon for Lukacs to come to the wall. "You're not staying out there."

In the beginning, when we were still raw with panic and misinformation, we made every effort to separate out the so-called "infected" from the rest of the community, thinking that they could harm us by way of proximity. But a man who is succumbing to the disease is no more dangerous than anyone else, and a single hollow-head is a manageable threat. If Gabor wants to spend his last hours under the canopy of his community, with his wife, no one here will stop him.

Marilyn arrives first, with her medical bag. She ushers Lukacs through after Olsen, then the sweep team locks the door behind us. She sits Lukacs on a bench at the end of the tunnel to examine him.

Word is already getting out that the scouts have returned and that one of them has been "converted" by hollow-heads. He isn't dying, but his life is ending, and by the time Marilyn has confirmed what we know, the man's friends have already gathered to greet him. To pay their respects. The crowd that is forming at the wall has come to say goodbye.

Lukacs's wife arrives at the same time that Owen catches my attention with a quick wave from across the wide street. I'm grateful for the distraction. I don't like seeing this part of it. It has been years since I could pretend to accept graciously the sympathy of others, even when it is not directed at me. Even when it is sincere, as it always is: everyone has been in those shoes, a hundred times or more.

"What's happening?" Owen asks once I come within easy speaking distance.

"Was there something you wanted?" I ask in return, not wanting to be dismissive but also not in any mood for idle conversation. But another part of me welcomed the distraction. "Sorry. One of our scouts is—"

When I hesitate, Owen says, "Oh. I understand. You let them through the wall? What I mean is: not everyone does that." He looks toward the building where his new apartment is being filled with furniture, as if to say that not everyone does a lot of things.

"Is Abigail settling in?" I ask to keep the momentum of the conversation.

"I think so. I'm sure she will."

"You could stay," I tell him. "I know you mentioned Macon, but that's a long way out."

"If I do, I'll have to earn my keep somehow. Back in Dahlonega I was—well, let's put it this way. I had advantages. My brother—" Owen stops, shrugs. When he continues, his tone has shifted away from the bitterness I began to hear. "I saw you have a crew that works on cars."

I have to laugh at that. "Not a crew so much as one man. If you're any good with that sort of thing, I'm sure he could use the help."

"I've changed a battery or two in my day." There is some levity in his voice again. "Back before, I was stationed at Fort Stewart, in the motor pool. I was there for all of a minute and a half, but I know my way around a diesel."

"Were you there when—?" I begin.

"Yeah," he interrupts. "I'm not really sure what the point was, but I was there even after the oil turned sour. We managed to put together a few technicals toward the end. You know what a technical is?"

I nod. "A jury-rigged gun truck." I tug on the lapel of my overcoat.

"Oh, yeah. You were Coast Guard? I thought maybe you found that coat. Anyway, we figured it was a terrorist attack, like poisoning the water supply. We got a hold of a few converted pickups and secured machine guns to the beds and thought we were going to rip the bad guys to shreds. Whoever they turned out to be. But they turned out to be us, after everyone got sick. Then Savannah happened. I know Savannah was near the end of it, but for us it was like—"

"Apocalypse," I suggest.

Owen continues as if he hasn't heard me. "We had eight technicals with three-man teams. That's all we had left, of trucks and people. Can you imagine that? Something like fifteen thousand people on that base, and at the end there was just the handful of us left. But we wanted to do some good. So we got in those technicals and rode hell-bent for leather to Savannah."

29

Savannah. The city that used to be my home, when I had a wife, and when I had a child. The city that introduced me to the new brutality and forced me to reckon with the person I needed to become. Perhaps Owen went to Savannah with the heart of a hero. For my part, I remember only the fear and the desperation, and the people who sacrificed themselves to get my daughter one more mile down the road. One more block. One more doorway. Until there were no more people left, and that last doorway was here.

We are interrupted by the arrival of Abigail and Phoebe. Phoebe gives me a long, piercing glance, as if to tell me that she knows about Lukacs but doesn't want to trouble the younger girl. Abigail, though not exactly cheerful, is at least nearly smiling.

Phoebe approaches Owen first. "I was going to show Abby the north fields. The chickens and the pigs. If that's all right."

"Yes, that's fine," Owen says. "You want me to come with you?" he asks Abigail.

Her expression becomes even more difficult to read.

"Then go on," he says. "It's all right."

As the two girls walk away, Phoebe making an attempt at conspiratorial banter, Owen sucks air through his teeth. "Some things you can't make right," he says. "Like Savannah. We got there, and it was too late, and it was a killing field. So when you can make something right, you have to, don't you?"

"Tell me about Dahlonega," I say by way of a reply.

"There's nothing for me to tell. They did all right by me for a while. But it's not the same anymore. You don't ever want to go to Dahlonega. Stay here, where it's good."

Owen leaves me to inspect his new apartment, and I am forced to confront the earlier development again. By now the crowd has thinned, most of Lukacs's acquaintances moving back to their routines. Only his closest friends will remain with him. The rest of us can't afford to spend all our pain on something that's a part of the new natural order.

Lukacs and Olsen have gone with Marilyn to the hospital, where I find them in the company of a few others, all of them in solemn silence. Gabor's wife is with him, crying into his shoulder and making Marilyn wait to speak. Gabor is consoling Cathy as well as he can, but I can see his strain. Though he must feel incredibly well in most respects—a mixed blessing from the disease that is taking him away—his brain is already beginning to dissolve into slush. This is making it difficult for him to form coherent thoughts.

We have seen this happen too many times.

"We need to make some decisions," Marilyn says when I enter, barely acknowledging my presence.

"I know," Lukacs says, gesturing to Olsen. "We already talked about it."

"He wants to go outside the wall," Olsen answers for him. "I can get Ernesto to let us borrow one of the cars. We'll go to the cache we left behind. I'll bring it back."

Cathy launches into a series of objections, each more frantic than the last, demanding that her husband stay in the Little Five.

"No," he insists. "I'm not going to make anyone go through that."

"I offered," Olsen says. "I said I would."

They are speaking around the harsh truth. If Lukacs stays in the Little Five until the end, someone is going to have to put him down after the change. Or he's going to have to kill himself, before it gets that far. Instead he is proposing to be left outside the community, to become a hollow-head and join another tribe. To be cast to whatever fate nature will provide.

Gabor sits down to take a few deep breaths. I can see the strain of concentration on his face. "I want this to be on my terms," he says, mainly to his wife. "I don't want to argue the time I have left."

"I'm coming with you, then," Cathy says. "I'll be with you at the end." Over the objections that Lukacs is about to make, she adds, "I'll keep safe. Olsen will be there."

They argue for a few more minutes while I watch, uncomfortable, but the compromise is a foregone conclusion. Lukacs simply hasn't the energy left to fight this last battle, and he agrees to let Cathy be with him until he is no longer conscious. He must know, surely, that she won't keep to that deal and will stay with him until he awakens in his new existence.

Our scouts are especially vulnerable to endings like this, as they spend more time beyond the perimeter than anyone else, but they are by no means the only ones who have lost their old lives to the hollow-heads. Most of the time, it's difficult for people to let go. Perhaps they hope that there will be a last minute reprieve. Perhaps they believe that their loved one will remember them, deep down, in the remnant parts of the brain that still function. The victims usually feel the same way. Only rarely do they choose another option.

When Olsen, Lukacs, and his wife leave the hospital to make their vigil outside the perimeter, Marilyn and I stay behind in the room alone. I know she wants to say something, but neither of us really needs to speak. We've talked about my daughter before, many times. And every time she insists, and I agree, that I made the right decision by not letting her suffer the way Lukacs will. But I'm not sure that Cathy will feel any worse now than I did then. I've come to believe that neither answer is the right one. But I can't say that to Marilyn. It would open wounds she was able to close when we parted.

Eventually, she does find her voice. "Is it wrong for me to be glad that you stopped going outside yourself?"

"I stopped too late for your liking."

That wasn't the right thing to say. Marilyn starts to busy herself with cleanup. I let the awkward silence grow until I've caused more than enough regret. Even so, as I am leaving, she pauses long enough to say, "I'm still glad."

When evening comes and the hours are up, Olsen and Lukacs's widow return with a small cache of parts and tools in the rear compartment of the blue biodiesel station wagon. Cathy is stoic, and when the Little Five decides to celebrate Lukacs's life with food and music until well past dark, she participates without apparent bitterness. I remain for a while, keeping the peace as mourners turn to revelers and make fools of themselves in public, but once the oil lamps are lit, I hand the task over to Luther.

Before I retire to my home, Ernesto Vargas intercepts me in the street to let me know that his partner, Belinda Braithwaite, has gotten word over shortwave radio that we will be receiving a trading caravan in a week's time. That takes my mind off matters for a little while. I bring the news back to Mayor Weeks, and his wife, Regina, demands that I dance with her at least once before I go.

I see Phoebe nearby and look for Abigail, but the girl isn't anywhere in the crowd. Neither is Owen. Perhaps they are settling into their new apartment and leaving Lukacs's wake to those who knew him. I am a little disappointed, though: I would have liked to know how well Phoebe is drawing the pregnant teenager out of her shell. But by the time I decline a second dance with the mayor's wife and truly take my leave of the party, I am exhausted from the weight of the day and go home to sleep.

As usual, it doesn't come easily. I sit at my breakfast table and read by the light of a strong candle, absorbing the trivia of a monograph from the 1930s on the forensic value of insects. It's only slightly more stimulating than the next book in the pile is likely to be, a college primer on basic economics. But I need this. I need to fill my head with unimportant things. Because at every turn of the page, in between every line, I think of my daughter, whose twelfth birthday would have been in five days. I would not be spending my restless nights reading alone in the dark if Jeannie were here. Or if I had not squandered the goodwill of the only person who kept me on the path after she was gone.

I think of Cathy and the countless nights ahead that she will have to spend in a cold bed, dreaming of her husband and the last time she saw him. And Abigail, whose young life has already seen too much horror. There must be more that I can do. More for the Little Five, more for Abigail. More for the people who rely on me to make their world safe.

Reading with bloodshot eyes in the dark of a cloud-covered night, it's hard to remember that I can't save everyone. And just as hard to forget.

DAY NINE, 10:00 P.M.

Convincing the last mayor to permit the construction of a still took some work, but eventually Thomas Cassidy was allowed to cobble together the parts he needed to make the moonshine that began his twilight empire. Now, on most nights, after the lights throughout the Little Five have been turned off to conserve batteries, the older citizens can be found inside Cassidy's Bar drinking his versions of beer and whiskey. Most of the younger crowd, the ones who were not yet teenagers when the collapse happened, don't have much interest in reclaiming this small slice of the old life, and they stay away, thinking us strange.

The bar smells of pig shit and goats: Cassidy keeps his animals in here after he closes down. It adds to the charm, along with the ridiculous plastic skull that frames the front door, but we don't come here for the atmosphere. We come to remind ourselves that we once lived civilized lives. We could be here on a weekend, after forty or eighty hours of hard work in an office somewhere, or in my case, working on a cutter off the Georgia coast. But there are no more offices, no more reports, no more managers or bosses or quarterly earnings. No more national waters. We dream of a future with these things in it—but the young ones do not. Perhaps I should be glad that we will leave this world to them, and not to our forebears.

But for now, on the nights that my brain won't shut off and my heart hurts, I need this place. I tell myself that I've moved forward, but the anniversaries hand-deliver the truth to my doorstep. I indulge in my sorrows for a night, and then wake up the next morning having pushed everything back once more. It's the way most of us live, and have lived for a decade, because the grief would be overwhelming if we did it any other way. My particular grief tonight is for Jeannie. I grasp at the good memories. First steps. First words. Seeing her mother in her eyes. Hugging close the echo of my wife, grateful for the chance to continue loving another person so fiercely.

Marilyn Trainor comes to me after I've been planted on my stool for an hour, staring at a Polaroid of Jeannie that I took on her third birthday. Marilyn nudges Kloves off the seat on my right. He and Pritch leave easily, finding an empty table near the back. They know why Marilyn is here. She slides her glass along the bar until it taps my own and says, "To Jeannie."

She knew my daughter only briefly, at the end. The memories she recalls with the click of her glass aren't the ones that dominate my thoughts, and in a way I'm thankful for that. She is remembering the path she helped me walk in the months and brief years that followed. To her, Jeannie doesn't represent losing the last pieces of my life before the collapse. For Marilyn, my daughter represents all of the things I never let go. The world that everyone else left behind is a world I've never been able to leave completely because the doors shut before me the last time I saw Jeannie's face.

Marilyn and I parted ways because I never managed to open those doors once I let them close. But she is not cruel. She could never be. She isn't trying to remind me of all the things that took us apart in the end. She saved my life; in exchange, she only wanted me to be present in hers. And I would like to think that I was, for a time.

"It's a good night," Marilyn says. "Too good to be having heavy thoughts."

I smile, knowing the dance. "They're not heavy," I reply. "They're diaphanous."

I don't tell her that the gears in my tired mind have clicked over to regrets beyond my daughter's short life. Marilyn's presence is never painful, but sometimes it isn't easy.

"No," she says, with a knowing nod and a glimmer of mischief in her eyes, "they're lugubrious."

I can't help but laugh. She must have been waiting a year to use that word. It works.

"It's a good night," I admit. "One of many. Look at what we've done."

"Jeannie is proud of you," she says. It's a surprise to me: she's never said it before, and we've been here every year for half a decade.

It's the regret that pushes me to ask, "And you?"

"Sam," she says. "Let it be a good night."

I let out a long sigh. This was the argument between us, always. The one that separated us in the end. She always knew my mind better than I did. She knew how to soothe me, and how to let me cope on my own. She saw, long before I became aware, that I was burying my self-repudiation in the work of protecting the Little Five. I couldn't save Jeannie; I had to save everyone else.

"You hold so tightly to how things should have been," she said at the end, "you forget how things are, and who is here with you." She told me that I mistook distance for strength, risk-taking for responsibility, and that I didn't understand her. Some days, like today, I think that maybe I still don't. That I cannot confide in her this weakness of mine is proof that she was always right about me.

And that's the uncomfortable truth. There has never been any doubt that Marilyn was, and is, proud of me. We couldn't have been together for as long as we were otherwise. But after Jeannie died, I ran from my loss by burying my head in the sand of work. I tried to see the world through Marilyn's eyes, and even now I strain for a glimpse of it in the shadows of Cassidy's Bar, but I can't be the person she needed. The one who only worries about the things that can be controlled.

"It's a good night," I say again, hoping she will believe me a second time.

"Get some sleep," Marilyn says tenderly. "The Little Five needs her chief."

And then she's gone, back into the shadows, back through the crowd of old men and women reminiscing about a world we still want to keep in our grasp. I put my daughter's photograph back in my pocket, as if to protest that I'm not one of them.

The door swings back open as Marilyn leaves the bar, letting in some of the full moonlight, and a newly familiar face enters: Owen, alone for the first time in days, looking for someone. For me, apparently. "Officer Luther told me you'd be here." He puts out a hand to shake mine. "I wanted to thank you again for everything you've done and for letting us in."

He glances around the room as if searching for someone else, then returns his attention to me. "Chief, I need to talk to you in the morning. It's important."

"Now is fine. We can go over to the station." I tap the side of my glass. "These don't really have the effect they once did."

"Maybe," he says. "Not just yet. There are some things I need to check first. To be sure." Before I can object, he adds, "But I can meet you at the station in an hour."

Owen turns and leaves as quickly as he arrived. Confused, I slip from my seat and follow him only a few paces behind. As my palm hits the door, there is a loud rifle crack from the street, and I burst out of the bar in time to see Owen crumpling to the ground less than five yards away. I reach for my own weapon but realize I left it at the station before I walked over here. My second instinct is to find cover and scan for the attacker, but in spite of the brightness of the full moon, there are too many shadows, and I see nothing—not even a hint of movement. The shooter may have been firing from a window or from one of the alleys. There is no way to be sure from my vantage. The most I can tell from the way Owen fell and where his wounds are is that he was shot in the back right side of the head, putting the shooter somewhere to my right.

Pritchard and Kloves are next out the door. Kloves uses his deep, carrying voice to make it clear that no one is to come into the lot until I tell them it's safe. Pritch finds me crouched behind an old bike rack, which isn't much in the way of cover, but the best I could find in a moment.

"Do you have your weapon?" I ask, and he shakes his head. "Get to the station. Bring Luther."

As Pritch rises to go, a loud, high pitched scream rattles among the buildings, echoing across the parking lot in front of the bar. Anyone unaccustomed to the sound would be forgiven for thinking that it was some hysterical woman's reaction to seeing a body bleeding out on the ground. But no one here is unaccustomed to the sound. It is too long, too loud, too uncanny.

"Fuck," Pritchard yelps, and he runs hard for the station.

"Where did that come from?" Kloves asks.

"Tunnel, I think." I do one last futile scan of the area before I stand and turn away from Owen. "Had to be. The echo." I motion for Kloves to step aside, and as the people in the bar come stumbling out, I address them as firmly as I can. "Everyone on the sweep team, get your gear and go to the tunnel wall. If you can't walk straight, go home."

All thoughts of the man on the ground are banished. We have a more immediate danger to address, even though it means losing evidence and the best chance of finding Owen's shooter. The only concession I can afford is to have Kloves bring Owen's body to the hospital. Then I face south and hurry to reach the station.

Luther and Pritch are outside when I arrive, both carrying crossbows and rifles. Luther tosses me a Remington and my holster, already moving toward the tunnel. "Pritch was saying something about a shooting."

The shrieker calls out again, more loudly this time. I had hoped someone would have taken the shot already. I curse under my breath. "It was Owen."

"Owen? Why?" Luther halts. "Has someone checked in on the girl?"

I grit my teeth. "Go," I tell Luther. "Make sure she's all right. Get her to the station. Put her in the cell to be sure. Keep her safe."

She hands over her crossbow and turns on her heels without a word.

By the time Pritch and I reach the tunnel wall, the sweep team is arriving behind us, their bows and crossbows at the ready. Most of these weapons were retrieved from the big box stores beyond the tunnel during the early days post-collapse, and they are a varied assortment of children's toys, sports equipment, and hunting weapons.

Half of the sweep team takes the high road atop the tunnel, next to the railroad tracks and the southern fence. The rest go down to the wall, onto the upper platform. Pritch joins the high road group with his rifle and I go to the wall, giving Luther's crossbow to one of the sweep team archers. I am a much better shot with a firearm.

Through one of the arrow slits at the top of the barricade I see the shrieker, just past the tunnel, out of range of the bows. Farther down the road, at the edge of the retail park, a mass of hollow-heads is moving toward the shrieker's call, which comes again and rattles my skull. "Come on, Pritch," I mutter.

The shot rings out and the shrieker's wailing is cut short. It collapses to the ground, exactly like Owen, and I shudder at the comparison. Both were men once.

At this distance, in the darkness, it is impossible to make out individuals in the hollow-head crowd, turning it into a single writhing mass of interconnected bodies, moving haltingly and silently toward the deeper darkness of the tunnel. The stench of them comes in like the fog over Kennesaw Mountain: sweat and blood and shit, mixed with the vapor of breath so vile that I feel like I'm swallowing dead rats each time I inhale.

Yet despite the smell, the worst is the silence. Perhaps it's some primal expectation of our ancient brains that predators must make a sound, a cry or a growl, any noise at all. The hollow-heads, for all their viciousness, are like the dead, giving us only their footfalls echoing in the tunnel. My chest tightens, and a sour taste percolates into my mouth. No matter how many times I find myself here, facing this, it feels like the first. Like the plazas of Savannah, where I frantically put myself between the hollow-heads and the civilians I couldn't save. I feel the guilt anew. I let it fuel me. I let it make me callous, if only for a moment, long enough to do what needs to be done.

There is a change in the horde, like the turning of a flock of birds, and the entire mass of hollow-heads begins to run, sprinting through the tunnel, grasping for the arrow slits of the upper platform. Half of the group has come through to the southbound side of the tunnel where I am posted; the other half, invisible to me now, is on the northbound side beyond the concrete median wall.

"Oh, fuck," yelps one of the newer sweep team members, and a bolt whistles down into a hollow-head's shoulder. The hollow-head opens its mouth wide in a silent scream and falls back into the crowd. The wall trembles, struck again and again with the force of at least two dozen enraged hollow-heads. They pound their open hands against the corrugated metal of the barricade, shove hard against the chained door. Some in the rear start to climb over the ones in front, pushing them down onto the asphalt.

We hold our ground, waiting, hoping that they won't find a weakness in the wall or manage to climb to the top, where there is enough room to squeeze through if you don't care about cutting open your belly. Even worse, too much pressure on the barricade may cause it to collapse.

Their tactics change a second time, part of a pattern we've seen over and over again. Six, then eight, pull away from the main group and rush for the far end of the tunnel. They know about the road above, and how to climb the shoulder to reach the much weaker chain link fence. They aren't planning; their reactions are more instinct than intent. But the effect is the same. At least Pritchard is prepared. Arrows and bolts punch into the climbing hollow-heads, forcing them back, killing two of them immediately. Two rifle shots make quick work of another. Its head bursts open in a cloud of red and it falls to the pavement below, skull splitting apart like a dry watermelon.

Penetrated by the deaths of their fellows, the last of the hollow-heads' glacial determination transforms into a burst of squirming, lunging, lurching. The barrier shakes beneath my feet and I shout to the others to remain steady, to hold their fire. I rest my trigger finger on the guard to keep my nerves from taking a shot I don't need to waste as the hollow-heads finally reach the arrow slits in numbers. Someone loses a crossbow to a lucky grab, and moments later I hear a groan of metal and the snapping of rivets as a section of the wall pulls away from the rest. It bends and falls down on top of the hollow-head who dislodged it, but there are three more to take its place, squirming into the opening. An older member of the sweep team, Jake Yanic, loses his weapon to a rough swipe of a hollow-head's arm, then falls back against the railing of the upper platform. I hear myself shouting for support from the other end of the wall, but Jake's nearest companions are already trying to pull him away from his attackers. I look for an opening to shoot, but there are too many of our people in the way.

Jake lets out a muffled scream. A spray of blood splashes against the corrugated wall and the man collapses in front of his teammates, who lose their grasp on him as the hollow-heads drag the body toward the gap in the wall. Even as they attempt to leave with their prey, they can't resist biting chunks of flesh from his neck, hands, and face—any exposed part of his body. The revulsion hits me like a punch: the thought of being torn open by dull, carious teeth is sickening. And the knowledge that Jake is dead is only marginally tempered by knowing that he won't have to suffer the loss of his mind.

More of the hollow-heads try to come through the breach, but they press up against the ones trying to drag Jake back, giving the rest of the sweep team an opportunity. A stream of bolts and arrows splashes against the frenzied cannibals, but the chaos prevents most of them from hitting in the places that matter: the neck and chest. My rifle is a bolt-action Remington 700 SPS with a four-round magazine; it won't do me any good at this distance, against this many. I drop it to the platform and draw my pistol, which I've kept with me since the Coast Guard: a SIG P229 with a fifteen-round magazine, loaded with .40 S&W hollow-point rounds that I salvaged from a house a few weeks after the collapse. I shout for the sweep team to get the hell out of the way, and they scatter off the platform, jumping down to the rough gravel below to continue the fight from the ground.

I ignore the clanging of my moral alarm as I raise the weapon and aim for the nearest hollow-head, which is chewing on Jake's left cheek as it yanks his arm toward the gap. The first shot rips across the back of the hollow-head's neck, severing the spinal cord. The next shot is higher, into the chest of the naked, dirt-covered man behind her.

The third shot paralyzes an ancient-looking hollow-head as it climbs over the two dead ones. It falls on its face, arms reaching out to pull itself toward me. The fourth shot obliterates the skull. Shots five and six, and my ears are ringing, and two hollow-heads fall from the platform, where they are killed by the sweep team.

I take shot seven on the move, going forward, pressing the advantage of my intelligence. These creatures don't react like human beings: they don't flee at the sound of gunfire. They don't retreat when their numbers are thinned. If they have any thoughts at all, they are of nothing but meat, and they don't care which meat is hurting them the most.

The hollow-heads below, on the outside of the wall, are now too few to climb up to the gap. The last two that made it onto the platform die as quickly as the others, but I use up four more rounds to make it happen.

A shriek rattles in the tunnel, catching me by surprise and making me feel the exhaustion of the fight more strongly. But it's a distant shriek, farther out, and it redirects the attention of the remaining members of the horde below me. Like a cargo ship turning in harbor, the crowd of hollow-heads veers away from the wall. They wander off to follow new prey, slow and shambling, leaving us to our grief and ambiguities.

Carpenters arrive with a temporary replacement panel for the wall, and I climb down from the upper platform to give them space to work. The smell of blood saturates my senses. I need to step away from this place.

No longer focused on the immediate problem, however, I am again confronted with tonight's unexpected reality. Luther is waiting for me at the bottom of the ladder, blood drying on her hands and arms. "It gets worse," she says after I tell her about Jake Yanic. "I went to the apartment. Someone broke in and must have left just before I got there. It didn't look like anything was taken, but there was a struggle in the bedroom. The girl was stabbed. I got the docs in there, but she was already dying. I left them working to save the baby, if they could, but—" She shakes her head, arms akimbo, trying to process what she saw. "Jesus fucking Christ, Chief."

The full moon accuses from its height, a reminder of our inadequacies. The streets are dark except for the silver reflections. In ten years we lost more than just the ability to keep the lights on. We lost our way, our methods, the expanse of knowledge beyond what is passed on from mother to daughter and father to son. I can hold the wall and fight off the monsters at the gates, but no one had the chance to teach me how to be a detective. Everything I know I learned from books.

"Get Pritch and Kloves out with the sweep team. I want them checking every inch of fencing and barricade. They're looking for a point of entry, or an exit."

"You're thinking someone from outside killed them," Luther says, recovering herself. "Someone from Dahlonega?"

"That's the most likely explanation," I say. Owen wanted to believe that no one would come after him and the girl; he wanted to convince me, at least, that we weren't putting ourselves at risk by letting Abigail stay. But clearly he was wrong. And yet—the way that he was wrong doesn't make sense. Wouldn't their pursuers want to bring them back? I could even understand Owen's murder as revenge for taking away the prize. But Abigail's death doesn't fit. If her abuser was anything like men I've known—men like my father—she was a trophy, and her unborn child was a possession.

"I'm going over to where Owen was killed," I continue. "By now it's probably useless, but the apartment will keep, assuming you secured it."

"Yes, and I'll get the perimeter check started," Luther says. "Kloves is still at the hospital. I'll grab him on our way to the north end."

Luther leaves me to my frustrations. The remains of Jake Yanic's body have been brought down from the upper platform, laid on the sidewalk, and covered with a tablecloth that quickly soaks with his blood. I don't want to be here when Jake's children arrive. After Lukacs, I don't yet have the strength to cope with another mourning. I'm thankful for the excuse to go.

Blood still stains the parking lot blacktop where Owen fell. A dozen neighbors have gathered in the street to hear news of the tunnel incursion, trampling any evidence that would point to the shooter. As if conspiring with them to make Owen's death completely indecipherable, a light rain begins to fall. Blood washes into the gutter. Standing by the skull-decorated door of the bar, I close my eyes and try to reconstruct the moment that I came outside.

Owen fell forward, shot behind his right ear. I didn't see it happen, but the aftermath was unmistakable. That put his shooter down the street, possibly as far as the small plaza at the five-point intersection. I walk the distance, scouring the ground for a dropped casing. By the time I reach the plaza, the futility of the whole situation has made itself sufficiently convincing, and I kick at one of the planted trees. I am too tired, and it is too wet and dark. Like a petulant child, I sit down hard on the curb and shield my face with my hands.

This is on me. I should have been more careful. I should have taken precautions. Abigail should have been able to trust the safety of the Little Five. Death by hollow-head is a fact of life, and we understand it. We accept it, and protect against it, as a community. But when it comes to Owen and Abigail, matters are different.

I can't plead to my conscience that I was unaware of what could happen. Abusers don't let go: letting go is a loss of control. You can run as far as you want; hell, you can join the Coast Guard and take a post eight hundred miles away to start a new life with people who love you. But they don't let go, and they don't let you forget, until they are erased entirely from the world.

She was just a child.

I force myself to stand again, to focus the remainder of my energy. If Owen and Abigail's killer is the same person, he wouldn't have needed much time to get from the sidewalk to the apartment above the bar. There is a staircase around back, unseen from the street. Fleeing the scene wouldn't have been difficult, either.

Behind the row of old shops on the southbound side of Moreland is the road that goes straight south to the Inman Park enclave. Between our two communities is a nine-foot tall fence with what passes for barbed wire strung along the top. It exists not to keep our two neighborhoods apart, but to prevent an overrun of hollow-heads if one of our "fortresses" should be compromised. There is a gate, locked on both sides, that is just as formidable as the rest of the fence. If the killer escaped that way, Luther will find something: damaged wire, cut fence, broken lock. Something. She has to.

I climb the back stairs to the apartments above the bar, dreading what I will find in the unit that Owen and Abigail shared. Luther has scrawled on the door with a permanent marker in her messy script: "Crime Scene Do Not Enter." I allow myself to laugh at Luther's idea of securing the apartment, but she really didn't need to do much more than this. There is only one other apartment above the bar, occupied by Cassidy and therefore empty at the moment.

The door jamb has been broken, forcing the lock off the strike plate and splintering the wood around the knob. I push through into a small but comfortable living room. The tranquility of the space belies what happened here, but once I can see the hallway, the truth makes itself known. A long streak of blood is spread across the hardwood floor, from the back bedroom to the threshold of the living room. Following the trail leads me to where the attacker found Abigail in bed. Blood soaks the disheveled sheets and the particle board bedside table is in pieces on the floor. A hunting knife rests among the pieces, the handle just as red as the rest of it.

I step back to the doorway, only in part to preserve the evidence. The blood is dark in the silver light of the moon shining through the window, and my head swims in the quantity of it. Maybe it was quick. I can hope it was quick. But maybe she had time to think about her unborn child. Maybe she had time to pray that the baby would live.

My stomach heaves momentarily, but I catch it in time. I swallow hard and lock the memory away.

The killer could have come here first, then gone down to the sidewalk to shoot Owen after discovering that he wasn't in the apartment. Luther's implication that Abigail was killed after Owen depends on how quickly she bled out. If the girl was still alive when Luther found her, it certainly doesn't seem likely that she was the first one attacked. There is too much blood here.

And whoever killed the girl would have been covered in it. If I had been able to search the area just after it happened, I might have been able to catch him. The shrieker's interruption served as such a perfect diversion that I begin to wonder whether the killer had an accomplice: someone to bait the hollow-heads at the appointed hour, to distract me and my officers from the hunt. I feel like I've fallen into a trap I saw from a mile away. I shout a curse into the empty room and retreat to the kitchen.

I find a cloth to wrap the knife, hoping that I will be able to recover fingerprints from the handle. There are no courts, no juries, that will need such a thing as evidence, but if we do find the person responsible, I want to be sure. I set the knife on the couch near the front door and am about to go back into the bedroom when I notice the edge of a piece of paper protruding from under one of the couch cushions.

The small stack that I pull from its hiding place is a collection of pages covered in text from a mechanical typewriter. The contents are gibberish: random letters arranged into six-letter combinations, suggesting a secret code. Some of the pages look like lists, with two "word" pairs that could be names. Nothing about them is recognizable or decipherable.

I sit down and shuffle through the papers, conceiving of too many wild theories on no evidence, while the simple fact is that if these pages had anything to do with the deaths of Owen and Abigail, it's unlikely the killer would have left without them. They were too poorly hidden, too easily found. Unless the killer didn't know what they were or had no time to retrieve them.

The living room's mundane cleanliness, its antiseptic emptiness, is trying to convince me that nothing is wrong. That tonight hasn't been brutal, exhausting, and that I don't have to be responsible for solving two murders. I could use sleep, and the couch is comfortable, but I cannot forget what Marilyn said about the stripes of the whip on Abigail's back. She deserves every ounce of my energy. I fold the cipher pages into my back pocket and head across the street to the hospital.

Marilyn is seated at the front of one of the examination tables, her back to me, rubbing her eyes. On the table in front of her is Abigail, looking nothing like she did when I saw her here the first time. Her body is uncovered, and I feel an instinct to turn away, but I force myself to look even more closely. Abigail's belly has been cut open, adding to the blood that is caked on her face, chest, and arms. A pair of bloody latex gloves is piled inside-out on the floor near her feet, and to her right is another examination table with the tiny, lifeless body of Abigail's son.

The doctor, hearing the door shut behind me, turns and stiffens. Her clothes and hands are covered in drying blood. She may have been crying, though I don't expect she would admit it. Like all of us, she wasn't prepared for the sudden changes in the world around us, but by the time the Little Five had become my first post as chief of police, she had already distinguished herself as a steel-nerved medic. Then Dr. Colbart, her mentor, died. So it was Marilyn who was there with me when I lost Jeannie, and for a time afterward it was Marilyn who comforted me in my grief. But that was years ago now, when we both still felt young and had to find ways to express our feelings of overwhelming inadequacy—pretending we still had that luxury.

"Oh, hello, Chief," she says, as if using the words to bring her back to reality. Once again not using my name. "She was

49

unresponsive when we got to her room. We brought her back here as quickly as we could, and I performed a Caesarian section, but the baby was stillborn. He died in the womb. The man, Owen, is in the cold room in back. Jake's there, too."

The news exacerbates my fatigue, and I slouch into a chair to accept the quadruple tragedy. Marilyn starts to clean up at a water barrel in the corner, scrubbing the blood from her hands. "Do you know anything yet?" she asks with a commiserating tone.

I am grateful, at least, for her empathy. "No. Luther and the sweep team are checking the fences. I can't see one of us doing this. No one here even knew them yet."

Marilyn nods, but adds, "Wasn't Abigail starting to make friends with Regina's kid? She didn't really talk much, though, did she? I suppose it makes sense. You think maybe—?" She comes to my side and squeezes my shoulder with a half-cleaned hand. "Never mind. You look like you need sleep."

"I should wait for the fence check." I look at the bundled knife in my hands, wishing the world were different.

"I think I still have some coffee in the cold room. We haven't gotten anything since the last time the Covington traders were here, so it's not going to be very good, but it'll keep you awake."

"That sounds wonderful," I say, and watch her walk away, her dreadlocks swaying behind her. I don't recall her returning from the cold room; the next thing I know, the roosters are crowing again.

DAY TEN, 7:00 A.M.

The northern half of the Little Five is almost entirely converted farmland. The Carter Center, which we now use as the mayor's administration building, is at the far corner of the field that used to be a scenic wooded area, complete with foot and bike paths. A single row of houses separates the fields from the perimeter fence, and on the other side of the boundary are block upon block of abandoned homes. The road that used to be the main artery for this section of Atlanta, Ponce de Leon, is still clogged with the rusting cars and buses that survivors tried to use to escape the city. The Virginia Highland area to the north was overrun immediately after the collapse and has never been reclaimed, except for the occasional raid in the early years that depleted its drugstores and restaurants of everything valuable. A little farther north is the Emory University campus, which, for many years, was probably the most secure place in the city. But they ran out of food eventually, and some combination of internal division and external interference led to the whole zone being burned to the ground three years ago.

In other words, virtually everything from I-85 in the west to Clairmont Road in the east belongs to the hollow-heads. So it makes no sense at all that I am standing at the corner of Moreland and Freedom Parkway, an intersection in the middle of the corn and bean fields, staring at a damaged section of the perimeter.

Someone has cut the fence with wire cutters and bent the chain links outward, leaving just enough of a gap for a man to squeeze through. I squat down and look at the cut links, hoping to find some trace evidence—a piece of fabric, some blood—but there is nothing that I can see.

"This is an exit route," I say, leaning into the opening. "You didn't find any other gaps?"

Luther, who came to me this morning in the hospital shortly after the roosters woke me, rests an arm against the fence a few feet away, eyes half closed. Her voice is grainy with fatigue. "I've got some people checking again now that it's light. We didn't find anything earlier, but we didn't exactly have the best conditions." She crouches beside me at the opening. "Do you think the bastard is gone?"

"I don't know," I mutter, realizing that my uncertainty is only going to get worse the longer I investigate this. In the beginning, I was given this post because I was the only person in the Little Five with any law enforcement experience, however unconventional it was. And at first, that wasn't much of a problem. In the early days, before we had fully secured the perimeter, our problems were straightforward. Hollow-heads at all hours, looters and poachers mainly at night. There were a few people in the Little Five who really didn't belong, and eventually it was my job to firmly ask them to leave or throw them out if necessary.

Anticipating that someday I might need the kind of knowledge that would have come with time and study for advancement in the department, I hunted for books on law enforcement procedure and forensics. But none of those books were a decent substitute for experience—for having to go through investigation after investigation, stumbling your way at first, then getting to the point where you're not reaching foolish conclusions and making your partner look bad.

Having Luther, Pritch, and Kloves has been a relief, but also a burden in its own way. At least I went through the Coast Guard Academy. I had to teach my officers everything I knew, while at the same time trying to figure out what it was I needed to know myself.

Luther was the hardest to work with, and many times I came close to regretting the decision to let her put on the badge. After all, she didn't endear herself to me on our first encounter. Her father came to me seeking help for his troubled daughter: Adelaide would sneak out of the Little Five at night and take pot shots at hollow-heads with an air gun she'd found. When I confronted her, she said she was trying to clean the world. She even tried to shoot me, that first time.

Mr. Luther insisted that she was a good kid. It was only the collapse that had changed her, and the death of her mother at the hands of looters in the first days after the oil soured. A few days before he was killed outside the perimeter, Mr. Luther begged me to take her under my wing. She needed structure; she needed a purpose. Something that would let her vent her rage against the unfairness, the injustice, of our lives. He made me promise. So there really was never any question of her washing out.

When I finally let her join up and made this a four-person team, she was barely eighteen, so of course there were going to be problems. But there were also advantages. She hadn't seen enough cop shows, for one thing, which meant she didn't have any bad habits to break. Her young brain sucked in information like a vacuum cleaner, making her a much quicker study than Pritch or Kloves. She just didn't like taking orders or doing things the way that I told her to. She thought she had better ideas, and on the rare occasion that she was right, it only reinforced the impression.

Eventually, though, she grew up. She didn't have much choice.

"Someone could've gotten in over the wire, maybe." Luther stands again, looking up at the barbed wire running across the top of the fence.

"Maybe," I say, not moving. "But that's not exactly quiet. And you checked the wire, didn't you?"

"Of course, Chief. We didn't see anything laid over it, or any scraps of anything that got stuck. But like I said, it was fucking dark out."

We've had climbers in the past. Desperate people trying to get to safety, charging the fence and throwing blankets or jackets over the wire to keep from cutting themselves. They don't know that they can come to the tunnel wall to ask for sanctuary or assistance, so they try to get in without us finding out. But the fence makes a lot of noise when you're wriggling against it, and it's a lot higher than it looks from a distance. We find blood and body parts on the outside ground from time to time, where hollow-heads caught the climbers before they could reach the top. We don't like that it happens, but we don't have an alternative. The only way to keep out the hollow-heads is to keep out the survivors, too.

"You should get some sleep," I tell her. "I'll come find you if there's anything new."

Luther gratefully accepts the plan, and I leave the guard with a promise that I'll be sending someone to repair the fence soon. That task will fall to Vargas, who has the tools and materials for fence building.

The biodiesel enterprise began in the back of a camper van, looking for all the world like a meth lab, after Vargas and Braithwaite had cobbled together the equipment and ingredients they needed to make their first few batches of alternative fuel. I'm sure that someone, somewhere, figured out what happened to all the

54

petroleum. The last rumor, reported as fact by desperate people, was that someone had released bacteria that did something to the oil—ate it, changed it, no one knew. It seems as good a theory as any, and certainly no one here is in any position to say otherwise. Whatever it was, it was never fixed, and the scramble to replace the world's petroleum infrastructure wasn't quite fast enough. The pandemic arrived too quickly after the oil ended.

What remained after the collapse were the people like Vargas, Braithwaite, and Abraham. Young turks who found that they were now the primary bulkhead between survival and chaos.

In the beginning, Braithwaite was able to make batches of fuel in one-liter containers. Vargas spent most of his time converting motorcycles, cars, and even lawnmowers, replacing the gaskets and other parts that could be corrupted by biodiesel, until he had a small fleet of vehicles of various shapes and sizes. These he would trade to other groups for food, equipment, and supplies.

Eventually, the two biodiesel hackers accumulated enough equipment and chemicals to expand to a converted shipping container brought west from the Port of Savannah. They began trading with farther flung communities for vegetable oil, both new in bottles and the used sludge. In exchange, Vargas converted their vehicles, and soon there was a biodiesel network centered in the Little Five that supplied and supported most of the greater metro Atlanta area. It only grew from there.

Today, the Little Five has a functioning tractor and three short-range Volvo station wagons. Most of the biodiesel is used to run generators—which, in turn, supplement the solar generators that provide the bulk of our electricity—and to fuel the vehicles that allow other communities to trade with us.

The parking lot that Braithwaite likes to call her "farm" is occupied by rows of oil barrels and a building on the south side constructed out of the shipping container. Braithwaite does most of the biodiesel manufacturing herself, though she occasionally enlists the help of others involved in the Little Five's power company group, while Vargas focuses on rebuilding and maintaining the equipment and vehicles.

I find him working on one of the Volvos in the small square of the farm that still serves as a parking lot. The son of a diplomat, he was born in Honduras but moved to the United States when he was ten years old. He enrolled at Georgia Tech a year before the collapse and never made it back to Virginia, to his mother and stepfather. He likes to believe that his parents escaped to Honduras before all the good fuel ran out. I've refrained from pointing out that this doesn't put his parents in a very good light.

Vargas's English is lightly accented, but I've become so used to it that I rarely notice it now. Twenty-eight years old and one of the brightest men in the Little Five, he has played a crucial part in keeping our community alive and comfortable. I know that I can rely on him for anything I need; he tells me often enough. So when he sees me approaching, he stops tinkering with the Volvo, wipes his greased hands on his pants, and says, "What do you need today, Chief?"

I explain the situation, and Vargas stands up, shaking his head. "This is about Owen, no? Belinda told me. Terrible thing. She's in the lab and won't come out. But what can you do? You have to let a person grieve in her own way."

For a moment I'm surprised, though I shouldn't be. Vargas and Braithwaite have been together for as long as I've known them, and for as long as I've known them, they've not been exclusive partners. I suspect this is more her idea than his, but he goes along with it amiably enough. They both have had many lovers over the years, some fleetingly, others for much longer periods. Most of their polyamorous adventures have been with other members of the power company, but from time to time, Braithwaite at least has taken lovers from outside that social circle. I wasn't aware that she was sleeping with Owen, but it certainly isn't out of character for her.

Vargas packs up his tools, following me over to the shipping container. He opens a small shed attached to the main building and retrieves a section of chain link fencing. I knock on the door to the container, but Vargas tells me to enter uninvited: Braithwaite isn't going to answer. Inside, I find her hunched over a workbench, her flowing skirt billowed out around her chair, her bare feet propped against a crossbeam despite the cooler temperature within the lab. With one hand she mixes the dark brown contents of a large piece of lab glass, while in the other she holds up a half-eaten sandwich. She doesn't look up when I enter, focusing instead on a book on her table.

I call her name, and still she doesn't look up. "Good morning, Chief Edison," she says. Braithwaite's personality is usually a cyclone, energetic and chaotic and exhausting. Even if Vargas hadn't said anything, I would know that something is wrong.

"Ernesto says you and Owen were close," I say, trying to be circumspect. Braithwaite isn't the sort of woman who needs to be coddled, or demands censoring, but right now she isn't behaving like Braithwaite.

"I enjoyed his company," she says. She uses the crust of her sandwich to turn the page of her book and push her glasses higher on her nose. "Is there something you wanted, Chief?"

The shipping container is poorly insulated, and the solar panels lining the top and upper sides don't help with heat retention during the colder months. I feel the chill of the room in my lungs. The air is tangy and strange, as it always is, with the colliding smells of biodiesel and body odor and food.

"When was the last time you saw him?"

"Last night," she answers without delay. "We were here. That's the deal."

"What 'deal' is that?"

"My deal with Ernesto. The apartment is for us. For everyone else, we use the lab or their place. But the girl was there. So it had

57

to be here." She gestures toward a bare mattress at the far end of the container lab, then takes a large bite out of her sandwich and stops stirring her concoction. She sniffs the contents of the glass, turns another page, and remains completely uninterested in my presence.

"When did he leave here?"

"Couldn't say," Braithwaite says. "I had to get home, so I told him to lock up when he left."

"Was that such a good idea? Leaving him here alone?"

At that question, Braithwaite finally deigns to turn toward me. She sets down the remnant of her sandwich, and I catch a glimpse of the fire that usually flickers on her face. But only a glimpse. "Afraid that he might steal trade secrets? Come on, Chief, don't be ridiculous. There's nothing here to steal. Nothing I can't replace. And even if he was going to grab some of my things, where would he take them? Why bother?"

Defensively, I respond, "Just because it doesn't fit your logic doesn't mean no one thinks that way. Not everyone is as smart as you are."

Braithwaite slouches in her chair, chastised, and I regret what I said. It was the voice of a callous parent. A voice I've always been careful not to use. It comes too easily.

More thoughtfully, she says, "He said he wanted to sleep a little before going home. I didn't think there was any harm in it. But he must've changed his mind because I wasn't home more than twenty minutes when—" She takes a deep breath, and when she continues, her voice is higher, softer. "Oh, fuck, Sam, what happened?"

"I'm trying to find out," I answer. "I have to ask these questions. They're important. I don't mean to be—"

Braithwaite shakes her head. "No. It's all right. I understand. Thank you."

"Did he say anything to you about Abigail?" I press. "Did he tell you anything about her that he didn't tell anyone else?"

"I don't know. He didn't talk about her much. I don't think he cared for her, really. He said the baby wasn't his. He was very clear about that: the baby wasn't his."

"What time did you leave the lab?" I ask.

"Midnight, maybe? I don't know. I remember hearing—it. The gun. I figured it was a hollow-head at the wall. And then in the morning I found out what happened."

"How did you meet? Did he seek you out, or was it just by chance?"

Braithwaite furrows her brow the way she does when she's working on an engineering problem. "I guess it was by chance. He was talking to Ernesto about the cars. I showed him the process we use for the diesel, but I don't think he was interested in that. If that's what you're asking."

"I suppose it is," I tell her. "I'm sorry. About all the questions, and about Owen."

"It wasn't your fault," Braithwaite says. "You didn't know."

"I still don't know. But I'm going to find out, if I can."

I leave the container lab and head back toward the fence. As I am passing Cassidy's Bar, I see Mayor Weeks flagging me down from across the street. I am impatient to be on my way, but Weeks has a habit of being too insistent to ignore.

"Do you know what happened?" he asks, falling in step and allowing me to continue walking. My update is brief; I don't have much more than what he could have gleaned from Luther or one of the people at the bar.

"You don't think anyone else is in danger, do you?"

I tell him I haven't really considered the possibility. I've worked under the assumption that Owen and Abigail were the only targets. He seems satisfied with the answer and grips my shoulder momentarily. "Don't overwork yourself, Chief. The Little Five is still safe in your hands."

And then we part ways, Weeks heading off toward his office in the old Carter Center while I continue to the north perimeter.

Watched over by the sweep team guard, Vargas is using a portable welder to marry his patch to the chain link fence. The generator supplying power to the welder is making its loud, unpleasant chugging sound. Hollow-heads have begun to investigate the noise, coming down from Ponce de Leon in pairs and threes.

The sweep team guard, a midthirties former bank teller by the name of Tenclin, is a master with a bow. Standing on the middle rung of a metal ladder so that his shoulders are above the fence line, he watches the approaching groups down the length of a nocked arrow. His weapon of choice is a Strother compound bow that he has owned since he was sixteen.

"This was your idea, wasn't it?" I call to Vargas while he welds. I point to Tenclin.

"No reason to add unnecessary noise," he calls back.

I unsnap my holster and draw my service pistol. I don't like that it's becoming a habit. "You're joking, right?"

"That's done," Vargas says, flipping up the visor on his welder's helmet. He starts packing away his equipment. "They will not stop coming just because I have turned off the generator. They already know we are here."

Of course, he's right. The dozen hollow-heads that are coming down the middle of the road didn't even pause when Vargas shut down the generator.

Knowing what could happen, I scan behind them for signs of other hollow-heads lying in wait. If Tenclin or I take out one of the hollow-heads in front, that will start a cascade of frantic running. I will be very grateful if they don't have any friends joining them from the main road.

"There are too many for just one bow," I tell Tenclin. "You won't get all of them before they hit the fence."

"Yeah," he admits, "you're right. I'll get maybe six or seven." Then he smirks. "Where's your sense of fun?"

"Were you there yesterday? Did you see what they did to Jake?"

Tenclin wipes the smirk off his face. "Sorry," he says quietly and sets his bow on the top of the ladder. He draws a Colt Anaconda from his belt.

"Better. Don't shoot until they come within twenty yards. If there's a horde on Ponce, I don't want them spotting their dead and turning this way."

We wait. Most of the time, hollow-heads move as slowly as a normal person on a Saturday morning stroll. The difference is that they don't look at anything except their intended prey. They stare at us as they approach, silent, footfalls barely registering on the pavement. Tenclin's undisciplined finger is agitating against his trigger.

"Come off that ladder," I remind him, "or you'll break your neck when the recoil knocks you off."

He steps down, rattling the metal, and the hollow-heads react by focusing on him instead of Vargas. They converge like mice heading for a sewer drain. Some are better dressed than others, making it easy to identify when they were lost to the rest of humanity. The ones in polyester hospital gowns got sick first or were in hospitals when the disease struck. Some are in tattered pajamas, suggesting they were taken at home in the early days when people still thought the pandemic was the flu. The ones that are dressed well knew what was coming but couldn't bring themselves to end their lives.

I track their distance relative to an arbitrary paving stone about twenty yards out. Then, when the curious hollow-heads are inches away from my order to shoot, there is a loud shriek from the trees near Ponce de Leon. I shiver at the sound, but that sensation is followed by a wave of relief even before the hollow-heads fully react. First, they halt, listening for more. The shriek comes again, and they turn toward it, now facing away from us and shambling back toward the main road. I relax my grip and step back from the fence.

We wait a minute while the hollow-heads make their way back to Ponce de Leon, just in case something else on our side catches their attention. But nothing does, and I'm grateful for that. A second breach in as many days would exhaust the sweep team and make us vulnerable to a third.

"That was lucky," I mutter. I tell Tenclin he can head back into town, with a stern reminder that archery is not a hobby. Then I give Vargas's generator a friendly kick. "No bows, Ernesto. You know better. Unless you're bringing a whole line of archers, they're just not fast enough."

"Yes, yes," he says, collecting his portable equipment. He starts back to town, and I follow.

"How is she?" he asks. "You talked to Belinda, no?"

"It's hard to tell," I admit. "Has she not said anything to you?"

Vargas shrugs. "Like I told you, I haven't really seen her since yesterday afternoon when she told me she was going to be with Owen. Since then she's been holed up in the lab. So I am giving her space."

"Wait," I say. "You haven't seen her since yesterday afternoon? She didn't come home last night?"

Vargas laughs, offering me a wink and a grin. "I wouldn't know. I wasn't there, either." Then, more seriously, he adds, "Well, she must have. The bed was slept in. I like to keep it neat and square, but she can't be bothered. You know how she is. She's messy with all of her toys."

Vargas looks wistful for a moment. I am reminded that Braithwaite is more adventurous than he. "I'm sorry you're in the middle of all this," I say.

"I love her," he says with a shrug. "We all do."

It would be simpler to think that Owen may have been killed by one of Braithwaite's other lovers—an act unrelated to the things Owen needed to tell. That kind of murderer would be so much easier to track down than one dealing in codes and secrets and conspiracies. But the power company has been a carefree polyamorous community for years now. None of them would consider him a threat.

Yet as I walk back to my station, I see Micah Abraham approaching me with agitated speed. For a moment I consider that I may be wrong after all: as the head of the solar power group, he was one of the first of Braithwaite's partners apart from Vargas, and he has shared her bed on and off for years. Heavy-set, with dry tanned skin from constant work outdoors and only the fragmentary remains of a head of hair, he comes at me like a rhino. His yellow headphones and ancient cassette tape player jostle on his belt, slapping against his thick thigh.

Sweat stains the front and armpits of his tee shirt, and I can smell his body as he thrusts his hands against my shoulders, shoving me into a tree in the middle of the plaza. I tense up and almost strike back. I hold a hand up to separate us, but he doesn't go for me a second time.

"What's wrong with you?" Maybe there are motives among Braithwaite's lovers. The surprise of his attack is rearranging my thoughts.

"What is it now?" he growls loudly, his voice pitching up under the fat in his neck. Others in the street stop what they're doing.

"Micah! What are you talking about?"

He stabs a meaty finger in the air behind him, pointing at a nearby rooftop covered with solar panels. "I saw you from up there, going into Belinda's. I know you talked to her. Are you going to throw her out, too? It's always the same with you, Edison."

"This doesn't have anything to do with that," I tell him, but I don't expect him to listen. It has been years, and Micah still holds a grudge against me for forcing one of his partners out of the Little Five. He hasn't trusted me since then, and I haven't tried to repair the breach.

"It has everything to do with that," he insists. "We always got under your skin. And now you think she killed that stranger."

"You're not—" I start, but he doesn't let me finish. He telegraphs his punch with all of his excess weight, making it easy for me to

63

slip under, and my own follow-up just below his solar plexus takes the wind out of him.

He stumbles back, gasping, and I grab a fistful of his stinking shirt. I want to do more. I'm angry enough. "And it's always the same with you, Micah. The last time we danced this dance I had to lock you up for a week. Is that how this goes again?"

He pushes at me, separating me from his shirt, but doesn't take another swing. "It should've been you that got shot," he mutters as soon as he has his breath back. "Don't take her away from me, too."

The pathetic whine in his voice softens my aggravation. Like Braithwaite, despite his age, he's still something of a child. "What makes you think I'm going to take Belinda away? All she's done is answer questions. Despite what you think, I don't care what any of you do. It's not my concern. What is my concern is how you're behaving right now. Making threats. But I'm going to be charitable. I'll assume I'm the only target of your frustration and that you're not going to throw a punch at anyone else. Don't make me regret it."

Kloves stands in the entrance to the station, watching us. I wave him over and tell him to escort Micah home and to make sure he doesn't come back out until he's calmed down.

"Are you sure, boss?" he asks.

Abraham was the same way the last time. Fury and frustration, then a long stretch of silent hurt, until he came back to himself, and the only lasting mark was his mistrust of me. "He's not really going to do anything he can't take back. Are you, Micah?"

"Fuck you."

Kloves nods, as if that were confirmation. He grabs Micah by the elbow and urges him away. I watch them leave and try not to let Micah's accusations echo in my head. I made the right decisions. Most of the citizens of the Little Five backed me up. But the power company has always been insular and a little strange. Young and smart and necessary, they think of themselves as a world apart from everyone else. I don't let it get to me.

Luther is asleep on the cot in the cell when I arrive. I sit down at my desk and unfold Owen's cipher papers, pretending to make heads or tails of them. I must be making too much noise, because Luther wakes and gives me a sour look as she comes out of the cell. She makes a point of yawning deeply before she says, "Any progress?"

"Apart from getting Micah to throw a punch at me? If you want to call that progress." I shrug, not bothering to explain. "I need you to go back to the apartment," I tell her. "See if you can find anything there that looks like this." I hand her the cipher pages.

"Where'd this come from?" she asks. She shuffles through the sheets, wearing the same expression I must have had when I found them.

"Have you seen it before?" I ask.

"No, I don't think so. What is it?"

"I don't know yet. They were under a sofa cushion. I think Owen was planning to bring them to me. I'm guessing they had something to do with Dahlonega. There's probably nothing else up there, but it's worth checking."

Luther hands the pages back to me. She sighs her frustration and spins on her heels. "All right. I'll ransack the apartment again, and maybe something will turn up."

Again, I am alone, staring at Owen's papers until I can build up enough inner motion to get back on my feet. I've been approaching the problem from Owen's side; now it's time to look into Abigail. That path leads me first to Phoebe Weeks.

At this time of day, Phoebe will be with her mother, making sandwiches for people unwilling or unable to make their own meals. When I step outside the station, Regina's stall is being inundated by a good third of the Little Five's population. Some of them continue to titter about my fight with Abraham, probably embellishing it into some Wild West tale of revenge and avarice while they conduct their business in the street. Others whisper about Owen and

Abigail, though few ever spoke to them at length, and their interest is only morbid curiosity. Most, however, share stories about Lukacs and Yanic, weaving an oral history of the Little Five that we will pass on to the next generation.

Early on, the original leaders of the Little Five tried to rebuild the local economy according to sensible capitalist principles, but it didn't work. Our second, successful attempt became something that one of the power company people likes to call a "low resolution simulacrum of society." Everyone fits into his or her own niche, helping to maintain the Little Five however he or she can best contribute, and all of our needs are taken care of by those who can best do those jobs. Farmers, doctors, cooks, bakers, police, and so on. All the roles and responsibilities that an eight-year-old conceives of as the depth and breadth of adult reality.

To this we added our interactions with the outside world: the enclaves, communes, and neighborhoods that appeared around us. Some of them are urban, like ours, but most are rural. We provide bread, biodiesel, and the technical and mechanical expertise of our power company. Others provide food that we can't grow ourselves. From the Inman Park enclave and some others we receive the vegetable oil and cook fire leavings that Braithwaite needs to make her fuel.

All of this together explains why Regina is such a popular figure in the Little Five and elsewhere. There is a semi-truck operated by a town in Clayton County that we keep running and filled with biodiesel, and once a month that truck delivers bushels of wheat flour and other necessities for Regina's baking empire. Most of her bread then finds its way around Georgia, which in turn brings in more fresh and used vegetable oil. It would not be an exaggeration to think of Regina as one of our post-collapse commodity barons, alongside Braithwaite and Vargas.

Her daughter has grown up steeped in this responsibility. I find her handing out sandwiches to a couple of children at the front of the growing line, her bright smile shared with everyone equally. But I've known her since she was seven years old, and that smile is the one she learned from her stepfather, the mayor. She knows how to make her eyes look like they are a part of the expression, and right now her eyes are smiling much too hard.

I bypass the line and come to the side of the stall where Regina is removing bread from a basket. She notices me after a few moments. "Come around the back," she says to me just above a whisper, and I go to the entrance flap of the covered stall. She joins me outside, arms crossed as if to ward off the implications of my arrival. "Tell me you know who did it," she says, and her tone refuses to accept anything other than a yes.

"I need to speak to your daughter," I say, holding the flap open. "I need to ask her some questions about the girl."

"It's not a good time." Regina takes a step back, blocking my way, though I haven't moved any closer to the stall. "I'm trying to keep her busy. Talking to you isn't going to help. She doesn't know anything."

"You can't be sure of that, Regina."

"Yes, Sam, I can. They're just—" Regina turns her head, shutting her eyes as if deflecting a painful memory. "Abby was a child. I told Phoebe not to go prying into things that weren't her business."

"Can you at least tell me if Abigail said anything to you? Was she worried that someone would follow them here?"

The iron in Regina's eyes flickers and fades when the question sinks in. "So it wasn't one of us," she says softly. "Thank God."

"I didn't say that," I point out. "We don't know yet. But I'm guessing she didn't say someone was after her."

"Well—" Regina begins. Now she steps fully out of the stall and closes the flap. "Look, Sam, I don't want to get my daughter involved in this."

"If you know anything at all," I say. "It's important. You know it is."

"Well, you know Abigail spent a night at our place, before they got their own. They were in Phoebe's room, and it was late, and I was checking on the girls. And I overheard them, the two of them.

"I hate to say this, Sam, but sometimes it seems to me that you were lucky. With Jeannie, I mean. The world wasn't exactly lollipops and sunbeams before, but back then there were buffers between the good things and the bad. I made it my business to get in between and to try to do good. But I saw my share of horrors, and you know what it was like. It's so much harder now. You try to shield your child from the worst of it, but in the end, there's still that fence. Closed doors and high walls that we need to keep out the nightmares. And when something gets through, what can you do?

"I heard Abigail talking about what happened to her. She didn't go into detail, but she talked about the men. Phoebe knows enough. She's sixteen, and I taught her. She understood. I so desperately wanted to interrupt them, but I couldn't. Abigail deserved not to feel shame. Responsibility. It was as important that I let her talk as it was important that I protect my own daughter. Does that make sense?"

"Yes," I say, helping her to continue. I don't want to hear it; I don't want to remember Abigail's scars. But this is important, and this isn't about me.

"She also talked about when she was little." Regina's eyes shimmer with held-back tears. "She didn't know where she came from. She said she was 'taken.' That's the word she used. 'Taken.' And then she ended up in Dahlonega, though that wasn't the first place she went. They brought her to a house where she was both the housekeeper and—" Regina sighs hard through a tensed throat. "Owen was the man's brother. Owen didn't live there. He didn't know. Until later. But that's not the important thing. The way Abigail was talking, I got the impression—Sam. Sam. I don't think she was the only one."

DAY ELEVEN, 10:00 A.M.

During the night, nightmares came, dragging memories of Jeannie with them. In them, she was four years old, as she always is. She remains as she was when she was happy and safe. My heart aches more thinking of her that way, but I prefer it to the memory of her last hours.

There was a time when I considered being a parent again. But maybe Braithwaite and Vargas and the rest of their crew have the right idea. Permanence is no longer something that we should expect, or perhaps even desire. We lose more than we gain. I certainly don't begrudge anyone the desire for children, even in this place, but there is hardly a life to be had here. We are only biding our time before the end of all things. The hollow-heads will inherit the earth.

And perhaps they should. A society that permits its adults to abuse its children, simulacrum or no, does not deserve survival. It never did, but we were too invested in our own self-absorptions to know it. We kept ourselves entertained, living for weekends and vacations that only served to remind us that we were trapped in lives not of our choosing. We didn't understand just how unprepared we were to extricate ourselves from the filaments and knots of our pointless greed. When the old world's human monsters came, we did our best to ignore them. And when the new world's monsters came, we died.

And so our children died. Jeannie first. Now Abigail. And yet she, Abigail, died at the hands of an old monster: a remnant of that greed-drenched world we left behind us. We thought that by keeping to our boundaries, by not making an effort to fully restore the corridors between this community and the next, we would be safe. But we were already infected by another disease. Infected by human nature. From time immemorial, with no cure to be had. I wanted to believe that we'd changed, that our terrors made us better than we were. Maybe that was naïve. I should have known. I do know. There is no escape but survival.

Someone killed Abigail and Owen because they represented a hell that was meant to be kept a secret. A hell that is worse than the one filled with hollow-heads and shriekers: a hell that chooses its victims deliberately. And Abigail was not the only one. While we go about our lives here in the Little Five, a machine has been grinding up children into fodder for an insatiable perversion. Thinking of it makes me sick to my stomach, but ignoring it only makes me feel guilty. So I focus on my piece of the problem. I don't really believe that pulling a single thread will unravel the whole tapestry, but maybe I can lie to myself for a little while longer.

◆

A few hours after dawn, word comes over the shortwave radio that the trading group from Clarke County is arriving, in a caravan of two biodiesel U-Haul trucks and a battery-powered University of Georgia campus bus. Vargas brings this to my attention so that I can coordinate the sweep team to be ready for their arrival, but there will be little for me to do once the traders arrive. The mayor's office handles the operation, since Weeks set up most of the trading network in the first place. I handle security, but we've been doing this so long that everyone already knows how best to avoid a hollow-head incursion.

So, while the rest of the Little Five succumbs to the excitement of a trading day, scouring away the recent violence, I take the opportunity to walk the perimeter myself, as if my own eyes might find something that all the others haven't.

The only conceivable place where someone might safely come across the perimeter without leaving a trace is at the gate between the Little Five and the Inman Park enclave. But when I arrive, it is as I expected to find it: locked with the locks we have always used, and no sign of anyone having tried to pick them or cut the cables. As with every other section of perimeter fencing, there is a cluster of barbed wire topping the gate, and it hasn't been disturbed.

My counterpart in the enclave is doing his own sweep of the Inman Park perimeter when I arrive, and he strides over with that combination of friendliness and suspicion to which I have become accustomed from that side of the fence. Mikhail Barkov has heavy-lidded eyes and a face that struggles to produce any expression other than bored resignation, but he is more talkative than the other peace officers over there. "Chief Edison," he says with his strong Russian accent. His palm rests on the butt of his hip-holstered weapon, adding to the impression of a swagger. "Is there a problem?"

"Have you had any strangers visiting in the last week or so? Not a trade group, but an individual, or maybe two or three?" I wrap my fingers around portions of the chain link.

Barkov shrugs. "No one I think. But the gate has been closed, yes? No one coming or going this way except for the usual ones. For

the trading. But not strangers. Hey, didn't that one—Adelaide—
yes, I like her. Adelaide was checking the fence yesterday. Or was
it the day before that? I don't remember. That's what Andrew is
saying. Are you having a problem? Trespassing?"

"No," I say, taking a deep breath. "Some people were killed. I'm
hoping it was someone from the outside. They made a hole in our
fence, but I'm pretty sure that was a distraction. I thought maybe
they'd tried to flee through Inman Park. But that's looking like a
dead end."

"I will ask Andrew," Barkov says. Andrew McGovern is what
the enclave calls their "primary lookout." A nice phrase to describe
a sniper. McGovern spends his days atop the buildings of Inman
Park, watching the hollow-heads, shooting when he gets bored. I
suspect they've given McGovern that job because he's not the sort
of person you want wandering the streets, looking you in the eye.

"Thank you, Mikhail." I release the chain links and flex my fingers. "And give Amy my regards," I say, referring to Barkov's wife.

"You know I will do no such thing," he says, barely managing
a smile. "She would leave me for you given half a chance. You
Americans. Always so—what is the word?"

"Fickle?" I answer, laughing.

"Experimental," he replies with another smile. But his face
quickly regains a serious expression. "Americans. Russians. It is the
children who will teach us how to think now. Some of them do not
even know what a Russian is. Or an American. Do you remember
when all we could say was 'globalization?' Now it is something else.
Ah. Well, Chief Edison, I am talking again. I will say hello to Amy,
and you will say hello to someone who likes me, yes?"

"No one likes you, Mikhail."

Barkov laughs and wanders off, whistling to himself.

By the time I return to the main street of the Little Five, it is
almost noon and the caravan is well ensconced on Moreland, north
of the tunnel wall, which had to be swung aside to let the trucks and

bus pass. The citizens of the Little Five clamor around the dozen or so visitors to gather news and gossip from the other communities.

The leader of the Clarke County trading group is a gray-haired man in his late sixties, wearing dark sunglasses, by the name of Norm Ithering. I spot him coordinating the delivery of two heavy plastic barrels of some substance or other onto Braithwaite's hand truck. Mayor Weeks is speaking to him, but when he notices me he interrupts his conversation and waves me over. Mr. Ithering shakes my hand when I come into range.

"You remember Sam?" Weeks asks the older man.

"I do," he says. "Semper Paratus," he adds: the motto of the Coast Guard, "Always Ready." I am reminded that Mr. Ithering was once a member of the Army Reserve.

"Yes, sir," I reply. "It's good to see you again."

The mayor says, "Norm is leaving two of his people here for a few days, to help Belinda and Ernesto with some of their equipment. I don't know all the details, but you know how it is. Geeks and their toys. I thought you should know, considering—"

Weeks doesn't have to finish the sentence. I nod, understanding. "As long as they check their weapons at the door," I say, "it's not a problem for me. I'll let Luther and the others know, so there isn't any confusion."

"Yeah," Ithering mutters. Then, a little more loudly, "I'm sorry to do this to you, Sam."

"It's not an inconvenience. It's Belinda who's going to have to herd the cats, not me."

I look over to the farm where Vargas is talking to two men beside one of the Volvos: a black man with a bald pate and a Hispanic man with curly hair. Neither one looks a day over twenty. "Is that them?" I ask, pointing in their direction.

"Sure is," says Ithering. "It's Randall and Banderas. We'll swing back around in a week and pick them up. If they cause you any trouble, you let me know, all right?"

"Of course," I say, watching Braithwaite maneuver a blue plastic barrel over the curb. One of the men with Vargas, the one who must be Banderas, scurries to her aid for a moment, helping to keep the barrel from tipping onto the pavement. Braithwaite takes a step back, looking momentarily spooked.

I take my leave and wander over toward the farm. Vargas introduces me to Randall and Banderas, but the three of them seem to be more interested in the engines of the Volvos than they are in talking to the Little Five police chief. So I leave them to their work and move on to help Braithwaite with her supplies.

She thanks me for the assistance, then adds, "I'm sorry if I was irritable the other day. It's one of those things."

"You don't have to explain," I tell her. "You're doing better today?"

"Absolutely. I've been waiting for this stuff for a while. It's easy enough to get potassium hydroxide. That's really just quicklime and potash, which isn't hard to produce. Just burn down a few forests, and you can make as much of the stuff as you want." She laughs abruptly. "See, you use a lime kiln to make quicklime out of limestone. Then you slake the quicklime to make calcium hydroxide—"

She continues, but I tune her out until she finishes, "We can't do it all ourselves, here. So we trade for it."

"What do we give them in exchange?" I ask absently, my attention more on the visitors in the street.

"In exchange?" Braithwaite stops, sets down the hand truck, thinking. "Fuel, obviously. Parts, if they need them. The usual." She tips the hand truck back again. "We got too big to be able to do it ourselves. I didn't have a choice but to make these deals."

I help her lift the hand truck over the container threshold. "Well, I'm glad you found a solution," I say, not wanting to go down the rabbit hole of Braithwaite's strange guilts. I don't need to know the inner workings of her moral economy.

Phoebe intercepts me as I step into the street. "Can I talk to you, Chief?" When I stop, she adds in a whisper, "But I don't want my parents to know I'm talking to you. Mom would squirt blood from her ears."

I lead Phoebe across the plaza to the station, taking care to stay in the crowd, away from the mayor's eye. We go inside, and I offer her my chair, which she takes as if it belonged to her. She props her feet on the edge of my desk. She is putting up a good front, that's clear enough: Phoebe doesn't usually display such a brash, nonchalant attitude, especially with me.

"What did you want to talk about?" I ask.

"I know you were talking about Abby yesterday, with Mom. I could hear you."

"What did you hear?" I sit down on the edge of Luther's desk, watching the girl's expressions for signs of dissembling.

"I don't know. It doesn't matter. Did she say anything about Abby's scars?"

"She didn't, but I knew about them. What did Abigail tell you?"

She shrugs, protecting herself with a manufactured ignorance. I resist the urge to push her to answer directly. Instead, I say, "There was something specific you wanted to tell me. Am I right?"

Phoebe nods. "She told me that they were probably going to leave soon. She said Owen didn't think it was safe."

"Wait," I start, surprised. "He said it wasn't safe? Why? Was Owen afraid of someone in particular?"

Again the shrug, but this time it's an honest one. "I don't think she knew." Phoebe wraps her arms across her chest. "It's not like Owen was creepy or anything, but he made me nervous. I only saw him a couple of times, at the apartment, but he was always so intense. Typical scout, I guess."

"What?" I say, taken off the track. "What do you mean?"

"You know how they get. Twitchy and weird after they come back, for days, like they're still looking over their shoulders."

"Did he say he was a scout, or are you just guessing?"

"He didn't have to say anything," Phoebe answers, slightly offended. "And I'm not just guessing. He had a map."

❖

"He had a map," I repeat to Luther, standing in the doorway to Owen's apartment. "But you're sure you didn't find anything yesterday."

"I didn't find anything," she says, the petulance in her voice almost like Phoebe's. "I know how to do my job, Chief."

"I'm not implying anything," I say. "She said it looked like a scout's map. A real pre-collapse map, with pencil marks all over it. She didn't get a good look at the marks, but she said there were numbers and circles. He was marking locations."

"Were we marked?" Luther asks, stepping inside. She goes through the motions of checking every cupboard and drawer, though I can tell she doesn't have her full attention in it. She's done this already, and she's confident she didn't miss anything.

"Phoebe didn't know. But if it was a map of Atlanta, and if Owen was a scout, was that why he was here?"

Luther pulls the shade off the lamp on a side table and looks within. "You don't scout places where people are. You scout where they're not. For food and supplies."

"You're right," I admit. "They don't go into towns. They don't try to cross fences. That's just asking for trouble. And you don't bring a pregnant girl with you on a scouting trip."

"If he was expecting to leave, maybe he was making a route. Planning it out." Luther throws up her hands. "I don't see anything here. Really, Chief, I checked every corner. There's no map."

I enter the apartment, heading for the back bedroom where Luther found Abigail's body. The scene is as I left it, with blood soaking the sheets and streaked across the floor into the hallway. Luther stays back, arms folded, leaning against the open door, while I lift the mattress and feel underneath. Then the dresser and the remains of the side table. Luther's irritation at my distrust of her is beginning to show in the set of her mouth, so I halt and nod with defeated approval. "Agreed. There's nothing here."

But a sudden realization snaps my attention back to the dresser. Then to the closet, also empty. "There's literally nothing here," I say. "Not even clothes. Not even the clothes she was given after they arrived. She was dressed when you found her?"

Luther's expression is quizzical, and her answer delayed. But she recovers as she realizes what I've just noticed. "Yes," she says.

"She slept with her clothes on?"

Luther says, "It's not that strange, is it? If you're on the run, or if you're twitchy from being on the road for who knows how long, wouldn't you sleep in your clothes, too?"

"Except our assumption has been that she was attacked in the bedroom by someone who broke in. But a break-in is loud. And the kind of person who sleeps in her clothes is the kind of person who wakes up when something nearby makes that much noise, like a gunshot from the street below. She wouldn't be caught in the bed. But if she knew her attacker, maybe she let the person in. Fully dressed. Killed, fully dressed. And then the killer could take his time making the place look like it was broken into. The blood in the hallway isn't from when she was taken out. It's from when she was brought in, after she was attacked."

"But she didn't really know anybody here," Luther says. "Maybe she knew Phoebe, a couple others. And what the fuck, Chief? Why would any of us want to kill a pregnant girl?"

We go down to the street as the trading excitement is dying down. The trucks have been moved off Moreland and the bus is parked in the biodiesel lot. The dozen-plus visitors are mingling with the people of the Little Five, making conversation and finding partners for all the drinking, dancing, and screwing that will happen after the sun goes down tonight.

Knowing that later the place will be too busy to hear myself think, I step into Cassidy's Bar, so I can get something to eat and continue to grind the gears in my head.

I sit down at the bar and the bartender offers me fresh meat from the traders. Grilled turkey with a side of tomatoes, green peppers, and olives. I lose myself in the meal for a time. After I finish, I pull out Owen's encrypted pages and flatten them on the bar. The top sheet is the most daunting: the six-letter combinations are spread across from margin to margin, daring me to decipher them.

The man beside me leans closer when he sees what I've spread out. Leonard Furness is a long retired high school math teacher, so I'm not surprised at his curiosity. But his reaction rocks me back in my seat. "Now that's a strange thing to see all these years later. That looks like a numbers station transcript. Where did you get it?"

Before I can answer, he slides the top sheet closer to himself. "These aren't printed. They're typewritten. How old are they?"

I admit that I don't know, but they must be new: the paper is fresh enough to have come from a recently opened ream. "You said it looks like a numbers station transcript. What do you mean?"

"Well, that can't be right, can it?" Furness puts the page up to his nose, scrutinizing it in the weak light. "There aren't any stations left. They went down when everything else did. And what would be the point?"

I don't have an answer to that. If I did, I might have seen what is now so obvious. Numbers stations were the conspiracy theorists' unicorn, back before the world changed: they existed, but they were rare and inscrutable. I knew about the ones sourced in Cuba, in part because they were once or twice mentioned during briefings about drug interdiction. Beyond that, though, they had little to do with me and my work, so I paid no attention to them.

But I knew what they were, or at least what was claimed about them. They delivered messages via unsecured radio transmissions, using virtually unbreakable encryption that had its origins in the

Second World War or earlier. Communication between spies and the handlers in their home countries could be made out in the open, and no one listening in would be able to understand a word of it. But with the death of nations after the collapse, any spy still alive was out of a job. Furness is right: there shouldn't be any numbers stations still broadcasting.

His fingers move across the pages as if he were reading three lines at once. "Maybe it's not a numbers station. Of course, it can't be. It must be passed from person to person by hand. But then why in groups of six? There's no point to the groups of six unless you're doing on-the-fly manual error correction. And six is right on the edge. Most of the ones I used to see were four or five."

"Can you read it?" I ask, trying to disrupt his momentary solipsism.

"Of course not," he says, looking up, responding just as I expected him to. "You'd need the companion text that goes with it." Furness takes a drink of weak beer and licks his lips with a distant memory. "Back when I was in the CIA—did you know I was CIA? Hah. Those were the days. One of the problems they gave us was to help secure the communications of our spies in Russia. One-time pads were my favorite because they are information-theoretically secure. Perfect secrecy. Unless you have access to the companion pad, it is one hundred percent impossible for you to decrypt those pages."

"So I'm wasting my time," I mutter.

"Those pages are either the ciphertext or the pad of a one-time pad system. As I said, they're information-theoretically secure. What that means, though, is that in practice they're not as useful. You have to have a key that's at least as long as the message. Without computers to do the heavy lifting, making a random pad long enough for what you've got there would take days. More likely, though, the pad is an existing text, probably a book, shared between sender and receiver. Something rare that you won't be able to identify or find in any old bookstore."

Then, rolling back to his first question, Furness asks, "Where did you get them?"

I begin to explain the events of the last two days, until Furness interrupts with a new question: "Who was this Owen person?"

I start to offer what little I know of him, then realize that's not the question Furness is asking. I stop, look at the remains of my food, and say, "I don't know who he was. Was he a spy? I don't think that's why he was here in the Little Five. But that map he had and this encryption. Was he looking for someone?"

"He only had these pages?" Furness asks, sliding them along the counter. I say yes, but he doesn't respond for a while, only scrutinizes the gibberish again. "It all looks like one side of the encryption. But you can't do anything with just one side. You need both the key and the ciphertext. You have to add the letters together from the two sides to get the plaintext message."

"Owen couldn't have used it as it is." I slap the table with an open palm. "Damnit. This has to be important. But how, if it's unreadable?"

Furness thinks it over, then nods. "I suppose he could be a courier, but the security of a one-time pad depends on certain practical considerations. Numbers stations used them because you only had to worry about the physical copy of one side of the system. Anyone who knows anything about cryptography would know never to send ciphertext to a recipient in physical form. Using a courier isn't smart. Did he have a shortwave radio with him?"

I shake my head. "No. Those aren't very portable anymore, without batteries, and those are rare now. You'd need a hand crank or a generator, and he didn't have—anything like—"

The rusty gears finally begin to turn, scraping against one another and stripping the cobwebs from my eyes.

"You've thought of something?" Furness asks.

"Braithwaite," I whisper. "The trading network radio. Belinda Braithwaite has a shortwave. It's the only one in the Little Five, and it's right there in the lab where Owen was on the night he died."

◆

My chest burns with the embers of missed opportunities and the fear that I'm coming to the answers too late to do me—to do anyone—any good. Walking the Little Five at midday is not usually so precarious, so fraught with potential.

"What are you thinking?" Luther asks after I fill her in at the police station. "You can't believe Vargas and Braithwaite had anything to do with it."

"I don't know yet," I admit, drawing her across the plaza to the biodiesel farm. "If Owen got to the shortwave while he was with Belinda and sent a message out, where did it go? Did someone pick it up and discover where he was?"

Vargas and two of the trading group's mechanics tinker with the engine of their bus while the rest of the group waits aimlessly by the trucks. Luther and I intercept Braithwaite as she is crossing the street to the old gas station where the underground tanks of biodiesel fuel are kept.

"I have some more questions," I tell her, but her acknowledgment is terse and dismissive. When I press on, she stops and turns in frustration.

"I don't have time for this right now. Can't you see we're busy?"

Luther takes the woman's arm gently, preventing her from continuing on her way. "Are the trucks fueled up? Yeah? Then you can spare a few minutes. The boys are going to be a while, I'm sure."

Braithwaite's mouth twists into a brief scowl at Luther's phrasing. Braithwaite is as good a mechanic as her partner. She turns back, focusing on the empty gas station market, but she doesn't move. Her jaw clenches, releases, and she says, "It has to be quick."

The biodiesel farmer's distraction doesn't abate after we've gone into her lab for privacy. My insistence catches her attention, briefly, but once inside her lab she starts pacing back and forth along the narrow center aisle.

"You have a shortwave radio," I begin, hoping to give some context to my questions.

"It's not mine," Braithwaite interrupts. "It's Ernesto's. He knows how to fix it. I don't."

"You and Ernesto have a shortwave radio," I amend, remembering that Braithwaite prefers precision. "I don't care whose it is. That's not important. Focus, Belinda." I allow a long breath to temper my impatience, then continue, "How many people have access to it? Who uses it?"

"No one," she says with a scoff. "I mean, we're in contact with the trading network. But no one else uses it. And it stays in the lab. The only people who come in here are the people we let in. But what does that have to do with anything?"

Luther, moving in from the door to stand between us, rests a hand on Braithwaite's shoulder, as if to calm her down. "You didn't let Owen use it, did you? He didn't know about it, right?"

Braithwaite seems to startle at the questions. "What? No, of course not. It's in a cabinet. Over there." She points to a sturdy wooden armoire behind me, at the very end of the lab, against the wall. "It's not locked, obviously, but as you can see—"

"You wouldn't know it was there if you didn't already know it was there," I say, nodding. "How is it powered? Is it on a generator? Or solar?"

"It has to be solar," Braithwaite says, less agitated. "We don't know when to expect transmissions, so it has to be on all the time. A generator would waste fuel. It's wired to a panel on the roof of the lab. The cable goes out the back and up. You can see it there, in the gap between the cabinet and the ceiling." She gestures dismissively.

"Then it's not completely hidden. Someone could have found it if they'd been looking."

"Why would he be looking?" Braithwaite asks. Her agitation has risen again as quickly as it sank, and she is resting a hand on the door handle as if to tell me that her time is increasingly precious.

"Owen was here for a week before he died," I explain, "and in that time it would have been easy for him to learn there was a radio in the Little Five, and who had it. We all know it's here, in the lab, if not in that cabinet. There's no secret about it. If he wanted to transmit a message, he would have to get in here." Now it's my turn to gesture dismissively, at Braithwaite. "It's also no secret that you take lovers. That was his way in. And we're all friends here. We've all gotten used to leaving our doors open at night, as the saying goes. You keep the lab locked to the outside, but it never occurred to you to make sure he was outside before you left for the night."

"It was twenty minutes, at the most!" Braithwaite says abruptly.

"That's more than enough time," I say. "Owen found the transmitter, used it, and then went back to his apartment. And after that, he came looking for me. Now, I don't know what he was planning to tell me, but I'm guessing it had something to do with this."

I brandish the ciphered pages, which seem to catch Braithwaite's attention the way laser pointers used to catch cats.

"What?" she says. "No. I don't know anything about that."

The tone of her voice, previously so dismissive, has shifted to something resembling defeat. And my heart sinks as the possibility I had so feared crumbles into dust. Because it is eminently clear that Belinda Braithwaite is lying.

"Belinda. No." Luther is as surprised as I am.

"These weren't Owen's papers, were they?" Perhaps I can salvage this; perhaps it isn't worse than I feared. Braithwaite may not have had anything to do with the man's death, even if she was keeping secrets that the stranger uncovered. Or if she was involved, there may have been justification. Perhaps he was threatening her. I want to believe it. Not only for myself, but for the Little Five as well. We need her.

And yet—Abigail. What possible reason could she have for hurting Abigail?

"These weren't Owen's papers," I repeat. "They're yours. You've been sending encrypted shortwave transmissions, like a numbers station. He must have known that there was a station here in the Little Five, and he tracked it to you. He found the radio. He found this key, this one-time pad."

"That's not a key. I mean, it's not what you think," Braithwaite says, stepping back. As she shifts I realize I've been getting closer, my fingers tightening into fists.

"What do I think?" I blurt out, feeling my face get hot. Anger masks the sting of her betrayal. It takes all of my effort not to shake her. "I don't know what the fuck is going on here. Did you kill him, Belinda? Did you kill Abigail?"

"No!" she shouts back, gripping the door handle more tightly. "I did not kill Owen. I did not kill the girl. I would never do that! Sam. Jesus! I would never do that. You don't understand. You can't—Look. I have to go. It's important." She wants to flee. I can see it in her eyes and in the tension of her wrist. But she is looking at the gun in my holster. The gun I've never used on a rational human being.

Her glance works like a slap. She is afraid of me. Maybe she should be; maybe she deserves it. But I don't like the way it makes me feel. I give her a few inches of space. I tell Luther, "Open the cabinet. See if there are any more papers there. Anything else encrypted."

I can hear Luther moving behind me. Pulling at a drawer that must be locked for all the racket it's making. "Tell me what's going on," I say to Braithwaite.

"I can't," Braithwaite says, her tone approaching a whine. Her eyes well up, and her forehead creases with tension. "I swear, Sam, I can't. But I have to go. Please. It's important."

Luther pounds a fist against the armoire. "There's a locked drawer, Chief."

"Where is the key?" I demand.

"I can stop it if you let me go," pleads Braithwaite.

"Stop what?"

I hear three engines come to life outside: the bus and trucks belonging to the trading group from Clarke County.

"No," Braithwaite wails. "No, no, no. No!" As she shouts the last word, Braithwaite yanks hard on the door handle and propels herself down the stairs and across the lot.

After recovering from my surprise, I follow, with Luther on my heels and reaching to her holster. Braithwaite runs for the lead truck, knocking past Vargas as he looks up from stowing his pile of equipment. I shout for Braithwaite to stop, to explain herself, but she ignores me. She climbs onto the truck's driver side runner and pounds on the heavy metal door. The truck's brakes squeal and the vehicle lurches to a halt. The window comes down and Norm Ithering, still in his dark sunglasses, leans out just as I arrive behind Braithwaite.

"Please, you can't," she pleads, most of her breath still gone.

Mr. Ithering looks back toward Vargas. "Is there something still wrong? I thought we got it fixed."

Braithwaite turns away from the door, grabbing my coat. "They're taking one of the children," she shouts, directly into my face. "Addie, explain!"

I look to my deputy. "Do you know something?"

"No, of course not," she answers curtly. "She's raving."

Perhaps it's Luther's tone, or something else that Braithwaite has just now realized, but the result is the same: she seems to break, going quiet and still. "Check the trucks," she says. "You have to check the trucks."

I want to ask why, to pretend that I can't already guess. But Abigail was taken from her family, and she wasn't the only one. Belinda is afraid that it's happening again.

"Mr. Ithering," I begin, sidestepping Braithwaite and Luther to climb onto the truck's runner. "I'm sorry to do this to you, but I need to check the trucks, and the bus."

Ithering tenses. "She's gone nuts, Edison. We're not taking anyone's children. You know us!"

I wave over to the people at the tunnel wall, signaling for them to close the gate, and once they begin to comply, Ithering realizes I'm serious.

He turns off his engine, cranks the truck's parking brake. "All right. But be quick about it."

He comes down from the cab and informs the other drivers that they're going to be stuck here a little while longer. Soon the street is quiet again, with no rumbling engines to add to our agitation. Some of that rumbling is replaced by complaints from the trading crew, but there is a longstanding rule in the trading network: you obey the laws—and the law—of the communities you enter, or you don't come back.

Ithering unlatches the gate of the forward U-Haul and throws it up, letting in the midmorning light to reveal boxes and bags of food and equipment. While Luther keeps watch over Braithwaite, who is now sulking on the curb, Pritch and Kloves inspect every large container in this truck and the one behind. I check the bus and come up as empty as the other two.

The whole process takes less than fifteen minutes. It would be quicker still, but I insist on at least making a show of thoroughness, no matter how unlikely it is that Braithwaite is telling the truth. At last, I slap the side of Ithering's cab door, the signal for him to get out of the Little Five. The tunnel wall swings open and the three vehicles depart as quickly as such minor behemoths can.

The spectacle has gathered a quarter of the community along the sidewalks, some of them here to watch the inspections, but most come to gawk at Belinda Braithwaite. Once my immediate obligation is done, Mayor Weeks strides across the street to me.

"What the hell is going on?" he asks.

I glance over at the biodiesel farmer. Vargas is with her now, and the two are in some heated discussion, with Luther nearby. It seems neither of the two cares that the police can hear every word.

"I'll know more soon, and I promise I'll give you a full report. But right now, I think it's best to get Belinda into the station and start untying this knot."

"This is about the strangers," Weeks says.

"Yes. But like I said, there's still more to figure out."

I start to turn away, but the mayor touches my shoulder. "You can't really think Belinda is involved."

Throwing my usual familiar rapport with the mayor out the window, I reply, "I'm certain of it, sir. And it goes beyond just Owen and Abigail. But I shouldn't say more than that for now. When I have something to give the mayor's office, I will."

"This could be a mess, Sam. You know that. Belinda's not just anyone. You have to be absolutely sure."

Aloysius isn't referring simply to Braithwaite's status in the Little Five, as if that conferred to her some kind of persuasive power, or meant that the mayor would have to tread lightly. He's talking about the biodiesel. He's reminding me that responsibility for dismantling one of our community's primary resources will fall on my shoulders.

"I know."

DAY TWELVE, 4:00 A.M.

I spent the next few hours trying to interrogate Braithwaite, but after her initial break, she stopped talking to me. I considered bringing in Vargas to make her use her words, but Luther shook her head and said, "He was only making things worse. He doesn't know what the fuck is going on, not any more than we do, but I'm pretty sure he believes she did it. He was not being very nice."

So I spoke to Vargas alone, then the rest of the power company. I sent Luther to speak to Micah Abraham, who would only have seethed at me. It became clear that none of them were involved in whatever Braithwaite's been doing. Each one was more horrified than the next. Eventually I came back around to Braithwaite, but she still wasn't talking. She paced her cell and ignored me even when I felt myself starting to yell.

By early evening I gave up, took dinner from Regina, and fell asleep at my desk after telling the others to go home. I awoke twice, just long enough to see that Braithwaite was still awake and still pacing back and forth, talking to herself, her bare feet making no sound on the cold concrete floor.

Unable to sleep a third time, I considered what I knew and what I suspected. Braithwaite must have been the one operating the Little Five numbers station, transmitting the texts that Owen later took from the container lab. To what end, I still couldn't guess. Then I remembered the map that Phoebe saw and put the two facts together: perhaps it was a map of the receivers—and possibly transmitters?—of the encrypted messages. If that was the case, then it meant Braithwaite was part of a much larger network of numbers stations and, for lack of a better term, "spies."

At four o'clock in the morning there is a pounding on the locked front door and an animated shadow on the other side of the frosted glass. I get up with a start, shake free the fugue of my deliberations, and unlock the door. Aloysius and Regina Weeks tumble into the small station, Regina out of breath and Aloysius appearing sterner than usual. Before Regina has a chance to compose herself, the mayor says, "Phoebe hasn't come home tonight, and her friends haven't seen her."

Now, at last, Braithwaite reacts. She bolts to her feet and grabs the bars in front of her. "No, that's not possible. You checked the trucks!" She bangs the meat of her palms against the bars, making noise, and I wave a hand at her angrily to shut her up.

"When did you last see her?" I ask. I reassure myself: the Little Five is too small for anyone to go missing for long. Unless Phoebe went beyond the perimeter, she must be somewhere in the neighborhood, and no one living here is stupid enough to go beyond the perimeter.

"This morning," Regina says, trying to push past me to get at Braithwaite. "What did you do?" she howls at Braithwaite. "Where is my daughter?"

I block Regina from getting to the other woman. "I'll talk to her," I say, and my glance at Braithwaite is meant to tell the engineer that I'm not going to let her stay quiet this time. "You two, go wake up Luther, Pritch, and Kloves. Have them rouse the sweep team. We'll find her. I promise."

Regina doesn't want to leave, but her husband takes her gently by the arm and coaxes her out of the station. I blink away the last of my sleep and go to the cell where Braithwaite is gripping the bars hard enough to whiten her knuckles.

"I can't tell you anything," she says before I open my mouth. "I don't know anything. I don't know where she is. It's the truth."

"But you knew she was going to be taken," I point out.

"No. Not her specifically. But I was threatened. One of the Clarke people. Randall. He came to the lab, and he knew everything. Of course, he did. He said if you or anyone found out what—" She stops short, releases her grip on the bars. She hugs her chest and takes a step back, as if worried that I might assault her. I realize that my palm is resting on the handle of my belt knife.

"What did he know, Belinda? What the hell have you been doing, and what did Owen find out?"

"I relay messages. That's all. I swear to God. I receive transmissions from one of the other stations and repeat them on a different channel. You have to understand. Sam, they didn't give me a choice. We needed phenolphthalein. They had it. This was the only way they'd trade."

"Who are they?" I ask, setting aside the rest of her explanation for the moment.

"I don't know. But they're in different enclaves, towns, everywhere. The man who came to me at the beginning said he could get phenolphthalein for me. Phenolphthalein and just about anything else I needed. And we needed a lot." I can see Braithwaite becoming righteously defensive as she talks, her body language shifting. Tension building in her shoulders, but not out of fear. This is resolve. Justification. "We couldn't have made the biodiesel farm what it is today without their supplies. You think we got everything by giving them bread? Jesus, Sam. We needed what they were offering, and this was the only way!"

"You never asked questions. You never wanted to know what you were transmitting. You never considered that they'd have you over a barrel. You'd do anything for the next fix. This never occurred to you?" She is about to reply but I bang my hand against the bars. "Don't answer that. There isn't time. You're going to tell me about Owen and Abigail, and you're going to be held responsible, but not now. Right now, you're going to tell me what Randall said."

Braithwaite takes a deep breath, exhales it slowly. There is a glistening in her eyes that supports the truthfulness of her remorse—or whatever it is that she is feeling. Even now it is difficult to tell.

"I told him what happened. With the strangers." Braithwaite examines the floor. "With Owen and Abigail. He wanted to know what Owen had told. I said I didn't know. I told him I was sure he'd said nothing. You were lurching around in the dark." A fleck of spite in her eyes, and a weak tremble of momentary triumph, and she continues. "He said my assurances weren't good enough. I had to try harder to keep things quiet. He said that if anyone else found out, he was going to select one of the girls. That's the word he used: 'select.' And then he said, 'You'll never see her again.' He told me to think of her as a hostage. Keep it quiet, and she'd be safe. Let it out, and she'd be 'selected.' But you figured it out before I could fix things."

I resist thinking about that word, "selected," because I know what it's likely to mean. It means Abigail. It means abduction and torture and rape. The bite of a hollow-head would be solace, after that.

Selfishly, I tell myself it isn't fair. This shouldn't be my weight to carry. I got out; I got past. Why do I have to be the one to remember the bruises, the split lips, the broken bones? Or the pang of loss, the confusion, the impotent despair? I shouldn't have to relive all of that. Not here. Not in the dark.

But it does me no good to turn away. It does Phoebe no good. I lost a childhood, and I lost a daughter. But if I abandoned my post now, I wouldn't be a victim anymore. I'd be a monster. The Little Five is my responsibility. And while there have been people I could not save, and there will be others I cannot save down the road, another child will not be one of them.

So I bring my tired mind to bear. If we had any sense that Phoebe was missing, it stood to reason that we'd inspect the trucks. Randall and Banderas wouldn't take her out of the Little Five that way. Still, it's not safe to assume that the Clarke County traders are innocent. Getting out of the Little Five isn't difficult, but staying alive outside without transportation takes one's full attention. An unwilling fellow traveler creates numerous problems best avoided.

So Phoebe's abductors may have planned to meet up with the Clarke caravan well out of view of the Little Five. But there are few safe routes out of town. There are too many hollow-heads to the north. The southbound tunnel is too well guarded. A route to the east wouldn't be impossible, but too many of us are out there working the fields at all hours. That leaves only one good option: Inman Park. That neighborhood is directly connected to the Belt Line trade zone, a long and narrow—and easily protected—two-mile stretch that could deposit Phoebe's abductors well out of our reach within a matter of hours.

I check my holster, my sidearm, my knife. "If she's lost to us," I say, facing Braithwaite, "I swear I will feed you to a hollow-head."

I don't stay in the station long enough to listen to her reply. The moon is veiled by an overcast sky. No street lamps or car lights, only the flickering glow of lanterns in windows and the odd incandescent bulb powered by battery-stored bicycle and solar power. My magnet flashlight doesn't make much difference. Doors open around the plaza, and the members of the sweep team converge on the station, brought out by Pritchard pounding on windows. Even some of the power company join the search, defying the brush with which Braithwaite's betrayal has painted that group.

Still buckling her belt and tucking in her shirt, Luther arrives with Kloves. Her M1903 Springfield rifle is slung over her shoulder, bouncing against her hip as she comes to a halt in the street. "Give me something to do, Chief," she says, flexing her fists. "I'll wring that woman's neck if I can't find anything else to do with my hands."

My first instinct is to take everyone to the Inman Park fence, but I have to be sensible. I instruct Kloves to coordinate most of the sweep team to do a building by building search of the Little Five, on the unlikely chance that Randall and Banderas have holed up with Phoebe somewhere in the town. I tell Pritch to remain at the station and keep an eye on Braithwaite and send runners out if any news comes in.

I hook a finger at Luther. "You and I, we're going to Inman Park. We'll take Olsen, Wright, and Robb from the sweep team." I set a quick pace, jogging toward the gate.

There are always two locked chains on the gate between the communities. One of the locks belongs to the Little Five, the other to Inman Park. To pass through the gate one must have permission from both sides; otherwise, at least one of the locks stays shut. The Little Five keys are held by the mayor, Pritchard, and myself, while the Inman Park keys are held by our counterparts on that side. I don't recognize the locks that are now in place on the chains: someone must have cut the old locks and replaced them with ones that would pass a casual inspection.

I resist the urge to have Olsen recall the sweep team searching the buildings. There is always a chance that this is a ruse, to make it look like Randall and Banderas left the Little Five, the same way the breached fence was a ruse. I test the locks to confirm that they are secure, rattle the gate for a moment, and then remember Andrew. The enclave's primary lookout will be watching from atop one of Inman Park's tall buildings, off to the southwest, scanning the perimeter with binoculars. Even if one of the perimeter guards doesn't come by soon, I can count on the sniper to alert someone.

And yet, while that solves our immediate problem, it poses another: if Phoebe's captors came this way, how would they have avoided the sniper's gaze? If they intended to slip into the enclave and disappear in the crowd, they would have to avoid being spotted on their way in. Cutting the locks instead of picking them might save time, but there could never be a guarantee that Andrew wouldn't swing his gaze in this direction at any moment.

"I'll go get cutters," Luther says. She turns to leave but I hold her back.

"That'll get us in, but we've still got trouble," I say, rattling the gate again. "They may have had help on the other side. Possibly the lookout. We need to be careful."

Owen uncovered a hidden network of some kind: that's the best explanation for the map Phoebe described, and it accounts for Braithwaite's numbers station. She was hiding her role in plain view, after a fashion, and doing it well enough that I never had the slightest suspicion until three days ago. If that could be true of the Little Five, it stands to reason that the same could be true of Inman Park.

"Would Belinda know who it is?" Luther asks.

"I doubt she was part of the inner circle. She was lured into being a transmitter with the promise of biodiesel supplies. Whoever they are, they probably keep their identities as secret as possible, even among themselves."

Olsen gestures for my attention. "There are people coming this way," he says, then adds with his usual flat humor, "We could just ask them."

Three men and a woman, walking up the middle of North Highland Avenue, all armed. I recognize Barkov among them but don't know whether to feel relief or tension. The tightness in my chest releases, irrationally, when Barkov waves to me. My second thought is to mistrust his motives, but if I let myself go down that path, I'll have too many suspects and no allies.

Barkov calls out to me, "I have a good guess for why you are standing there like a baboon, my friend. I was right that they came from here."

"Two men and a girl?" I ask.

"A girl, yes," Barkov says, reaching the gate. "We know her. We know Phoebe. She is your mayor's daughter." He rattles the two chains. "What is this? Why are the locks changed?"

"There were two men with her," I continue.

"There is one man with her," he says. "A black man. They are together in the old parking station. He is threatening her, and we cannot find Andrew."

"Shit," I mutter, assuming the worst.

"You tell me what is going on and why you changed the locks."

"That wasn't us," I explain. "Two men abducted the mayor's stepdaughter and took her through here. They cut the locks and changed them, so they wouldn't be noticed. There's a lot more I should tell you but right now—"

"You want to rescue the girl and save the day," Barkov says with a sigh of fatigue. "Like Old West." But he shrugs. "Do you have bolt cutters? No?" He gestures to the woman next to him, and she hurries back the way they came. Barkov rattles the fence in front of me. "We are going back to the parking station. When you come, try not to get in the way, yes?"

I send Robb to gather up a handful of people from the sweep team. Barkov may not want us interfering, but I'm not going to sit on my hands. By the time the woman returns with the bolt cutters and breaks through the two replacement locks, I've already been joined by five more men. The ten of us follow the woman down North Highland toward the parking deck.

The multilevel parking structure sits behind what used to be a coffee shop, long since converted into a kind of cold storage warehouse for the enclave's food stores. Behind the parking deck are a few apartments, then a surface lot, and then the Belt Line trading stalls that won't see use until next summer. This gives anyone atop the structure a pretty good view of the area but doesn't explain why someone would hole up in a building with too many access points. Maybe Randall and Banderas aren't quite as canny as they led Braithwaite to believe.

The side vehicle entrance to the parking deck has been blocked off with construction site barriers. Barkov and the other peace officers are on the street side of the barriers, discussing some matter of hostage negotiation policy that no one ever expected to have to implement. Barkov takes one look at my crew and makes a face of both amusement and distaste. "We don't need an invasion, Edison. It is just one man and a girl."

"One man holding a girl hostage," I remind him, but his expression doesn't improve. "Tell us what you want us to do. This is your dance. But remember, she's our girl." After Barkov nods, I ask, "Has he made any demands?"

"Only to be allowed to leave," he says. "With your girl. Tell me what is happening here, Sam. He is not one of yours. I don't recognize him."

"He's with the traders from Clarke County." I want to explain the rest, but I don't have enough of the answer yet, and trying to pick my way through it now would only make Phoebe wait longer for rescue. "I don't know much more than that. He left the Little Five with another man named Banderas. They got through the gate in broad daylight without their heads being blown off by your man Andrew, who has gone missing. You tell me what you think that means."

"Shit," Barkov says, mimicking my earlier comment. He turns back toward the dark maw of the parking structure. "And she is not a simple hostage," he adds. "No one would have thought twice, even two unfamiliar men walking down Highland. But a struggling girl? So she is valuable to him. He will do whatever he can to leave here with her. Negotiation will be harder. He did not take her to keep himself safe. We cannot offer a replacement. She is his only real demand. Do you understand?"

Someday I will have to ask my friend about his life before the collapse.

"You think we are going to have to kill him," I say with no pleasure in my voice.

"Perhaps," Barkov says. "Probably." He slaps me on the shoulder. "You are a pessimist. We might make him believe that we will let him go. With your girl. Right now, he cannot see us from where he is hiding. He does not know that you are here."

Barkov and his people will have to convince Randall that they don't care about Phoebe, that they are willing to let the two leave just to get him out of their hair. But that depends on too many unknowns. Where is Banderas? Is Andrew, the Inman Park sniper, a part of their network? Any bluff we might attempt would be spotted as far away as a sniper rifle. It is a dangerous gamble, and I point this out.

"I have had someone talking to him for some time," Barkov says. "We did not know you were coming."

I suppress a strong urge to push past the barrier and confront the man myself. That won't improve the situation at all. We have no advantages here, except time. And even that may not be ours, if Randall is especially convincing in his threats, or Banderas has his own tricks.

"We need to find his partner," I suggest. "If he's still here. Maybe that will give us something real to trade."

I don't think Randall and Banderas came to the Little Five specifically to kidnap Phoebe. They came to solve the problem of Owen and Abigail. They took Phoebe as insurance and a reminder to give them what they want. That makes her valuable, but maybe not more valuable than one of their own. They've still made their point, even if Phoebe comes back safe and sound.

"You are volunteering?" Barkov asks. "Then go. But do not make trouble. You are not the police here."

"I know that," I reassure him, then signal to my group to move away from the parking deck. We gather in the street, shrouded by a darkness untouched by the weak street lanterns lining the sidewalks. Quickly I give my instructions. "The enclave is laid out in two roughly parallel strips. One strip is North Highland Avenue, where we are now. The other strip is the Belt Line market zone. The best way out of here is through the Belt Line, going back the way we came, then curving off toward Piedmont Park. Once you're out, you're in the open, and free and clear of pursuit. Chances are Banderas hasn't gone that way yet, but I want three of you scouting ahead anyway. The rest of us will do a sweep along North Highland. Check unlocked buildings. All the way down to the bridge over Freedom Parkway. But remember, this isn't the Little Five. Like Barkov said, we're not the police here."

DAY TWELVE, 6:00 A.M.

As the sky begins to turn to steel, Luther and I take point with Olsen, Wright, and three sweepers following a few paces behind. I unholster my service pistol and keep a two-handed grip on it as we proceed down the yellow line of North Highland. Olsen and Wright fan out left and right with the others, checking doors on both sides of the street. Some of the doors open, lantern light splashing out onto the sidewalk, bleary-eyed occupants making noise about the disturbance. But most doors remain shut, and unlike the Little Five, the residents of Inman Park seem to like locking their doors.

I blink hard against my fatigue. Luther, carrying her Springfield with the barrel in the crook of her elbow, grits her teeth and mutters, "She put us in a fix, didn't she?" When I snap a glance at her she says, "Belinda. Obviously."

"What do you mean?" I ask as Olsen returns from half a block down, shaking his head.

"I mean the biodiesel," Luther says. "Now what do we have to trade, if we can't make it without whatever that shit was she needed from these assholes? I mean—"

I interrupt, almost halting in the street. "You can't think she did the right thing, making a devil's bargain."

"But she didn't know, did she?" Luther says. "It doesn't matter now. If she was in any way responsible for those deaths, it's not like we can let her keep doing her job. So who's going to find another source? Who's going to be the one to get us out of the hole she put us in? There has to be another way, right?"

"God, I hope so," I mutter as we come into view of the bridge that marks the boundary of the Inman Park enclave. The bridge extends North Highland Avenue beyond the enclave's gated perimeter fence, an inversion of the way our own community closes off its southern border.

"Holy crap," Luther says, raising her rifle and gesturing to the rest of our team. I see it immediately after: the gate is open, rolled back completely so that the entire length of the perimeter across the bridge is exposed. In the dawning light I notice movement just beyond a pair of gutted Volkswagen buses on blocks perpendicular to the road.

I lift a hand to halt the team. I don't know the area well enough; I don't know how dangerous this section of the perimeter is. The slope down to the street below is steep, making it unlikely that hollow-heads could climb up to attack the fence, but the bridge is much less secure than our tunnel. And it is wide open. The buses are not a real barrier: I'd guess that the enclave uses them as baffles, to prevent hollow-heads from simply rushing across the bridge to strike the gate. But there is still enough room on either side for two people to walk abreast.

The wood and iron gate opens to the side, on runners, but someone has relocked the heavy chain to prevent the gate from being easily wheeled back into position. Closing the gate will mean getting much closer and making a considerable amount of noise. Without a better vantage, I can't tell how many hollow-heads are on the other side of the buses—or how dangerous it would be to try to secure the fence again. If even one shrieker hears us and reflexively calls out, there could be a horde on the bridge in a matter of minutes.

Just above a whisper, I tell Wright to run back to Barkov and tell him about the sabotage. I instruct Olsen to find a way to get on top of the buildings to our left, so I'll have eyes on the far half of the bridge. From here back almost a block, the old storefronts are a single contiguous building, which means Olsen can find a safe place to climb and then make his way quietly across rooftops.

But this also poses a problem. Back when the hollow-heads were new, everyone assumed that the best defense was to hole up in a building and wait them out. Groups gravitated toward urban areas with tightly-packed buildings, thinking them to be much more defensible than open spaces. But hollow-heads don't think like people do. They don't encircle; they don't avoid impediments. All of the assumed disadvantages of wide open spaces turned out not to be anything of the sort. And the enclosed streets, the locked buildings, the single-entry barricades—these became killing fields for the hollow-heads to enjoy. Hollow-heads don't run away. They don't frighten. They don't become claustrophobic. Confronted with a locked door, they break through a window without a second thought. And then a much-prized secured building becomes an abattoir. An unbroken street block, seen as an excellent way to control points of entry, is a funnel down which hollow-heads can find their panicked prey.

Inman Park enclave is a slaughterhouse waiting to happen, and as I wipe nervous sweat from my palms, I realize just how bad it's going to get. The Atlanta Medical Center, the eastern heart of the hollow-head infestation in the city, is only a few blocks west of where we're standing, on this very street.

The first sign of real trouble doesn't take long to make itself known. Two figures tumble around the front of one of the Volkswagens, both of them dressed in ancient rags that have seen too many winters. The two figures are male, tall, and gaunt like starving men. I have my weapon up and ready to shoot when I remember Randall and Banderas. The crack of the gunshot may spook them, alert them to our presence. I have no doubt that they are responsible for the gate being open. I'm sure they're paying attention to whether anyone notices.

Luther seems to have the same momentary hesitation, as she and the others look to me for guidance. It is a mistake, and we have all made it. Both hollow-heads stop their shuffling approach, open their mouths, and shriek.

"Fuck!" Luther shouts, and this brings us back to our senses. I fire the first shot, catching one of the shriekers in the chest. It slumps against the Volkswagen, its siren cry cut short like a needle pulled off a record. Three shots from other weapons miss the remaining shrieker; then a round from someone's revolver catches it in the face.

The sudden silence is deceptive. More shadows move behind the buses as a mass of hollow-heads arrive, expecting food. Something bangs against the far side of one of the buses, causing it to shudder. The metallic thump grows increasingly insistent as more hollow-heads press against the baffle.

"The gate," I shout, running the last few yards to the perimeter. I pull hard on the locked chain. I consider and then discard the idea of shooting at the lock or one of the links. Getting a bullet to strike dead-on would be next to impossible, and missing even by millimeters would only cause it to deflect in some random, dangerous direction. Had I known about the gate, I would have taken the officer's bolt cutters with me. Wright has gone for help, but he won't be back before the hollow-heads have passed the fence.

I count our numbers and our bullets. There may be at most a hundred rounds among us, but probably a lot fewer. We're not going to be able to hold off any sizable group. Certainly not from our exposed position in the middle of the street. We're going to have to retreat, but even the best shooters can't hit the side of a barn door when fleeing for their lives. I glance around, looking for Olsen, and find him at the end of his climb atop the nearest building. He drops to his belly and pulls a small pair of binoculars from his pack.

The hollow-heads are coming around the Volkswagens now. I tell the others to take up positions, and we fall into place in a practiced, fluid movement, making a shallow arc across the width of the street. Luther and I remain in the center. Olsen uses scout signals to describe what he sees, and I feel the blood run from my face when his last signal is "dozens."

I wait, tensed, weapon raised. The hollow-heads didn't see their scouts go down, which is why they haven't reacted with their typical pattern of enragement. They stumble over the bodies, a few of them even dropping to feast, but most ignore the shrieker corpses. If we shoot now, they will certainly notice, and they will react with the speed and aggression that we saw in the tunnel, back when all of this began.

The first spilling of blood within view of the hollow-head mass will mean that we've already lost the fight. No containment will be possible, unless we have overwhelming numbers. We have to wait until we have reinforcements.

Already the citizens of this street are rousing themselves in the early morning, responding to the shrieks and gunfire. Doors open, heads peek out, and within minutes there are people streaming onto the sidewalks, heading away from the open gate. At the same time, Luther and I pull our warding semicircle back along the blacktop, still unwilling to shoot again. Now that there are civilians in the streets, it would be even more dangerous to bring out the hollow-heads' wrath. I hear Luther muttering under her breath as she pivots her rifle from one hollow-head to the next. A steady stream of curses, repetitive, meaningless. The words rattle me, and I have a strong urge to tell her to shut up, but I know she needs to release that anger.

Wright returns, coming up to my side and hooking a thumb back to show me that Barkov has sent some of his people. One of them has a bolt cutter, but she doesn't try to use it. It's too late for that now. "Any word on Phoebe?" I ask between clenched teeth.

"No," Wright answers without equivocation. "Barkov is pulling his people away from the parking deck."

I share a glance with Luther: we know what's going to happen next. Randall will escape with Regina's daughter, perhaps with Banderas and the sniper as well. And right now, none of that matters, no matter how much the bile in my throat insists otherwise. Phoebe is my responsibility, but these people shouldn't be collateral damage. I want to leave them. I can't leave them. Groaning with the decision, I tell Wright to help with the evacuation of Inman Park.

The Little Five has never been breached like this before. We have contingencies, and some semblance of a tactical plan, but it all boils down to the simple mantra of escape. I've never heard of a community surviving an incursion of any size, and based on Olsen's continuing frenzied signals, I'm sure this one is significant. The hollow-heads shamble forward, blank expressions punctuated by wide stretches of open, gap-toothed mouths blowing fetid breath.

We have no options. All we are accomplishing now, stepping backward from the slow tide, is staying within range so that if they decide to give chase we will be close enough to kill them. But not enough of them. Back at the tunnel, there was only a small gap in the wall that the hollow-heads could exploit, and they managed to break through and rip apart a member of the sweep team. This is horrifically worse. This is Savannah all over again.

Olsen rises from his position and hurries back down, stowing his binoculars. I gesture for the sweep team members of my group to go with Wright, leaving only Luther, Olsen, and myself at the vanguard. To my left and right I see men and women rattling doors, gathering up those too stubborn or sleepy to get out on their own. Behind us, the street fills with quietly fleeing citizens, some carrying prepared luggage, but most moving quickly in hastily thrown-on clothes. Families. Young children, bewildered. Some with mouths held shut by their parents, wriggling against the affront to their right to panicked screaming. Then ahead of us, to the right side where peaceful-looking houses are nestled in small, prim plots of grass, a door opens, revealing an elderly couple dressed in night clothes, silhouetted against lamplight from their hallway. Somehow that house was missed, or no one answered.

Now it is too late to retrieve them. Hollow-heads are within yards of that front door, and as soon as the light pours out onto the sidewalk, eyes turn. The couple keep their wits; I'm grateful for that. They step back and shut the door in moments. But the noise was loud enough to attract more attention. More hollow-heads turn to follow the sound, and soon the façade of the pleasant two-story home is swarming with hungry bodies. Glass breaks: a front window. I am reminded of the futility of hiding indoors.

Suddenly, gunshots sound from inside the house. A revolver I can't identify and what must be a Glock. The householders are fighting back, together, as their deaths approach. Again I'm grateful: they are shooting inside the house, which keeps the bulk of the horde unaware. But it can't last. Soon a wave of agitation ripples out from the house as the man and woman scream their last moments. The agitation spreads across the mob, and I can see, with excruciating clarity, the exact moment that the search for food becomes a frantic lust for whatever kind of vengeance these mindless creatures can feel.

Our three-person shield won't hold them back. Gulping down the disgust, I fire two shots into the nearest hollow-heads, then turn away with a shout to the evacuees: drop everything and run.

Luther throws her rifle onto her back and echoes my urgency, screaming, "Go! Go!"

In movies, the heroes always took lazy shots behind them as they ran, hitting their targets every time, but we would only be wasting bullets. Unless we shoot them in a vital spot, hollow-heads ignore their wounds until they bleed out and collapse. And a bite from a dying hollow-head is no less dangerous than from the other kind.

The screaming, panicked confusion rises from the civilians as the mob presses into the street, spreading out into the gaps between houses, an impenetrable wave of predation. I think I see Amy, Barkov's wife, at the back of the evacuation. She and other stragglers, some still trying to keep their possessions, lose ground against the threat, too lost in their own confusions to heed us when we shout for them to just let go and run. I kick a rolling suitcase out of one man's grip, and he turns back to retrieve it. Before I can grab his arm to drag him forward, a hollow-head wearing the remnants of a Sunday best suit lunges at him, biting the right side of his face. His scream is cut short by the gurgling of blood.

Like breakers against the rocks, a leading-edge portion of the hollow-head mob collapses against the dying man, rending his flesh and opening a gap between them and the rest of us who are still fleeing. I wish I knew his name. The man's unintended sacrifice may have saved lives.

But not all of them. Fed by a panic of the uncanny, some of the civilians on the sidewalks have stopped to pound on doors, screaming to be let in, or have crashed their way through unlocked entrances. Clusters of the horde follow them, snatching the foolish and unlucky.

The street in front of the parking deck where Barkov barricaded Randall is swarming with the enclave's defenders. They have set up a defensive line, most of them wielding automatic weapons that they must have scavenged from an army base or police armory after the collapse. But they can't shoot: there are too many civilians in the line of fire. I shout for the evacuees to drop to the asphalt or run to the sides, but very few listen to me, and those who do quickly regret their decision and climb to their feet or continue running directly toward their protectors.

Memories of Savannah interfere with my concentration: desperation, futility, no sense of control over anything that was happening around me, trying to keep Jeannie safe. Everyone panicked. Bad decisions piled on top of one another, compounded by the certainty that each next step would pull Jeannie away from me. Her body held tight to my side, every muscle straining to hold her steady while I ran. For the first time since my wife died, I cried out of fear. Hated myself for the weakness. And lost every sailor and civilian I had promised to protect, except one.

I can't let that slaughter happen again. I walked out of Savannah with one child in my arms and the blood of a hundred on my boots. Not here. Dropping to one knee, I begin shooting into the asphalt, scaring the evacuees into fleeing the crazy person with the gun and clearing a space between Barkov's men and the oncoming horde. I use every bullet, but it's worth it. I fall flat to the ground as the rifles explode in front of me. Hollow-heads drop behind me. Some fall only a few feet away, blood and air gurgling from collapsed lungs, liquefied brain matter spilling like applesauce onto the pavement. I tell myself, convince myself, that I don't recognize any of the dead. And perhaps I don't, but I have to safeguard my sanity, just in case.

I wait until the noise has quelled. A glance behind tells me that most of the horde has been dispatched. The survivors feed on their dead, giving the riflemen time to reload their weapons and herd the evacuees. I hear Barkov shout for everyone to get onto the Belt Line path and head for the football stadium at the far end of it. I climb to my feet, look around, and see Olsen on his side, clutching his bleeding leg. A dead hollow-head lies less than a foot away, blood in its mouth.

"Damn," Olsen says when Luther helps him up. "Tripped in a goddamn pothole," he adds, trying to laugh.

Luther says, "Chief, I'm taking him back to Marilyn. You're going to be fine, Olsen."

"Bullshit," he mutters. "I've got maybe a day, and you know it."

"She can put you in the freezer," Luther says, giving Olsen a shake. "Clean the wound. Keep your fever down. It might not—"

"Fine," Olsen says. "Fine." He looks at me, his eyes telling me that he knows the truth. Hollow-heads spend their days eating fresh and rotting meat. Without antibiotics to treat an infected wound, the cocktail of bacteria in a bite is enough to send even the strongest people into septic shock.

I nod to my friend. "All right. Luther, take him back to the hospital. I'm staying here. Maybe there's a chance Randall hasn't gotten far, and I can convince Barkov to—"

I am interrupted by a shriek echoing between the buildings around us. It sounds muffled, constrained, but not by distance or walls. It's much too loud for that. Barkov notices as well. "Where is that coming from?" he calls to his people, and some of them fan out to search for the source.

The surviving hollow-heads who were eating their dead perk up at the sound of the shrieker. They look in our direction, stand and begin shambling toward the noise. Barkov gestures for two of his peace officers to finish them off. The shriek comes again, exactly as before, and I realize that we are listening to a recording. Like the open locked gate, Randall's partner Banderas—or the sniper, Andrew—must be behind it.

Now I hear different screams from the far side of the parking deck as evacuees begin fleeing back toward us. Leaving Luther and Olsen, I hurry to round the corner. The Belt Line runs parallel to the main road at this point, and because the miles-long stretch of walkway has been secure for years, there is no gate or fence here. Only a low hill rising to the pavement defines the boundary between the Inman Park enclave and the public strip of land. The nearest gate is five hundred yards down the Belt Line, past the hollow-heads that are now beginning to tumble down the hill from that direction. We are being surrounded.

The recording of the shrieker blares again, agitating the hollow-heads further. They move faster now, with more attention, coming onto the street and making their way past the parking deck. The barricade erected by Barkov's men diverts the horde away from it, keeping them on the short road toward North Highland Avenue.

I can see that some of Barkov's peace officers want to shoot despite the crowd. Their own agitation is increasing, especially after the adrenaline rush of slaughter. They're good people, but they're not used to this. I've been here before, and even I am having to focus on keeping my finger off the trigger, though it wouldn't matter, anyway: I'm out of ammunition.

Barkov's usually impassive expression has tightened. "What have you brought to my town?" he growls at me, pulling me away from the approaching horde. I can see the gears of his mind spinning as he looks left, right. To our left is the bridge gate, where more hollow-heads are beginning to gather. To our right, around a bend in the street, is the gate to the Little Five. There could be safety there, but there is an unwritten rule between communities. He knows it; he doesn't want to remember it.

I grip Barkov's jacket sleeve and wrench his thoughts back. "No," I say firmly. "You can't. We can't. That fence won't hold back a mob this size."

The people of Inman Park have gathered like coagulating blood in the center of the main street, trapped between two horrors. If a horde ever broke through the Little Five's tunnel, at least it would be faced with a wide-open space with plazas and small crop fields. Here, there are only buildings, fences, and panicked civilians. And more prerecorded shrieking, coming from up the street in the direction of the Little Five. I'm sure of it.

"What choice do I have?" Barkov says, shoving me away. "There is nowhere else to go!"

Already we are being pushed into the street with the others. Already the civilians have realized the only remaining avenue of escape. A few of them break from the group and run in the direction of the Little Five. There is nothing I can do to stop them. The gate isn't locked. They pass Luther and Olsen around the curve of the road.

That fence won't hold. A small group of hollow-heads would break against it, but a mass this size would pile up, turning a mound of bodies into a ramp. And the wire at the top would tangle only the first few hollow-heads to try.

The shriek again. "Fuck!" I shout. Then, "I have an idea." I pound Barkov on the back to get him moving. "Evacuate to our side. But be careful. It's a small gate. Don't let everyone jam up. You'll end up getting people crushed. I'm going to try to keep the hollow-heads away from the fence."

Barkov stares at me for a long moment, probably wondering when I went insane.

"I have an idea," I say again. "I'm going to find the speakers."

Before giving Barkov the chance to respond, I run, but Olsen flags me down as I approach. The strain of trying to hurry with a gash in his leg has started him sweating. I tell myself that it isn't fever—not yet—but it doesn't help. I swallow around the lump in my throat.

"I'm slowing her down," he tells me. Luther supports him under one shoulder, keeping the weight off the wounded leg, but despite her strength, they aren't moving nearly fast enough to get away from the hollow-heads.

"Luther, get him into one of the houses." I don't have time to explain. "They're going to walk right past you," I say. "Trust me."

Without waiting for objections, I continue up the incline of the road toward the source of the shrieking. As I get closer, the echoes resolve themselves and reveal their origin: the last multi-story apartment building on the street before everything turns back to single-family homes with pleasant front yards. I realize too late that I lost my flashlight somewhere in the retreat.

The building is unoccupied and has been for a while. The windows and doors are boarded, though a service entrance at the side has been forced open. Before entering, I check my weapon and remember that I used my last bullets getting civilians out of the way of the firing line. I have only my hunting knife.

The shrieking comes again. The sound is unnerving, uncanny, like the scream of a demon. As I make my way to the stairs I distract myself by trying to figure out how Randall and Banderas managed to get a hold of something like that. How they managed to play it back.

I stop on the second floor, one floor below the source of the sound. I wait for the shriek to come again so I can use it to mask my approach. There must be someone in the room with the speakers waiting for a signal, or a set time, to shut off the machine; otherwise the sound would continue looping until every hollow-head was crowding around the building.

There is a door at the top of the stairs. I think it's safe to assume that the speakers are in an outward-facing apartment, which would cut the options down to three. And if it were up to me, I'd pick the apartment farthest from the stairs.

I hear footsteps below me. I swing around to see Luther, alone in the shadows, hurrying to reach me. Just loudly enough to be heard half a floor away, I hiss, "What are you doing here?"

"I figured out the same thing you did, and you need me more. Olsen's got help. You've got a knife." Luther hands me an old M1911A that she must have gotten off one of Barkov's officers. She keeps her Springfield rifle slung on her back, preferring her G27 Glock.

"Don't be trigger-happy," I remind her. "If it's Banderas, we're going to need him alive."

Luther nods, and when the shriek pierces the air, muffled by concrete walls, I push open the door. We hurry across the unadorned, echo-laden corridor as quietly but as quickly as possible. The shrieking stops before we reach the door, but I'm certain it's the correct one. I test the handle and find it locked, which is disappointing but not surprising. And shooting the lock won't help. I know from my training years ago that pistols don't do enough damage to the mechanism to break it; they only jam the lock more.

"Banderas," I call out, "we know you're inside. You have nowhere to go."

I hear movement and voices on the other side of the door: more than one person in the apartment.

"We only care about the girl," Luther adds. "Surrender easy, and we can exchange you for her. No one has to get hurt." She shrugs at me and whispers, "Worth a shot, right?"

"It's too late for that." The unfamiliar voice is loaded with amusement and contempt. "They're long gone." Someone on the inside keys the lock and the door swings open, revealing an empty apartment and three men, one of them dead on the floor, soaked in blood.

I recognize Banderas as the man who opened the door. Micah Abraham is by the back windows, tending to a set of portable speakers attached to his ancient tape player and a cobbled together battery pack. A glance at Luther, who interviewed him after Braithwaite's arrest, tells me that she can make no more sense of it than I can. I thought he was harmless; I thought his only involvement was his hatred of me.

What else have I missed?

"Arrest us," Banderas says, "lock us up, do whatever you think you have to do. But if you want to see that girl again, you're also going to do exactly what I tell you."

I take the threat as bluster and ignore it. Banderas has already admitted that Randall fled with Phoebe. Following the kidnapper's instructions in a world without cell phones isn't likely to bring her back. So I'll take the easy capture and worry about the consequences later. I tell Luther to deliver Banderas and Micah to the station and secure them until I return.

As they leave, Micah gives me a look that seems to apologize for what he's done, but I have no more sympathy for him than I do for Braithwaite. They should have trusted us. They could have confided in me. Maybe I would have found another way. They wouldn't have had to make unholy bargains.

And even if I couldn't have fixed it, at least I would have known what was coming. Maybe Owen and Abigail would still be alive and in Macon, with people to look after them. Away from here where they were never safe.

DAY TWELVE, 8:00 A.M.

The surviving population of Inman Park is amassed now in the middle of Moreland Avenue like their own kind of horde. A few have suitcases and bags, but most are still dressed in night clothes. Some are shoeless, with blood-streaked feet cut by the uneven and unmaintained asphalt. The majority are in shock, either in tears or staring back at their former homes with expressionless faces.

My heart breaks when I see Barkov again. He is moving slowly through the street, carrying his blood-covered wife. For a moment I have hope that she is alive, but when I reach him to help carry her, I see that the gash in her arm is deep enough to sever an artery. The last of her blood is seeping off her clothes and onto the asphalt.

We set her down in the shadow of one of the plaza's trees. I don't even try to find words. Barkov's usual easy manner, which I've always assumed masked a stoic inner life, is gone. What's left is the raw meat of a personality much darker than I imagined. There is nothing I can say to him. If he blames me for his wife's death, for stumbling my way into letting Randall and Banderas escape to Inman Park, I will have difficulty disagreeing. The best I can do, the least that I owe him, is to meet his gaze, then leave him to his grief.

Mayor Weeks has found the surviving leaders of the enclave and is in deep discussion with them. Passing by, I overhear ideas about how to direct the sweep team to finish clearing out the enclave's streets as quickly as possible—if it is possible. The work is difficult and dangerous, tempting a frenzy at every footstep. That is a task that should involve me, but I have other, more pressing responsibilities. The refugees are alive and safe for the moment. They don't need my help.

Luther is waiting just inside the door of the station, finishing the dregs of a cup of coffee, watching the cell. The Little Five's station was never meant to hold more than one person at a time, but now Braithwaite, Banderas, and Abraham share the cramped space.

"It's done," I tell Luther. "I was able to get across the rooftops, close to the bridge. I played the tape as long as I could." I drop the cassette on my desk. "Most of them are heading back the way they came now."

Braithwaite's expression has hardly changed. She seems not to care that the others are near. She sits on the far edge of the hard cot, staring at the floor. Abraham's demeanor shifts from confusion to anger when he notices that I've entered. He comes to the bars and grips them like a malefactor. Banderas stands in the shadows, arms crossed as if waiting for me. He looks up when I close the door, and I see nothing but satisfaction in his eyes.

It's clear which of the three I need to interrogate first. If I start with Banderas and he refuses to talk, that will embolden Abraham to try the same. I'm not going to get anything new out of Braithwaite, by the look of her. Abraham is the most fragile. He lets his anger and fear do stupid things on his behalf. Maybe they will make him talk.

"Where are Pritch and Kloves?" I ask Luther as she sets down her coffee cup. "And how is Olsen?"

"I just sent them to the fence. I figured you'd want eyes on the 'heads. Olsen's with the docs. Last I saw him they were bringing him to the walk-in fridge." She shrugs. "I don't know."

Acknowledging Luther with a nod, I unlock the cell door and gesture for Micah to come outside. There is a storage closet to one side, which will have to suffice as an interrogation room for now. I drag two chairs with me as I usher Micah into it, then direct him to sit down. His jaw tightens as he watches me take my seat. He makes an effort not to fidget.

"Right now," I begin, "I don't care about why you're involved in all of this, or how much you hate me, or what your justifications are for being part of a kidnapping and a near slaughter. So we're not going to talk about any of that. All I want to know is where Phoebe's being taken."

"Why the fuck would I tell you anything?" Micah says, spitting the words as if to compensate for his bewilderment. "You're the reason all of this is happening."

"I'm not responsible for this," I say. "And pointing fingers doesn't put you in any kind of a good position. Your actions today led to the deaths of I don't know how many people. Good people. Neighbors."

"How do you think it's going to be when we can't make diesel anymore?" Micah retorts, leaning forward.

"I get it, Micah. Belinda made some kind of a deal with these people to provide the chemicals she needs. In return for what? Favored nation prices on everything she produces? There's nothing terrible about that. That's a deal anyone would have been happy with." I know this wasn't the real agreement, but either Micah won't take the bait, or he doesn't know the truth.

He leans back again, crossing his substantial arms over his belly. "If she could have trusted you, you'd know enough not to look into the girl and where she came from. Hell, you might've killed the two of them yourself." He emits a strangled laugh. "Fuck. It's my fault, isn't it?"

"How is it your fault?"

"Because Belinda stopped trusting you after Amanda. Because I told her what happened, and what you did, and why she was gone."

"Amanda is gone because she was stealing food," I say, though I shouldn't reopen old wounds. I can't afford to distract him.

I'm thankful that he doesn't pursue it. "Yeah, well," he says. "Belinda stopped trusting you. We all did. If she hadn't, she might have told you everything. Asked your advice. Tried to find a way out. Something. I don't know. Or even if it had to go down the same way, at least you'd be on board, and when the strangers came—"

Micah's body seems to compress into the chair. "If we didn't let Randall get away, they were just going to come with more people. We were going to be right back at the beginning. At least this way Belinda has a chance to make the deal work again." His eyes, shining and hard, rise to meet mine. "But you won't allow that to happen, will you? You and your fucking black and white cop morality."

I hear the door to the station open and muffled voices in the main room. I consider stopping the interview to check on Luther but decide against it. Micah is too close to telling me what I need to know.

"That depends on what the deal was," I say, though I can tell from Micah's expression that he doesn't believe me.

"Phoebe isn't retribution," Micah says. "She's just the first."

"The first what?" I blurt out, but before I've finished the question, I know the answer. Enough of it, anyway, to see the parts that matter to the Little Five. Owen told me that Abigail wasn't from Dahlonega. When he fled with her, he took a marked map

117

with him. A map that must be related in some way to the numbers station that Braithwaite set up for Randall's people.

"There are going to be more," Micah continues, ignoring my question. "Maybe all of them, since they're pissed off now."

Human trafficking. An immovable certainty settles itself deep inside my chest. And the weight is more terrible than anything I've been imagining. Regina told me: there were more. Abigail wasn't the only one. I've been so naïve.

I push aside all pretense at understanding. "Where did they go, Micah? Where did he take her? To Dahlonega?"

"Oh," he answers with a growing defiance. "You're going to hunt him down and take her back? And then what? They're just going to come again. I told you that!"

"We can protect ourselves. We've managed so far. We've never been breached by a horde." But that's just a deflection. I don't even believe it. Humans and hollow-heads behave differently from one another. A fence might hold back a mindless animal, but not men with vehicles and guns.

"Sure," Micah says. "Chief Edison, shield of this shining beacon of civilization. Do you have any idea how much biodiesel we supplied them with? Fuck's sake. They must have a whole fleet of trucks." Then, for a moment, he relaxes. He shrugs. "Besides, I don't even know. We've only ever seen them coming with the Clarke County traders. But that doesn't mean shit."

As if to punctuate Micah's words, a scream penetrates the closed door. The first person I see when I crash through it is Mikhail Barkov, gripping a knife in one hand while the other holds Banderas's wrist against the top of my desk. Blood spurts from the wound where the man's left ring finger used to be.

Banderas thrashes, but Barkov has all the leverage. His captive crumples against the side of the desk, knees hitting the handle of a drawer. As I reach for my weapon, Barkov shouts, "Answer the question, and I'll take you to a doctor."

I shout his name in response, raising the weapon Luther gave me in Inman Park. Luther, still standing by the door, fumbles for her own sidearm.

Banderas looks at me, both relieved and pleading. The color is leaving his face, most of it still splashing all over my desk. Barkov glances in my direction. "Let me do my job, Edison."

"Your job?" I repeat. "It's not a job, it's just revenge. You're going to kill him! He's not going to tell you anything. At most he's going to lie, and that won't get us anywhere."

Barkov allows himself a chuckle. "American squeamishness. If we don't find his friend where he tells us to look, we will take off his balls and feed them to him. He won't lie."

"This isn't your concern." Watching Barkov's expression over the sight of the gun makes me falter. I've never shot a man who wasn't hollow.

"This man killed my wife," Barkov insists. Although his tone is level, calm, his accent is thickening. "And he did it on orders from someone else. I want to know who."

"It's the same people who took Phoebe," I explain, looking at Banderas again. His breathing is becoming labored. "I can get the answers another way. Let him go."

Barkov doesn't move. He keeps the knife poised, blood coagulating on the blade edge. Banderas struggles to get his feet under him, and I can see that he has regained some of his composure now that I'm nominally on his side. He glares at Barkov. "Go ahead. Take another finger. You don't have any authority here."

Out of the corner of my eye I see Belinda Braithwaite moving toward the open cell door. She isn't trying to leave; she's trying to get a better angle. Her eyes aren't on Barkov or Banderas. She is watching Luther.

And Luther is watching her.

Luther says, "Put down the knife, Mikhail. I won't ask a second time."

I feel Micah pushing against me, looking over my shoulder, filling the doorway with the stink of his sweat. "Shit," he mutters. "You have to let him go," he says, and I assume he is speaking to Barkov until he adds, "Chief. Please. She's gone. Leave it be."

Micah's callousness is a calculation. Braithwaite's earlier catatonia came from the same place. They both knew that my success meant the Little Five's suffering. Finding Phoebe can only end the same way. They are taking a broader view of things. But I refuse to do that. Phoebe deserves more from me than that. She deserves more from everyone. She is owed every effort to keep her safe, to give her a life without open wounds.

"I will get the answers my way," I tell Barkov. "I already know generally where to look. He needs a doctor." Barkov shakes his head almost imperceptibly, and I add, "I will get justice for both of us. For the Little Five and for Inman Park. For Amy. Right now, you have to look after your people who are alive. You can't do that if you're locked up or dead."

Barkov looks briefly behind him, catching sight of Luther's weapon. He lets out a long sigh and releases Banderas's wrist, sheathing his knife on his belt. The prisoner stumbles back, clutching his bleeding hand to his chest, trying to staunch the flow of blood with his fingers.

I don't see sorrow in Barkov's eyes as he turns away from his quarry. I see a practiced deadness that he must have used many times in his former life. "You are making a mistake not taking my help," he says. "Come find me when you change your mind." He leaves the station as calmly as if he had just paid a parking ticket.

The moment that Barkov is outside, I move toward Banderas. "Luther, go fetch Marilyn. Tell her to bring her kit."

Braithwaite says, "Addie."

I look up. The two women are locked in a silent conversation, eye to eye, from across the room.

"I can't," Luther says, but it's not clear what she means, or who she's talking to.

"Luther," I insist. Then I realize that she still has her weapon raised. She begins to bring it down as Banderas moves to sit in my chair.

"Holy mother of god," Micah says. "Bel, you never said—"

"Not now," Braithwaite says sharply. "Addie. Think about what you're doing."

Luther twists her head as if to deny something, but the movement is tortured, conflicted. Braithwaite continues, "It's too late now. Maybe I can renegotiate. But we're not going to get Phoebe back. And if we try, they'll only come for more. And they won't listen to me. You have to know it's true. We've talked about this. Don't make it worse. We have to let him go!"

I should say something. I should intervene, interfere, find a way into Luther's head. But my mouth is dry. Too many pieces have fallen into place for one day already. My mind reels at the realization that there were more pieces than I could see. Pieces I should have known were missing. I don't know what to say to make her stop. I don't know if the words exist.

Braithwaite and Abraham don't own rifles. I don't even think they know how to shoot.

Luther was the one to find Abigail dead. I trusted her description of what she saw. But Abigail must have known her attacker. There were blood streaks on the floor. Signs of a struggle in the expected places.

But she wasn't killed in her bed.

She was killed when she answered the door and let Adelaide Luther inside.

It had to be that way. Micah's self-pitying complaint only makes sense in this light. When Braithwaite couldn't trust me anymore, she had to find someone to help her hide the truth from me for all these years. It had to be someone close. Someone who could step in, get in the way, if things ever went south. Someone who could do her dirty work without getting caught.

"Luther," I say. "Don't."

Braithwaite doesn't let me turn Luther's head. She pushes harder: "How do you want this to be, Addie? Maybe I should tell the chief about where you go at night. What you do. About all the people who have died because you can't control your urges and lead the consequences home with you. Maybe I should tell everyone about what you did to your father."

Luther takes in a sharp breath. "No," she says. "I'm done. Chief, I tried. I swear I tried." She looks at me with a heartbreaking mixture of defiance and regret, then fires the gun. Banderas's face blooms with red as the back of his head splatters onto the fabric of my chair. As I run toward her, she pulls her gun in close, bringing the barrel to her mouth.

I don't reach her in time. Her skull obliterated, she crumples to the floor as my fingers grasp uselessly at her jacket. Seething with anger, I train the gun Luther gave me at Braithwaite, then Micah, both of whom have started toward the door, or toward my dead deputy. It doesn't matter which anymore.

Through a rising wave of grief, I manage to shout for the two of them to return to the cell and shut the door. I cock the hammer for the effect it will have on them. They don't know guns; they used Luther for that.

I have known Adelaide Luther since she was a teenager, a kid. I thought I had changed her path. I made a promise to her father. Another promise broken. Maybe the Little Five was wrong to give me this post.

I shake off the doubt. There is still work to do and no one else to do it. Phoebe is gone because of compromises I never would have made. Perhaps if I had given Luther better guidance, not thrust her into a role for which she was not prepared, she might have understood that such compromises are never acceptable, no matter how many secrets you have to give up.

But we were tainted from the beginning, when Braithwaite made the deal to keep the traffickers on the other side of the fences. In exchange for chemistry beyond my understanding, needed to make even more of the fuel that they would use to destroy families and towns and the last remaining bricks of the world's moral foundation. And in trade for that, Braithwaite received protection for the community, and the shackles of participation through the numbers station she maintained.

Then Owen changed the equation. Whatever his experience was in Dahlonega, it taught him what to look for, and he uncovered Braithwaite's complicity. So Braithwaite used Luther to silence the threat, leveraging whatever she knew about my deputy to get her to commit murder.

But that wasn't enough for whoever has Braithwaite in thrall. Randall and Banderas were sent to make sure she finished the cover-up. They used Abraham's resentment toward me to secure his cooperation. Phoebe was supposed to be insurance.

The more I play out the scenario in my baffled mind, the more I want to have let Barkov do his job. And then let him move on to Braithwaite, and Abraham, and cut them into pieces. Leave them as food for the hollow-heads.

◆

I find Mayor Weeks at the Carter Center, where he has moved his meeting with the Inman Park leaders. I wait impatiently in his office, marveling as I always do at the large oak desk and the wall-to-wall bookshelf displaying hundreds of academic works as if they were bricks. Weeks once told me this collection is only a portion of the one he used to have, back when he was a professor. Even so, compared to my collection, this is the Library of Congress. Running my fingers over the titles brings a certain satisfaction, and some relief, while I wait.

When he finally arrives, I rush toward him. "I think I know—" I begin.

KEVIN A. MUÑOZ

He interrupts. "You're going to get her back," he says, as if expecting me to be on the fence.

"Yes. Of course. If I—"

"No, Edison. I mean you. *You* are going to get her back. We have the peace officers from Inman Park. We can make do while you're gone."

"That's what I came here to say," I tell him. "I thought I was going to have to convince you to let me go, and not just send people from the sweep team."

"I love Phoebe like she were my own," Weeks says. "And after today, I don't trust anyone else." He chews on this for a moment. "I couldn't face Regina if I had to tell her you were staying behind."

"I'm going to need—"

"Anything. Take it." Weeks sits down hard in his leather chair as if suddenly exhausted. "We can survive almost anything, Chief. But not the children. Not losing children."

◆

Marilyn rests a hand on my shoulder as I stare blankly at the two bodies laid out on her table. Night is falling, and burial will have to wait for tomorrow. Under better circumstances, our dead would be put in the walk-in refrigerator until morning, but Olsen is there now, fighting for his life and mind. Another casualty of my blindness.

"What are you going to do?" Marilyn asks.

Mikhail Barkov, as enigmatic as I've always known him, reacted to the news with his old humor. I thought he would be angry at me for wasting his chance, but he only shrugged and waved it away. Now, standing across from us on the other side of the table, he says, "We are going to find this Randall, yes?"

"Yes," I say. "Braithwaite and Abraham are too terrified to talk—they think this is only going to make things worse—but I've figured out enough to know that our best chance is to head toward the Clarke County community. Tomorrow morning. I don't want to travel in the dark. Mayor Weeks has agreed that I can be spared. You, me, Kloves. And—"

I pause. Now to broach the subject that brought me here to Marilyn's hospital. "We need a doctor with us," I continue. "The enclave's doctors are here. They can take over operation of the hospital while we're gone. I could really use you, Marilyn."

She lets out a soft laugh. "I'm not posse material, Sam."

"We're not going out with a full complement of soldiers and scouts," I explain. "It has to be small, so we don't attract the wrong attention. But with small comes dangerous. And we don't know what condition we'll find Phoebe in. I'd feel a lot better with a doctor along."

"Then take one of Inman's docs," Marilyn says, stepping away from me. A shadow covers her expression. "I haven't been outside in years."

"I need someone I can trust," I point out. Barkov looks like he might object but keeps his silence.

"Is that all?" she asks distantly, covering Luther's destroyed features with a sheet. She points at Barkov. "I want to talk to Sam alone."

He nods and moves away, inspecting the tools and devices on the other side of the room.

"Please tell me this isn't the old argument again, Sam. I'm not going to be drawn into your obsessions."

"That's unfair," I tell her, surprised. "I haven't been outside in over a year. I don't take those risks anymore. I listened. It was too late, I know, and I understand. But eventually, Marilyn, I listened. It's not like you to be callous."

My response surprises her, too, and she acknowledges it with a shake of her head. "No, you're right. But I'm not like you, either."

"I'm not asking you for heroics. I'm asking you to help me save Phoebe."

Marilyn clicks her tongue and furrows her brow in an expression that I used to know more intimately. She's looking for excuses. But she recognizes what she's doing. Unlike me, she has never succumbed to lies she's told herself.

"I know," she says. "Of course. But whatever you have to do when we find her, when we find them, I don't want any part of it." Now she looks at me directly. "I understand what you're probably going to have to do. And I'll find a way to be okay with that. But I don't want any part of it."

I dare to embrace her, feeling the familiar warmth against my arms and chest. I want to tell her that I still love her. That I wish every day I could be the person she needed.

But I can't. I'm not. So I say only, "Thank you."

◆

I pack a change of clothes into a small duffel bag, then the few amenities I keep at home. Toothbrush and toothpaste, our only defense against infections of the mouth. A bottle of hydrogen peroxide, to ward off the terrible potential of even the smallest cuts. And then there is Micah's recording of a shrieker's call to hunt. I shove the tape into an outer pocket: it may be useful again.

But that only takes twenty minutes, and I am still too restless for sleep. So I sit at my kitchen table and try to distract myself with a book. It doesn't work. My thoughts keep turning to Phoebe and then to Jeannie. And from her to my wife. She has been gone twelve years, and all I have left of her is a single photograph, which I slip out of my pocket to help me remember her face.

She would have known what to do long before this. She would have had all the answers. I can see it in her eyes. She is smiling, in the middle of a laugh, looking at me instead of the photo booth camera we used to commemorate our engagement. Two women more deeply in love than I ever thought possible for me. So deeply that I can still feel her warmth on my face.

But she is gone, and it feels like forever. Like I am alone in the world. I lost her. I lost Jeannie. Now Owen. Abigail. And so many others before them. I don't even know most of their names.

But she would have known what to do. So I slip the photograph back into my pocket, keeping her close to our daughter, and pray that together they will help me find a way to bring Phoebe home.

PART TWO

LONG ROADS
AND OPEN SKIES

DAY THIRTEEN, 5:00 A.M.

Sleep is fitful. In my waking hours, reliving the memory of gunshots, I become fully aware that the Little Five is not the place I thought it was. Braithwaite's compromises and Luther's murders have made this irrevocably apparent, forcing me to recognize that I haven't truly known the Little Five as my home since my daughter died.

Maybe that's why I want Marilyn with us when we go on the fool's errand to rescue Phoebe Weeks. For a time, she was a vestige of sanity and sensibility, and losing her made me even more needful of human connection. That need let me trust more than I should have, to fill the empty space that she left. I knew better, but I didn't care.

I rise before dawn, unable to justify thrashing about in bed any longer. I stumble over all of the books that didn't help me move quickly enough to reach an answer before its consequences came through the gate. Somewhere among my shelves there are maps of the state, probably close enough to current reality to be useful, and I spend the next ten minutes fumbling in the dark until I find them.

Once dressed, I hoist my pack and head down to the street, the roosters reminding me that I've already wasted half an hour. I want the Little Five to look different, to feel different, but it's the same place it's always been, until I reach its center. The refugees have set up a makeshift camp in the middle of the street, using tents and sheets and heavy boxes. Most of the people are still asleep, and those who are awake sit outside their temporary homes, warming themselves by barrel fires with empty looks in their eyes. Only a few of them acknowledge me when I pass.

At the hospital I almost expect to find Luther waiting for me with Marilyn, but I catch myself in enough time not to be overly shocked at the sight of her demolished body on the table. Marilyn is nearly finished wrapping her in a linen sheet. She covers what was once Luther's face with the kind of clinical detachment that comes only from practice.

"Olsen isn't doing well," she says. "The wound's deeply infected, and this morning the fever started. I hate leaving him like this." For a moment, I'm afraid that Marilyn is going to back out, but after a silence she adds, "Inman's doctors can treat him just as well as I could. Probably better." Then she smiles as if to wash away her self-pity. "You're going to need me more than he does. I'm going to finish up here. You should go in and talk to him."

Olsen is laid out on a cot in one of the walk-in fridges that used to hold restaurant inventory. Without refrigerant, the room isn't as cold as it would have been before the collapse, but the insulation makes it possible to keep the place cooler than the rest of the building. The man shivers under a pile of blankets, more from his own body's struggle than from the temperature. His face is pale, and the bandages that cover his leg seep.

"Chief," he says, his teeth chattering. "You have to take care of me. The doctors won't do it until I'm gone. But you know better."

"No, they do," I say as neutrally as I can. "You could still pull through this."

Olsen coughs out a laugh. "Maybe. I just don't feel like I'm getting better."

"No," I admit, "and you don't look like it, either. God, I'm so sorry this happened." I don't know what else to say. Everything I *could* say would only be a repetition of things I've said before. Ten years is a long time. The platitudes grow stale after a while, though offering them never gets easier.

"You know, I'm sure it's just my imagination, but it feels like my head is getting lighter." He laughs again. Blood appears on his teeth. "Of course, it's not really. The slush is still the same weight, right?" He reaches out to grip my arm. "Leave me a gun. Please. You know they won't do it themselves. And I can't ask them to. But I don't want to wait six hours. I don't want to wait, knowing."

I set my borrowed M1911A on the floor by the cot. The doctors from the enclave will probably remove it as soon as they see it, but I need Olsen to know that I care. With everything that's been crumbling around us, it's more important than ever.

◆

We bury Banderas first, in an unmarked grave behind the north end townhomes, near the fences. Then Luther, with more respect, despite the revelations of her last day. Kloves lowers the makeshift casket himself, then piles the dirt alone, while a small crowd watches. The rhythm of the shovel sinking into the earth, then sliding across open space, feels like time ticking away. I remind myself that Phoebe is somewhere beyond the fences, afraid, and that Luther helped put her there. I give Luther as much time as my anger allows, then turn away to lead Marilyn and Kloves to the biodiesel farm where Vargas is waiting with the white Volvo.

I might have expected anger from him, or at the very least resentment, but his brief acknowledgement, "Chief," is the extent of his dismay. Vargas opens the trunk hatch and lightly pounds the side of his fist against a pair of short barrels in the back. "You have ten gallons in each barrel. Station wagons aren't the most efficient, but this, plus what's in the tank, should get you wherever you need to go."

Regina and the mayor come across the street as Barkov and I are packing the last of our supplies into the back of the Volvo. I make promises as they make their goodbyes and wish me luck. I tell them that they will have their daughter back soon; that this whole terrible affair will end, and our life in the Little Five will go back to the way it was.

"We must go before we lose the morning," Barkov reminds me. He assists Kloves with the last knots tying our gear to the roof rack.

Vargas hands me the keys, whispering, "Bring her back," and I am not sure if he means the car or the girl. Marilyn and Kloves settle into the back seat while Barkov rides to my right with weapons on his lap, at the ready. The sweepers at the tunnel pull the wall open, then close it behind us as I slip the car out of the shadows under the train tracks.

Back before the collapse, it wouldn't have taken more than an hour and a half to reach the Athens-Clarke County line from the Little Five. In the first days, when the people of Atlanta started fleeing the greater metro area, they jammed the interstates and highways, turning the I-285 loop around Atlanta into a permanent parking lot. Interstate 20, which runs from the border with Alabama out to the sea, didn't fare much better, and it took a surprisingly long time for the surviving communities to clear the abandoned cars. From what I've heard over the years, there are still large sections of state road that are impassable by anything larger than a motorcycle. Luckily, I-20 is traveled often enough that the greater majority of the obstacles have been moved, and trucks can cross old Georgia with relative ease, assuming there are no hordes blocking the path. Hollow-heads are attracted to the sound of engines.

I drive slowly past the abandoned Edgewood shopping center, with its smashed windows and overgrown sidewalks. Squatters tried to take back the shopping center a few years ago and discovered what we already knew: big windows are not defensible, and unless you're willing to live in the parking lot, places like this are a death trap. Most of the food and supplies were raided, by us and by others, in the months following the collapse. Shopping centers are not the boon everyone once thought they were.

A dozen hollow-heads wander near an old mattress store, purposeless, it seems, after having gorged themselves on a deer. The blood streaks are still fresh on the sidewalk, and the animal's mangled head is in the gutter. The hollow-heads notice the Volvo, turn toward us as we pass, and begin moving in our direction. They aren't a threat, but I'm still glad to be past them as we go over the hill and head down toward the entrance to the interstate.

There is no familiar movement on the road. Even after ten years, it is strange to experience the near-total abandonment of a city. Wildlife has reclaimed the streets, alongside the hollow-heads rummaging for food in the dark corners. A pack of dogs edges warily away from them, no doubt having learned the hard way that they are no longer on friendly terms. I almost laugh out loud realizing that I've used the left turn signal to get onto I-20. The *click-click-click* of the switch is a comfortable memory.

The interstate is a different environment. Abandoned cars have been pushed to the center of the highway and off the sides, leaving a wide path open for trucks. But even with the cleared path, it takes over an hour to reach the outskirts of Conyers and the end of the first leg of our journey. I pull off the highway at Exit 82, expecting to head across the overpass and then up Highway 138 to Monroe, but as I reach the top of the exit ramp I see a reflection flash at the intersection a moment before both front tires blow out. I brake hard and the Volvo skids to a halt, the front wheels grinding against the pavement.

Immediately Barkov hands me my SIG P229 and passes a shotgun back to Kloves as he pushes Marilyn's head down against the back of my seat. I open my door slowly, sliding out behind it, keeping myself marginally protected by the metal. Most bullets will go right through a car door, but they're too valuable to be wasted on shooting at a target that isn't completely visible.

A glance behind me confirms what I suspected: a spike strip laid across the road, dragged out of position by the Volvo's front tires.

Barkov mirrors me on the passenger's side. I watch my side of the landscape, across the overpass, but I see no people, not even a hollow-head. Behind me, down the ramp to the interstate, the road is as abandoned as every other stretch. Minutes pass until Barkov and I agree that no one is waiting to ambush us: a standoff like this is pointless, and anyone waiting for us would have the clear upper hand, even after announcing their presence.

I haven't been in this area in almost a decade, but I know that there is a community here. Reports from the Clarke County traders have always suggested that the group is small, barely subsisting, with few resources, but I don't know how much I can trust that information now. It's possible they were the ones who set the trap, though Randall is more likely.

I stand up straight, motioning for Kloves and Marilyn to stay in the car. "Be careful," Marilyn mouths. I shut the door to help her feel safer. Barkov moves away from the car, walking south across the intersection toward one of the shopping districts of Conyers, but he halts a dozen yards from the Volvo.

"I think they are long gone," he calls back to me, lowering the shotgun.

I relax my grip as well, holstering my pistol and joining Barkov. "I should have been paying closer attention."

"Now we know they expected us to follow," he says, ignoring my comment. "It will be much harder."

I knew it was a possibility, but I suppose I hoped for a miracle. "We're going to need new tires. There's a spare, but only the one. We could head back to the Little Five, but that's eight hours away on foot."

Barkov points down the hill to the shops. The boarded-up restaurants, retail stores, and gas stations on either side of the highway look abandoned, but that could be only appearances. Glass is harder to protect than lumber, so even an inhabited storefront would look decrepit.

"No fences," my friend says, as if that were enough.

"You think there's no one here," I offer.

"I think they will be hard to find. At one time there would have been too much here to pass up. But it is very open, and you remember what it was like, yes? Everyone wanted walls. They thought walls made them safer."

"If there's no one here," I point out, "or they stay in hiding, we won't be bothered. We'll do a search for usable tires and be on our way. I doubt Randall's people would have taken the time to make sure we couldn't find replacements. And if there are people here, we'll deal with it. It makes no sense to walk back to Atlanta for another car."

Barkov agrees, and after a few more minutes of searching, we're both satisfied that the Volvo will be secure long enough for us to retrieve the tires we need. We debate whether to bring Marilyn along with us on the search for tires: leaving her with Kloves would keep her safe, but Barkov and I could use the extra eyes.

Marilyn steps out of the car and shoulders one of our backpacks, stocked with enough food and water to last us the rest of the day, then shoos us along impatiently. "I can make up my own mind. Let's go. You insisted I come along. So I'm coming."

We head into what was once a typical example of southern suburban sprawl, full of oversized parking lots and short, expansive standalone shops.

Kloves is the first to point out that most of the abandoned cars here either have flat tires or none at all, victims of a decade's worth of looting and decay. The tires that have survived tend to be premium models that wouldn't fit a ramshackle Volvo from thirty years ago. Although he's no mechanic like Vargas, Kloves has the best eye of all of us for these things, so he hurries ahead to check the wide flatland of asphalt while the rest of us take a slower pace and aim down the center of the highway. There is bound to be a garage, tire center, or lube shop along the main drag, and if we're lucky we'll find one that hasn't been completely stripped.

A quarter mile down the road, Marilyn notices a pair of large birds sitting down in front of a chain coffee shop. "Carrion crows," she says. "My mother called them that. Here they're called buzzards. You never used to see them in this area."

We called them turkey vultures growing up. They mean something big and dead, but I think none of us are prepared for what we find. I assumed it would be a deer, or a dog—maybe even a hollowhead, though they tend to be eaten by their own kind. Instead, it becomes clear as we approach that two people were chained to the cafe's patio fence and left to die. One man, one woman, both stripped naked.

Barkov is the first to become alert, drawing his weapon again and watching the nearby buildings. Marilyn hurries forward as if there were anything she could do for them. I see Kloves approaching from the direction of a ramshackle Christian tchotchke department store, just as tense as Barkov. He's raised his shotgun to his shoulder, and he walks almost backwards toward us.

The turkey vultures scatter when we get within a few yards, squawking their discontent. "This is recent," Marilyn calls over to Barkov, who nods an acknowledgment. She crouches down by the woman's body. "Carrion crows don't eat anything that's started to rot."

"And they were alive when they were chained," I add, pointing to the marks on the wrists where the chains dig in.

The bodies look young, possibly early twenties. The faces have been obliterated by the birds, and both abdomens are torn open, but the rest of the flesh is largely intact. I move the woman's body to one side and reveal a series of angry welts and evidence of whipping going back months, maybe even years. The man has no such marks, but even my untrained eye can tell that his right leg is broken just above the ankle. That must have happened shortly before he died, since the bruising hasn't spread beyond the site of the break.

"Just like Abigail," Marilyn says, disbelief in her voice. "Who would do this?"

"They were tortured, then left out here to die," I mutter. By the time Barkov and Kloves have tightened their perimeter and are within talking distance, my anxiety has doubled. "We need to find the tires and then get the hell out of here. It's not safe."

"This is barbaric," Marilyn says, crossing her arms as if to ward off what she's seen. "Sexual trauma on the female. Bruising, cutting. Mutilation."

"Could it've been the birds?" Kloves asks.

"No," she answers. "It was a knife or a scalpel. The cuts are too clean."

"Let's just find the tires we need and move on," I repeat.

Marilyn meets my eyes. "It's okay," she says, just above a whisper. "We can take a minute."

But I remember Abigail's wounds, and what may be coming for Phoebe if I don't find her soon. However much these two victims deserve our attention, Phoebe deserves mine more. "I can't," I admit, and she doesn't press me. So we move away from the torture scene with our eyes on the stores across the parking lot. There are a few hollow-heads wandering around the shopping district, but most of them look starved and slow. None of them are shriekers, and we avoid them easily.

As I expected, there is a tire store just over a mile from the intersection where we left the Volvo. Unlike most of the other buildings nearby, it hasn't been boarded up, which makes me hopeful that no one thought it to be of any value. Once we are inside, however, we realize that most of the useful contents have indeed been carried off. A single stack each of emergency spare tires and car batteries remains in the back storage, and while Kloves is sure that a few of the tires will work on the Volvo, I am still disappointed that we aren't going to find better.

I take Kloves's shotgun, and he hoists two tires under his arms before we head back out. Barkov suggests taking along a hand-powered air pump, but I point out that Vargas already packed one in the car, along with the single spare tire.

We begin the trek back to the Volvo, but as we step outside, a voice to my left shouts, "Hold it right there!" Without hesitation, I raise the shotgun—and Barkov his pistol—but we are already surrounded by men appearing from behind cars and around the sides of the building. All seven are carrying hunting rifles. All seven look rough enough to be the ones who tortured the two victims at the coffee shop.

A couple of the men chuckle to themselves while a third shakes his head and addresses Barkov. "Now, don't get yourself riled up, son." His South Georgia accent is thick. I step forward enough to keep Marilyn behind me.

"How should I be?" Barkov says.

"Shit," the man replies, sounding disappointed. But that disappointment changes quickly to satisfaction. He leers at me. "Well, we might get one good one. Don't matter. The nigger boy looks like a good mule anyway."

Kloves doesn't react except to loosen his grip on the tires.

"What do you want?" Barkov asks sharply.

"Son, you're going to keep your mouth shut, and tell your mules to come quietly."

"Which one? Mouth shut or give instructions?" Barkov's defiance unnerves me almost as much as the men pointing guns do.

My palms go slick on the shotgun. I want to tell him to shut up, not to make it worse, but even that could go badly.

The spokesman for the group chews on this for a few seconds, then almost nonchalantly gestures to the man at his left. "Stuff a rag in the smartass."

"No," Barkov says immediately. "You are not going to do that. You think you outnumber us, but look at what we are carrying."

The leader casts glances left and right, as if to count his numbers. Then he says, "Son, we have seven rifles pointed at your head, and you're threatening me with a popgun."

"No, I am aiming a Browning M1911A automatic pistol with .45 ACP rounds at your head. I am not—what's the word?—*partial* to this particular weapon. It is old and slow. But I am fast, and my trigger finger is strong. Also, I know my firearms. My friend here is holding a double barrel Stoeger Coach, twelve gauge, loaded with bird shot. That shotgun will maim or blind no less than three of you, foolishly standing so close together. And all you have are an assortment of cheap hunting rifles meant for children that you have had difficulty keeping clean and in good condition. I think maybe four of them will not fire. But that is not what matters. What matters, *son*, is that we are both pointing our weapons at *you*."

The other man turns the idea over in his head, and for a few seconds it seems as though Barkov's bluff will work. But then he smiles, and his confidence returns. There is movement to my right, and with a glance my heart sinks. Five more men have arrived from behind the shop, and they look even more eager than the ones in front of us.

I want my friend to have another trick up his sleeve, but he says nothing. I half expect him to open fire. I prepare myself for the possibility of having to gun down rational men. But even Barkov can't talk his way clear of a posse this size, and I have Marilyn to think about. In the end, we comply.

DAY FOURTEEN, 1:00 A.M.

I can only assume that by now the Volvo has been dismantled by our captors. Our weapons were confiscated, along with the two tires and my wristwatch. A guard was posted outside, and hours passed before we heard anything more. Food in the form of metallic-tasting canned meat came shortly before nightfall. Just enough to keep our stomachs from complaining.

It must now be after midnight. At least it feels like we've been here for half a day. I can't see the moon through the window, and there are no working clocks in the building. Kloves and Barkov are asleep by the front door, but I'm certain they will wake instantly should anyone rattle the door's chain.

I can't sleep. My thoughts race too quickly, and there are too many of them to control. At the moment, I am turning the scene at the coffee shop over and over in my mind. They weren't travelers like us. The wounds on their bodies suggested intimacy. Their murderers knew them and were angry in very specific ways; they were sexually tortured.

The woman's marks weren't the kind that an abused wife gets at the hands of her husband. They were the long stripes of a bullwhip or singletail. And the man hadn't been marked in that way.

I remember what the leader said to his companions: they might get "one good one" out of us. To them, women are nothing but commodities to be traded. No better than biodiesel or bread. Confronted with that kind of callous, selfish calculation, I find it difficult not to wander down Barkov's path. But I will not be an executioner. I let my father live.

Yet I cannot help but remember my relief, my sense of release, when I learned that he was dead.

Marilyn comes to me out of the darkness, finding me seated on the floor with my back against the sales counter. She slides down next to me and grasps my arm. Her touch brings back fragments of my life after Jeannie, and I shiver both with recollection and ill-timed desire.

"What are they going to do, do you think?" She whispers this as if there were any threat of overhearing—as if that even mattered. Still, her voice is steady and unafraid.

I don't want her to have to think about it. I try to find some answer that doesn't hint at the truth, but there isn't one. Marilyn is the most vulnerable one of us: a young black woman surrounded by racists and rapists is unlikely to come out unscathed. They spoke to Barkov because he was the only one they might have conceivably respected, but they were disappointed to learn he is Russian. That means every last one of us is expendable to some degree or another.

Useful only as labor, perhaps. Or as merchandise for exchange. I assumed that Randall's people set the tire spikes in the road, but it could well have been these Conyers men.

And yet the woman they murdered was young and white and probably attractive when she was alive. She wasn't used as a "mule." It's much more likely that she was a "wife" in the loosest of senses: a woman kept only for sex. For children, possibly. I can imagine a scenario much like the one that befell Abigail. The dead woman's partner may have been another Owen.

I can't believe that this is the nature of the world now. The Little Five can't be the only remaining sanctuary, the only simulacrum that isn't thoroughly broken. But perhaps I'm being naïve. Perhaps I am not admitting the truth so as not to feel like a child again, powerless, overshadowed by the edifice of a father's anger.

So I don't answer Marilyn directly. I don't want to be the one to tell her that we are probably no more than goods for sale in exchange for bodies more to their liking. Instead I say, "They won't do anything. They aren't going to get the chance."

"Sam," she says, chiding me. "You know what I think about heroes. And I don't need to be protected like that. I'm not that breakable."

"I know," I concede. "I do. But I shouldn't have gotten you into this. You didn't want to come."

Marilyn smiles. She touches my cheek softly. "I told you, I can make my own decisions, too."

Barkov stirs, rising to a sitting position, then standing as if there were no transition from sleep to wakefulness. "Edison, it's time. Come with me."

"Time for what?" I ask, rising and stretching my back.

"Time to leave," he says, then leads me into the back storage area where we found the tires. He points to the tower of car batteries stacked like cases of beer, nearly to the ceiling. "What do you see?" he asks.

It takes a moment or two for my eyes to adjust to the deeper darkness, but I understand what he is getting at when he starts counting. "There are too many," I say, almost whispering. "And they're all still neatly stacked."

Most batteries will die within four or five years without exceptional care. What's more, it's necessary to charge them regularly to prevent them from going flat, even if you aren't using them. This pristine stack of batteries in the back storage of a tire store tells me that the people who live here, the ones who took us captive, may not have a working vehicle. Then I remember that they took the tires from Kloves. They didn't return them to this room: they took them away. They don't intend to strip the Volvo. They intend to use it.

"Your car must be close," Barkov says. "It is too exposed where it was. They would have brought it back."

"I don't see how that helps us," I say. "We still have a guard, and the door is chained shut."

"They are not smart," Barkov answers with a smile. "The back door used to be locked electronically." He walks to it, lightly tapping the silver studs of the industrial-looking keypad. The lock is not engaged. "This leads to the garage. That door may be chained. But there will be tools in the garage that I can use to pick that lock or break the chain. Then you will go find your car and bring it here. But it must be soon, before the morning comes."

I open the door a few inches, peering out into the darker gloom of the garage. "And it has to be me, doesn't it?"

"Yes. Because they won't shoot you if you get caught."

But that triggers another thought. One that he is not going to like. "So you'd agree that they were talking about the network. They're part of it."

"The human traffickers, yes." Barkov has said the words I couldn't bring myself to say. "What you described to me is very much like what we used to see, back before all of this. In Eastern Europe, in some cities, they were on every street corner. Some traded in workers. Others in prostitutes."

I try to block out images of Phoebe. I'd guessed all of this already. "The men here trade the people they capture for—what? Women of a certain age?"

Barkov nods. "That is what we saw at the cafe, yes?"

"Yes," I echo. The abused corpse, the long-term torture. It matched what I expect would have become of Abigail had she not

145

found someone to take her away from Dahlonega. "This puts us a lot closer to finding Phoebe than we were before."

Barkov clicks his tongue and gives me a rough sigh. "I know what you are thinking. But we do not have the numbers. We do not have the weapons."

"We could take the guard," I point out. "We might not need anyone else. Just someone to push us in the right direction. I assumed Randall was taking Phoebe to Clarke County, but that was only a guess based on where the truck came from. If he was picked up by someone else, we could be going in completely the wrong direction."

"Cowboys," Barkov mutters, though not bitterly. "The guard will not know anything. But we can use him as—"

"Leverage?" I finish.

"There is a chance that it will not work," he says with a lecturing tone. "The man they killed with the woman, I think he was one of their own."

"I'm sure you're right. I know this isn't going to be easy."

"It may be impossible," Barkov says. "But we do it anyway." He leads me through the door and into the cavernous garage behind the storefront. Because the darkness here is more complete, we move slowly and carefully until Barkov tells me to hold still while he searches for the tools he needs.

It strikes me as odd that the Conyers enclave would have no vehicles. They have easy access to the biodiesel farm in the Little Five: a trip down the interstate would put them on our doorstep. Our Volvo can't have been the first car they intercepted. Perhaps they have a collection hidden away somewhere, in various states of disrepair. Even so, I don't recall hearing of any trade between the power company and the Conyers group. So if they are mobile, they must be getting their batteries and fuel from some other source. Or they simply don't care and haven't moved from this area since they took it over.

Barkov interrupts my frustrated game of connect-the-dots with a light touch on the shoulder. "I have what I need. Come." He leads me past the garage bay door to the smaller door at the far end of the garage. Here I can barely see my hands in front of my face, but Barkov seems to have no difficulty opening the door an inch and working his tools into the outside padlock. After less than a minute he announces success.

Moonlight floods the space as he opens the door. Ahead of us is a small stretch of parking lot separated from the rest of the asphalt sprawl by a grass-covered median. Barkov moves right, and I move left so that we will be flanking the guard when we come back around to the front of the building. During the brief time that I am alone outside, my heart races. I feel the weight of solitude, the weight of cool air and darkness, of quiet. I feel like I'm the last person alive in the world. I scan the lot for signs of danger and notice two hollow-heads who weren't here during the day. I hold my breath.

The Christian tchotchke store we passed on the way from the interstate is barely visible, its large orange sign looming less prominently in the night's moon-silvered obscurity. There, just below it, is the familiar white profile of the Volvo.

I come to the last corner of the store and dare a peek at the guard. He has the air of an eager, unprofessional militia member: standing stock still, rifle gripped in both hands, completely exposed in all the ways that matter. Emulating something he may have seen in a movie or on television when he was a child. Only an idiot guards prisoners by facing away from the cell. There is too much tension in his body, which means he is more tired than he knows. Standing and waiting is more exhausting than most people suppose, and keeping still for so long will have prevented him from realizing how sluggish his muscles have become.

I hear a hiss from the other side of the storefront: Barkov creating a diversion. As expected, the guard turns in that direction, lifting his rifle a bit too slowly. Taking advantage of the opportunity, I hurry the last few yards and throw my arm across his neck as Barkov reveals himself just a few feet away. Barkov disarms the guard immediately and the hapless fellow stops struggling almost as quickly. He whimpers as he pleads with me not to hurt him.

"I saw hollow-heads," I tell Barkov.

"Then we will be quick, and we will be quiet." Barkov puts his face uncomfortably close to the guard's. "The nice lady doesn't like a mess. When I ask you questions, you will answer them."

For effect, I put a little more pressure on the man's neck. He makes an effort to nod. Barkov checks the confiscated rifle and the expression on his face confirms that he was right about its condition. "Where are the rest of your people?" he asks.

The guard points weakly at the tchotchke chain store up the road. Barkov nods, then asks his next question. "How many of you are there?"

"Twenty-three," the man answers breathlessly.

Barkov lifts the butt of the rifle and cracks it across the guard's nose, which makes an unpleasant sound and begins to bleed. I ignore my distaste and cover the man's mouth before he can make more noise. Even participating this much makes me queasy, but doing less won't get us what we need, and objecting will only make it take longer. With every passing second, I expect to hear a shriek behind me.

Barkov asks again, "How many of you are there? Not including the women you rape."

I smell urine as the guard trembles under my grasp. He whines his reply: fifteen. We learn more details in rapid succession. His replacement is coming at dawn. The group's leader is named Orwell, and he lives with two captive women in the pizza parlor adjacent to the tchotchke store. The man who spoke to Barkov earlier is his right hand and an all-around thug, Frank Keadley. Then a stroke of luck: this guard is Keadley's younger brother.

"What have they done with our weapons?" Barkov asks, but the guard doesn't know. He assumes they must be with Orwell, but his brother never tells him anything important.

"Does Orwell have guards? Is he protected?"

The man shakes his head tentatively. "I don't think so. His—wives. That's all. No one's allowed to keep guns except my brother. I only have one because I'm watching you."

"And what about your brother? Where is he?"

The guard gestures toward the tchotchke store again. "Inside. He's inside."

It doesn't take much longer for Barkov to be satisfied that he knows all he needs to know. I pull on the front doors as far as the chain will allow and speak to Kloves through the gap. "Keep Marilyn safe for me. Don't come outside just yet. There are hollow-heads nearby."

"What's going on?" Marilyn calls out from the middle of the room.

"We'll be back soon," I call back in a loud whisper.

"Sam—" she starts, but I let the door shut before she finishes. Right now, I don't have the luxury of doubt.

We lead the guard toward the stores, the rifle at the back of the young man's head. I don't feel sorry for him: he is part of a group that rapes, tortures, and murders women, and is exponentially more complicit in the human trafficking network than Braithwaite ever was. I don't care that he's a kid, barely twenty, too young to remember much of what it was like before the collapse. His moral world may have been shaped by his brother and the people he follows, but he could have said no.

I can see the remnants of a cook fire outside the entrance to the department store. It's a telling detail: the pizza parlor next door would have ovens with good ventilation, but it must be reserved for Orwell and his concubines. It is an expression of inefficient power, much like the badly preserved and undistributed rifles, and it means there's not likely to be much backlash if we go after Orwell. So I hope, anyway.

Barkov halts us twenty yards short of the department store's doors. Unlike most of the other buildings nearby, this one has intact glass across the storefront. This gives the people within a clear view of any dangers coming across the parking lot. That might explain why there is no barricade protecting the enclave, but it means there must be some other defensive measure that I can't see.

"Where is the gun?" Barkov asks, keeping the guard between us and the storefront windows.

"What gun?"

I have the same question. Barkov gestures behind him. "The walls of these buildings are shot through. You have a machine gun emplacement. It can't be on the roof because the parking lot is not full of holes. So it must be on the ground. Where is it?"

"It's—it's inside," the guard answers. "The boss keeps it there until we need it."

Even more inefficiency. They fight off hollow-heads, the occasional poacher or thief. They don't have a bunker mentality against intelligent adversaries, and it must never have occurred to them that they might need one someday. They don't bother with small arms upkeep because they don't need it. They have a machine gun.

"Lookouts?"

The guard points to the roof, to the right of the store sign.

"Call for your brother," Barkov says in a tone that offers no room for resistance.

Immediately, the guard hollers up to the unseen men on the roof. "Get Frankie! Tell them it's Ben. It's important."

A few minutes later an oil lantern sways across the interior of the store, casting a spiderweb glow on the windows. The door opens, and the spokesman comes out with two of his associates flanking him. The first words out of Frankie's mouth are, "Jesus fuck, Ben." He is carrying my P229, wielding it like an action hero, with no control. He tries to keep it on Barkov, then on me, but his brother is too close to both of us, and he must know he doesn't have the training to make the shot.

Barkov is no more impressed than I am. "I am going to ask you some questions now. If you stop answering them, or if you lie, your brother's face will be a stain on the ground."

"Jesus fuck!" repeats Frankie. "We're going to kill every fucking one of you. Then we'll find where you came from and kill them, too."

"How do you get your girls?" Barkov asks, shrugging off the threats.

"Fuck you, you fucking Russian—!"

Barkov doesn't give Frankie the opportunity to finish his insult. Ben's head explodes with a deafening crack, and the boy's body flops forward like a rag doll. A mist of blood and brain and bone billows outward in front of us, and the choked scream from Frankie sounds as if it has been muffled by the foam of his brother's head. Before the body has fully settled to the ground, Barkov is moving forward, stepping around the corpse, the rifle still poised to shoot. Frankie, bereft of sense, rushes forward, and Barkov swings the rifle stock around to catch the thug on the side of his head. He crumples a few feet from his brother, rolling in pain and anguish. Barkov puts a boot on Frankie's neck and aims the rifle at the two remaining men.

"Fetch your boss," he says without a hint of anxiety. "In twenty-eight seconds I am going to crush his windpipe. Hurry."

He begins to count. As the two men rush away, I am unable to take my eyes off the remains of Ben's brain on the blacktop, and I vomit wetly onto the pavement around his feet. As I spit out the sick, Barkov turns away as if to limit my humiliation. I silently thank him for the courtesy.

"Take your gun," he says, kicking it away from Frankie's weakened grasp. "The boss will ask for us. He will give us answers."

When I don't respond, he reaches down and picks up my P229. He forces it into my hand. "It had to be this way, Sam. This man was not going to talk. He felt protected. Orwell will not feel protected now. He will talk."

"You're going to kill him, too," I say, meaning Frankie. I may have all the anger necessary to do it myself, but I don't think I have the will. Seeing Barkov's ruthlessness up close again has made me less hungry for retribution.

"You remember your CIA? The enhanced interrogation. The renditions. You know all this? You Americans were so indignant. Do you know what we called our intelligence agency in the Great Patriotic War? SMERSH. They say it meant 'Death to Spies.'"

As if to authorize Barkov's response, the door to the pizza parlor opens. No one comes outside, and no one stands in the doorway.

"We do this my way, yes? This is how we get back your girl. This is how we hurt them for what they did to my wife." Without waiting for my acquiescence, Barkov reaches down and lifts Frankie by the collar, forcing him to stand and walk ahead of us. He sets the rifle on Frankie's shoulder, lacing his free arm behind the man's back and through his elbows so he can't use his hands. I follow a pace or two behind with my SIG at our captive's head.

The pizza parlor's lobby is lit with candles and a few old gas lanterns that haven't been cleaned in years. The room is jaundiced, and the man seated at the booth at the far end is even worse. His mass presses into him, his girth too significant to be held easily between the back of his bench and the table. He is wearing a stained, worn bathrobe and a pair of slippers that are two sizes too small for his fat-laden feet.

"Boss," Frankie says in a whimper, but Orwell ignores him and snaps his fingers for Frankie's two thugs to shut the door behind me.

"What do you want?" Orwell asks. His voice is tight from the rolls of jelly pinching his neck. "Your car is outside. But you're still here."

As we come closer, I notice that Orwell is clutching my Remington with one hand as it lies on the cracked red vinyl of the bench. His stubby fingers leave grease on the stock.

"Where do you get your girls?" Barkov halts a few yards from the booth, and I turn to keep an eye on the two guards behind us. They both look rattled and confused, unlikely to cause trouble, but I'd rather be watching them than the interrogation.

"You've got two already," Orwell replies, and I hear his bulk shifting on the vinyl seat. "Don't get greedy, boy."

"Take your hand off the rifle," Barkov says. "You are smarter than your little men, and you know that I don't care about killing you. This Frankie is not here as a bargaining chip. He is here as a shield."

The silence is heavy, like the moment after a thunderclap. I taste the bile in my mouth and throat. With my back to Barkov and Orwell, I can only guess at the fat man's reaction until he replies with agitation, "His name is Ravana. Or that's what they call him. Just 'Ravana.' We haven't seen him. Only his people."

Another silence as Barkov waits for Orwell to continue. When he does, his throat is squeezed nearly shut with audible panic. "We get them in exchange for workers and cars. People pass through here all the time. We just—" I'd almost attribute his hesitation to shame, if I didn't know better. "We just hand them over, and they give us the ones we want. They come from everywhere."

"That is not helpful," Barkov says without any hint of irritation.

"I don't know anything else! I don't know where Ravana is. When they leave they go northeast. That's all I know. Northeast on the highway. Towards Monroe."

"And Clarke County," I whisper.

"They come once a month to pick up. They bring ours every six months."

"And did they come yesterday or the day before? Do you know a man named Randall?"

"I know Randall," Orwell says. "Him and his buddy. They're enforcers. They only come if they have to. We haven't seen 'em in a year. And they sure as hell weren't here yesterday. What the fuck is this about? Who the fuck are you?"

"Tell me about the bodies we found. How many women have you killed?"

"Look," Orwell says, and I can hear him squirming in his seat again. "It's not like that."

"Sam," Barkov says, his eyes remaining fixed on Orwell. "This is when you step outside."

"I should stay. You might—"

"No," he interrupts. "I will not. This is not for you."

As Orwell listens to the exchange his agitation grows. The vinyl underneath his bulk squeals its own objection.

I shouldn't leave. I know what Barkov is going to do. But these men only care about themselves, about whatever sadistic pleasure they can derive from another's misery. They embody the filth that I've been wading through for days. I'll learn to live with the guilt of scraping them off my boot.

So I leave the interrogation to Barkov and move to the front of the store. A small crowd of onlookers has amassed in the parking lot, keeping a superstitious distance but clearly wanting to know what is happening within. Frankie's thug friends are torn between their obligation to look out for the boss and their strong desire to get the hell out of the building. I gesture with my weapon, nudging them toward the door, and follow them outside.

The crowd is behaving very differently from our first encounter. One of their number is dead and two are under threat, leaving the men to watch me with helpless confusion as I swing my sidearm across them. They are not carrying weapons.

If Frankie's brother—whose body has not been moved from its gore-painted spot on the pavement—was right with his count, then there are two abducted women in Orwell's headquarters and six more in the department store. The boss can protest all he wants about appearances not matching reality: I need to see for myself what they've been doing.

I match Barkov's cold voice and find it easier than I'd like. I point to the man showing the least shock and say, "Take me to the women you bought." Sensing some hesitation, I gesture in the direction of Ben's body. "He refused, too," I say as nonchalantly as I can.

My chosen guide accepts the lie eagerly and separates from the crowd, leading me to the department store doors. I keep him a few paces ahead of me and glance behind me every few seconds to make sure we're not being followed. I steal a glance at the Volvo as we pass and note with some annoyance that our supplies have largely been removed.

The interior of the store is darker than Orwell's hovel. There is an equal number of candles and lanterns, but they are illuminating a space at least four times larger. Most of the aisles and displays must have been dismantled years ago to make way for a ramshackle, largely public living area. There are cots and bare mattresses set against the side walls and an eclectic array of chairs, sofas, and futons in the center. Storage lockers that may have come from a faux upscale import store are stuffed full of equipment and discarded knickknacks, while the more useful junk is laid out on the few shelves that the inhabitants decided to keep. I recognize most of our things stacked in a pile to one side, not yet sorted through.

In spite of my anger at what's been going on here, I can't help but pity these men for living in near squalor. I want to ask them why they never thought to move to nearby houses. Part of the answer may be what I see shrouded in shadow at the far end of the store: a rusted out technical with a creatively secured Browning .50 caliber M2A1 machine gun in pristine condition, looking much like it must have done when it was built back in the early 2010s. Boxes of ammunition are stacked in the corner nearby.

My guide stops at the stockroom door to the left of the improvised gunwagon. "Through there," he says.

"Go back out to your friends," I mutter. He doesn't hesitate, moving away as if I were on fire. Once the man is well out of range, I push open the door.

Immediately I'm assaulted by the smell of sweat and the gasping of half a dozen unseen people. A gas lamp winks to life and the glow illuminates a horror. Ten mangy-looking futon mattresses are strewn across the room. Six of them are occupied by nude or virtually nude women, all of whom have been shackled by one ankle to heavy rings screwed haphazardly into the walls.

The oldest of the women could be my age, though she looks like her years have been much longer than mine. The youngest can't be older than twenty. All of them are emaciated, the worst case showing every single rib like a wind-whitened skeleton in the desert. They are covered in dirt and grime. Three have shaved heads, with the beginnings of new growth; the other three have longer hair, matted and tangled. All of them are blonde and fair-skinned, presumably selected by the men to conform to a racist rejection of color even among the women they choose to victimize.

I shut the door behind me to keep their captors on the other side, ignoring the stench that I trap inside with us. They've been living in it for who knows how long; I can handle a few minutes. I holster my weapon and show my hands. They have no reason to be afraid of me, surely, but I can't assume that all of them are sane. I don't know that I would be, in their position.

A few steps farther in and I can see blood on the mattresses. Two of the captives have bleeding sores and cuts on their arms, legs. The others are covered in bruises, scabs, and scars.

"You're safe," I say. "My name is Sam. No one is going to hurt you."

The woman nearest to me, the young one, begins to cry. I kneel down to her. The others react by retracting their bodies a few inches away from me, a couple of them whimpering. I hold my hands out inoffensively in front of the crying woman for a few seconds, then reach for hers. I clutch her fingers firmly. "What's your name?"

"She's Madison," says the woman I've pegged as the eldest. "She won't talk. She doesn't talk anymore."

I nod, recognizing a shadow of Abigail in the younger woman's eyes.

"What's happening outside?" asks another of the women. She slides closer to me, to the edge of her mattress and the full reach of her chain. "We heard a shot."

"We're going to get you out of here. I'm not alone. I have friends with me." I speak to soothe them; the words themselves don't matter. I don't think about how I'm going to deliver on the implied promise, or what we're going to do after we've taken them away from this hell. I only care that they understand they are safer now.

"Did Jamie send you?" asks yet another. Her voice is rough and wounded.

"Jamie's dead," says the eldest, sparing no pity. "You remember." She turns to address me. "Sam. My name is Clara. Forgive me if I'm not being grateful enough, but I have to protect my girls. Don't give them hope if there isn't any."

The sound of a rifle shot penetrates the walls of the captivity, followed by a long scream and another shot that cuts it short. It doesn't take much to guess that Barkov first killed Orwell, which must have burst Frankie's eardrum, then killed Frankie.

"We're going to get you out of here," I repeat, and this time I know it's true.

◆

I leave the six women, and the two who were held by Orwell himself, in Marilyn's care after Barkov and I are certain the remaining men are not going to be any kind of a threat. Kloves gladly stands watch over them, though the robust racism Frankie exhibited seems not to extend so deeply to the rest.

This leaves Barkov and me to decide their fates, and the fates of the eight women. Quietly we walk to the coffee shop where the tortured bodies are still tied to the fence, and as we take them down and lay them on the cold pavement, we debate what to do with the survivors.

Barkov doesn't come right out with his suggestion, but I know from the look in his eye that he wants to scrub this city clean of its infection. When I confront him, he admits, "It would be the safest for us. They have lost their leaders, but they are still dangerous. They had a radio. I destroyed it, but they may have contacted this Ravana. They will surely try now, if they haven't already."

"They may not even make it out of Conyers alive," I say, looking back to the group of now-timid men corralled outside their Hobby Lobby home. Saying this, I realize that my solution—simply walking away—could be just as much of a death sentence for them. Perhaps my hands would be clean, but I would want to wash them just the same.

"You may be right," Barkov responds. "That leaves us with the question of those women. If the ruffians are not going to survive, what do you think will happen to them?"

"You're not suggesting—"

"Sam," he says, with a breath sounding almost paternal, certainly condescending. "They are in no shape to take care of themselves. If we leave them here, they will only be abused again. We cannot take them with us. The humane—"

"They aren't dogs, Mikhail." I turn away from the bodies.

Barkov lets me have silence for a time. Then he says, "Your sentimentality puts us in danger."

"Is that what you think this is? I know why you're here. Revenge for your wife's death. Do you know why I'm here? Why Marilyn is here? If we let these women die—"

"There is no room in the car for all of them and us."

"Then one of us will have to drive back to Atlanta," I say. "We do not leave them here. This is not a discussion."

"I'll take them," Marilyn says. I turn at the sound of steel in her voice but see the anguish in her eyes.

"No," I say. "If this has shown us anything, it's that we need you with us. If we find Phoebe like we found these women—"

"Yes," Marilyn says. "Of course. But there are doctors back home who can look after them. I won't have to stay. If it's really not safe here, you could keep walking north on the highway, and I'll find you. As long as you stay on the road, I'll meet up with you in just a few hours. And besides, it can't be anyone else. The three of you can take care of yourselves out here. I'd just get in the way."

Though I am reluctant to leave Marilyn on her own, I remember what she said at the tire shop. It's not my place to tell her what to do or demand that she let me protect her, no matter how difficult that prospect is.

"This is not a good idea," Barkov says. "But if you are insisting—" He shrugs, acceding to the plan without another word. While he and Kloves rearrange the contents of the Volvo, I address the assembled Conyers men.

"We are leaving. What you do next is up to you. You will tell no one that we've been here, or we will be back to finish what we started." This time, I have no difficulty channeling Barkov's Russian bluntness. It's easier than asking myself if I could actually follow through. "If you leave this place, you will not go west. You will not go near Atlanta. And if we meet you again in any place where this is going on—" I gesture toward the women that Marilyn is coaxing toward the car—"we will shoot you like we shot the others. You don't get a second chance. Not for this."

Barkov, Kloves, and I hoist heavier packs, filled with some of the supplies that wouldn't fit in the station wagon, and head north behind Marilyn toward the interstate. We say our temporary goodbyes, and Marilyn turns left onto the ramp, heading back west toward Atlanta. I expect to see her again before the sun is at its peak, but the crawling sensation in my chest makes it difficult to trust that I will.

I walk resolutely, aiming for the city of Monroe twenty miles away, letting the others pay closer attention to the scenery and potential threats. We should be halfway there by the time Marilyn returns to us. I spend my time coming to terms with what we've done in the last few hours. I didn't try to stop it. They were monsters.

But they were also men.

I don't want to become the sort of person who accepts what we did as necessary, as justifiable. That's a compromise just like all the others, a compromise I can't allow. I joined the Coast Guard because I wanted to save people. I'm still that woman. I have to be.

DAY FOURTEEN, 12:00 P.M.

When I was younger, still in the Coast Guard, I might have found this long walk with a heavy load bracing, even enjoyable. I had habits back then that I now find unpleasant to contemplate: waking up at dawn and running five miles before breakfast is the one that comes immediately to mind. But I've kept fit and capable, owing in part to my post in the Little Five and in larger part to a shame at my own flirtations with bodily slovenliness. I just no longer consider exercise a form of entertainment.

The long walk offers me the chance to think about better memories and better times. A life filled with courtships and miraculous weddings and expectancies, before births and deaths took away the brighter lights of my world. And then the flicker of new light in Marilyn, who gave me what passes for hope in this unmapped country.

But she needed someone who didn't spend every waking moment looking for the wrong kind of closure. I wish that I could turn back and see that the answers glistened in her eyes, but it's too late. The candle has gone out.

"Hollow-head," Kloves announces, and we all halt.

It's a man, looking healthier than most of his kind, wearing clothes that haven't seen more than one winter. He can't be much "older" than six months. Still, he shuffles slowly across the road with the characteristic gait of a hollow-head, his arms hanging slack at his sides. The lower half of his face is caked with drying blood.

He is crossing at a broad intersection, moving from one gas station toward another diagonally across the street. There are only sparse trees in all directions except the way we came, with empty parking lots in front of squat convenience stores. No fences anywhere to be seen. One hollow-head in an area familiar to us is nothing to worry about, but none of us have been here before, or at least not recently enough to remember the terrain.

And sure enough, glancing down past one of the gas stations, I see a gathering of hollow-heads working their way toward us.

"Shit," I whisper. "It's a shrieker." It has to be: it's in the lead. Its partner—they always travel in pairs and trios—will be nearby. Hurrying as carefully as we can, we back away, looking to hide behind a low brick T-shaped building on our left. It was once the diminutive Walnut Grove fire station, and has two garage doors, one half-open, that provide us with good cover. One of the truck bays is empty; the other holds a white and red heavy rescue vehicle.

And then I hear the engine. The Volvo is coming up from Conyers, out in the open, with its early 1990s V-6 groaning like it wants to be heard. I step back out from the garage and wave my arms, trying to get Marilyn's attention before the shrieker finds its target.

She either sees me or sees the hollow-head: she swerves left, coming toward the fire station, the barrels of biodiesel strapped to the roof swaying. The garage door is too low: the Volvo, with its payload, won't fit through. Marilyn crushes the brakes and squeals to a halt just outside.

"Get in!" she whispers loudly. I glance toward the intersection: the shrieker is moving our way, head swaying left and right, tracking the sound of the engine and the squeal of the tires. The horde following it is coming up to the edge of the gas station, only a few dozen yards from the intersection.

"No, wait," I say, holding out my arm to keep Barkov and Kloves from leaving the safety of the dark garage. "We won't get through in time."

There are too many hollow-heads. I've seen panicked drivers floor their accelerators like action heroes, believing that they could ram their way through. But bodies don't react to impacts the way they did in the movies, flying over the windshield and out of the way of the tires. More often than not, struck hollow-heads will fall down in the road. One or two can be crushed under the tires of a heavy car, but more than that and the car won't have enough clearance. The front axle will run aground on a mound of bodies, and in an instant, the car will become a death trap, and then a coffin.

I have another option. Before the Coast Guard, I worked a few summers as a volunteer firefighter as a way to get out of my hostile home. I remember how commercial garage doors like these work. I gesture to Marilyn to keep the car running and duck back into the garage. Blinking to make my eyes adjust to the shadows, I look for the double chain to one side of the door.

"Kloves, pull this down and keep it down." I hand him a single chain with a wooden ball at the end. When he pulls, the gear at the top of the door locks into place, and I pull hard on the second, looped chain. The panel door begins sliding up.

It's noisy. It takes time. Every pull on the loop chain clears maybe an inch, generously. I don't have the upper body strength for an extended pull; when Barkov takes over, the door moves fractionally more quickly.

I keep watch on the horde. The shrieker—and now its partner as well, coming up from behind the gas station to join its companion—is shuffling across the street to the sidewalk in front of the fire station. As soon as they see us, they will alert the group, and there's nothing I can do about that. A glance at the door tells me that we aren't going to get Marilyn inside and the door shut before the horde learns we're here.

I hear the squeak of the Volvo's brakes and Marilyn slides the car into the station. Barkov lets go of the chain, then Kloves, both of them no doubt assuming that the door will drop when there is no longer any pressure on the gear. But it doesn't work that way.

"Reverse!" I hiss to Barkov, and the two men take up positions again. Barkov pulls hard on the loop chain in the opposite direction. The panel door starts to draw down, inch by inch.

Marilyn jumps out of the car and comes to the door. She grabs the gear lock chain from Kloves, who takes over for Barkov. A little more speed now. Barkov joins me, flexing his oil-stained hands.

"There is no way to make it go faster?" he asks.

"There is," I admit. "Though it will be a lot harder to keep open later."

The shriekers make the decision for us. They cry out in unison and the horde turns toward the fire station. I nudge Barkov back inside the station and tell everyone to stay away from the entrance. The panel door still has four more feet to clear before it's closed: more than enough space for a hollow-head to enter, and they are more than halfway across the intersection now. The shriekers are even closer.

I tear into my backpack and find the magnetic flashlight. I shake it twice to give it just enough power, then switch it on and sweep the light across the top of the door, near the gear. "That," I say, pointing at a brake pin on the side of the gear opposite the chains, roughly the shape of an Allen wrench. "We need to pull that out."

I tell Marilyn to keep pressure on the gear lock chain while I hunt for something to use to reach the pin. There is a long brush hook attached to the side of the HRV, and I hand it to Kloves, the tallest of us.

"They're on the sidewalk," Barkov informs us. I don't take the time to look. I shine the light on the brake pin again, and Kloves reaches up with the hook, tapping the pin out of its seating.

"Let go," I tell Marilyn, and as soon as she releases the lock chain the panel door slams down. The noise is almost deafening in the enclosed space, but not so loud that we can't hear the shriekers reacting with a second alert.

The station is in darkness, except for the weak LED glow of my flashlight. The weight of exhaustion from the long walk and lack of sleep hits me at once, even as adrenaline floods my body. My hands shake. The flashlight's beam flickers across the garage door. I lean against the Volvo's rear hatch, steadying myself.

A minute later, we hear the first rattling thump of bodies against the door. Long fingernails scratch the metal, seeking a way in.

"What now?" Marilyn asks with a surprisingly controlled voice. "Isn't this the situation we teach kids never to let themselves get into? Trapped inside a building surrounded by hollow-heads?"

"I'll check the doors," Kloves says, retrieving his own flashlight. "Let's hope we're trapped."

He heads off into the darkness. The rest of us look for places to sleep on the floor. Given the choice between dust and grease, we pick dust and bed down in the corners of the garage.

After Kloves returns with an all clear, Barkov claims first watch and promises to wake me in two hours. But I don't sleep at first: Marilyn sits close to me and rests her head against my shoulder. The warmth is welcome in this place, which reminds me of the first months after the collapse, when most of us who survived did so by finding what few safe places remained. Warehouses. Schools.

Jeannie and I spent three nights in a movie theater with a hundred other people, all of whom are dead now.

We were refugees in our own land, sharing a solidarity that few of us had experienced before. Whatever else was going on around us, however terrifying and terrible it became, we were comforted. We were not alone.

Marilyn is not alone. Neither am I. The conflicts that came between us can't touch the warmth of her body resting against mine. They can't make me anything other than grateful that she is here.

My eyes open eight hours later. Barkov never woke me: Kloves spelled him instead, and they took two-hour turns by the doors, listening to the perpetual soft thumping and scratching. I try to build up some indignation, but I am thankful, and I can guess as to why Barkov let me sleep. Marilyn remained at my side the entire time, one arm and one leg curled over me.

"All right," I say, dusting myself off once Marilyn stirs and sits up. Three flashlights illuminate the garage, and I can see for the first time the scope of what we have to work with. The Volvo takes up only a small portion of the left bay. The heavy rescue vehicle is in the right bay.

I stare at it for a long moment, then realize why it's bothering me. "This shouldn't be here," I tell the others. "We're in Walnut Grove. This HRV comes from Conyers. Someone brought this one here, after the collapse. If it wasn't too long ago, it might still run."

Almost too hopeful, I climb into the apparatus on the passenger side. Kloves examines the dash and driver panels, not making heads or tails of most of it, I'm sure. "Keyless ignition," I say, pointing to the round black button just above the gear selector.

Kloves pushes it. There is a momentary squeal, then a sputter, and the HRV rumbles to life, loud in the enclosed space.

"Shit," Kloves says. "Can you drive it?"

"I can try." We must both be thinking the same thing: an apparatus this big and heavy isn't going to be impeded by a horde of hollow-heads. We could drive right through them without worrying about getting an axle caught. "The fuel tank is at a quarter. I'm not sure how far we'll get. And the diesel we brought with us will probably take this beast twenty miles."

"Then let's be quick," Barkov calls from the ground. "Transfer everything to the truck." Kloves jumps down and goes to help him.

"Can't we tow the car?" Marilyn asks.

I slide into the driver's seat. "Not easily," I answer. "She'd shimmy all over the place. The only way we can keep the car is if someone drives her out right up against the bumper of the truck."

"I'll do it," Kloves announces.

I reject the idea out of hand. "It's too dangerous. The HRV is big, with high windows. We'll all be safer in the cab."

"The fuel won't take us far enough," he says. "We're going to need the Volvo."

I shut my eyes and take a strained breath, the choice and its consequences like a weight on my chest. But he's right: we're going to need the Volvo to get back home.

"We should try," Barkov says, "but get everything onto the truck just in case."

I feel our luck changing when I open the first compartment on the driver side of the HRV. I drag out a diesel-powered portable AC generator and fill it from one of our barrels, then hunt through the rest of the compartment for power cables.

Barkov is watching me with suspicion. "Things just got a lot easier," I explain as I attach the cables to the garage door control panel on the wall. "We can power the door opener. It'll take seconds instead of minutes to lift it."

The commotion within the garage has started attracting the attention of the hollow-heads. I can hear them banging more loudly and in greater numbers. No doubt most of them wandered off while we were asleep, but they've returned in force.

After finishing with the control panel, I cut off the engine and help with the transfer from the Volvo. The HRV compartments are still full of assorted rescue equipment: small tools, first aid and paramedic kits, a rotary saw. A treasure trove, under other circumstances. I pull everything out as quickly as I can to give Barkov space to load our fuel barrels. Flashlights bounce and sweep across the back of the garage like searchlights.

It takes us less than an hour to make everything ready, but by now the horde has fully re-formed outside. I can almost feel the weight of their numbers through the garage doors, which shudder and bulge with the pressure.

When we are finished, Marilyn faces the banging door and says, "Maybe we should wait. They could wander off."

"That might take hours," Barkov points out.

"And we don't have that kind of time," I add. "We've already wasted so much. And there's no guarantee that more won't come. We don't know how many of them are in this area."

But I have to admit: I still want another option. Some way to avoid the danger that I'm putting my friend in. "Augustus. You can still change your mind."

He answers by way of getting into the driver's seat of the Volvo. "As soon as you start to pull out, I'll swing the car into the truck's bay and come up on your bumper."

I start the HRV's engine. Marilyn and Barkov come into the cabin. Barkov stows our spare weapons on the floor.

"Are we ready?" I call out to Kloves. He responds affirmatively. I hop out of the driver's seat and punch the button to open the panel door, then hurry back to my spot. I shut the driver door as the first twilight spreads into the garage, revealing all of the dust and grime we kicked up while we were here.

Hollow-heads begin crawling under the door, then ducking under it. We wait. They spill into the garage, and we wait. Marilyn clutches my arm. I can't pull forward until I'm certain the panel door is above the level of the apparatus or I'm liable to jam it in place.

The two shriekers sound their alert unnecessarily, but the noise unnerves me enough to make my foot twitch over the accelerator. My fingers grip the steering wheel until my knuckles turn white. Bodies fill the space around us, scratching and scrambling at the sides of the HRV. Despite the weight of the apparatus, it shudders under their constant writhing.

I can see Walnut Grove now. The two gas stations, the houses down the street. The intersection.

"Shit," I hear Kloves calling out. In the right-side mirror, I see hollow-heads already swarming around the easier target. I can barely see Kloves through the windshield. "Get moving!" he shouts, and I can barely hear him.

I put the truck in gear. The hollow-heads I can see through the front windshield seem to pause at the sound of the gearbox. The crowd is five deep. I won't be able to ease the HRV out slowly. I'll need as much force as I can throw at them.

"Go, go, go," Marilyn mutters.

I jam my foot down on the accelerator and the apparatus bucks beneath me. We jerk forward and the front of the truck pushes hollow-heads out of the way, then down. The truck's massive tires roll over them like they were pillows. Instinctively I squeeze my eyes shut for a moment, hating the sound and sensation, but there's nothing else to be done. This is necessary. Everything hinges on the Volvo being able to drive over the carpet of flattened bodies.

The truck growls out of the garage. Kloves swings the Volvo around until it's partially obscured by the HRV's shadow, and otherwise invisible behind the truck.

I pull a hard left and scrape hollow-heads off the apparatus with the side of the building. I hear the scratch and whine of paint transfer. Now I can see the Volvo again out of my mirrors. Kloves miscalculates and crunches the fender against the load-bearing pillar between the two panel doors.

The Volvo is stuck, its front end snagged on the pillar. Hollow-heads swarm over the car and the tires jam up against a few writhing bodies. I halt the HRV, waiting for Kloves to back up and try again, knowing that any sizable gap between us is going to trap him just as firmly.

Arms reach up to scrabble at my side window. More shrieking. I have almost no visibility behind me and begin to feel claustrophobic.

"We're going to lose the car," Barkov says, not stating the harder truth.

Another pair of shrieks. And then it gets worse. A second horde appears from the same direction as the first, moving quickly to join the hunt, though not yet at an all-out run. They haven't yet seen the frenzy of the hollow-heads around us, who have reacted typically to the crushing deaths of their companions.

Kloves pulls the Volvo into reverse and forces it back against the far wall of the bay. The gap fills.

I feel helpless. I need to do something. I go for my door, but Marilyn yanks me back, and Barkov shouts, "No sense in both of you risking your lives."

I reverse as well and try to push my way back to connect with the Volvo's fender. Now it's my turn to miscalculate, and I travel too far, too fast. The rear of the HRV parts the hollow-heads like a cigar boat through surf and slams into the front of the white station wagon. The hood goes up. I hear glass breaking.

I can't see what's happening. The Volvo is now in my blind spot. But I have to do more; this was my plan. My error. Ignoring the protests, ignoring the danger, I shove open my door, pushing away the few hollow-heads that still attack the truck. I move to drop down to the pavement, then catch sight of Kloves crawling out of the Volvo through the broken windshield.

"Boss!" he shouts, waving me back into the cabin. He climbs onto the roof of the station wagon. "Go," he says, as the horde around him floods over the top of the Volvo.

I close the driver door. I pound the wheel, then grip it hard. I jam my foot down, and the apparatus bucks again. I want to stop, turn around. But looking into my mirror I know it's already too late. I plow the truck through the second horde as it enters the intersection. I keep my foot down, wanting to slaughter every last one, but content enough to splatter a dozen brains on the asphalt.

The three of us do not speak a word until we've reached Monroe and turned onto Highway 78, heading for Athens. When words do come, they come from Marilyn.

"I've changed my mind. I want to be there, Sam. I'm going to be there when it's done."

DAY FIFTEEN, 6:00 A.M.

We stopped a few miles short of Clarke County, just after nine o'clock, once the darkness had wrapped around us. In Monroe, Barkov and I brought the truck's tank to half full with the barrels taken from the Volvo, and by the time we stopped for the night, the tank was already below a quarter full again. As I'd suspected, we weren't going to make it back to the Little Five in the HRV unless we happened across some more biodiesel.

We have all lost loved ones to violence before. Parents, husbands, wives, children—worse losses than dear friends. There is no one in the Little Five over the age of fifteen who doesn't remember someone who never made it this far. Most of the world didn't make it this far.

It doesn't make the loss of Augustus Kloves any less painful.

We stir ourselves awake at dawn when the sun shines through the large windshield of the HRV cabin. I climb out of the cabin to check the area for hollow-heads, and when I see none nearby

I gesture to Barkov and Marilyn that it's safe to step down. We relieve ourselves in the high, overgrown grass at the side of Highway 78.

A family of deer moves skittishly across the road a hundred yards away. In my youth, growing up in the urban northeast, this would have awed me. But it's too familiar a sight now to receive much of my attention. At most it tells me that there aren't any hollow-heads hiding among the trees up the road.

At last, Barkov speaks. "I have never been to the Clarke County community. Do you know where we will find them?"

I shake my head, rubbing the sleep from my eyes. "I visited Athens before the collapse, but not since. I know there was a group holed up in one of the UGA dorms, but the university was a big agriculture school, so they may have moved nearer to where they grow food. There'd be enough research buildings around that they could set up a decent community."

"We can't drive through Athens in this," Marilyn says, knocking on the side of the HRV. "Unless we want to be obvious."

"They may not know we're coming," I say, "or they might have been expecting us to show up yesterday, or the day before. But we can't assume any of that. If we go the rest of the way on foot, it could be another day before we find anything. There's a loop around the town that I think we should take in the truck, and if we see anything promising, we hide the truck and go the rest of the way on foot. Take what we think we'll need."

We agree to this plan, having no other to replace it, and get back in the cabin. I continue driving east until we come to a large gas station on the outskirts of the city where there are still a few buildings, most of them single story. The area is covered in grass and trees, with rusting cars shoved to the grassy median. Ahead, there is a turnoff toward the loop, and farther beyond that is what looks like the very edge of Athens proper. I confirm again that Barkov and Marilyn are on board with what I've proposed, then take the turn.

Phoebe is close. She has to be. We can't go much farther: we don't have the diesel. If we don't find her here, I don't know what's next.

The approach to the southern arc of the loop around Athens is devoid of human presence. There is only a divided four-lane highway surrounded on both sides by trees and overgrowth so thick that we'd need a machete to pass through. Then another turn, and we are on the loop proper. We pass an enormous hardware store sign, orange and gray against the green of the trees—and then nothing again.

More deer, and clans of possum and armadillo. A sign informs us that we have entered Athens-Clarke County. But even the overpasses, which give us a slightly broader view, don't provide any evidence of human life. Even life that once lived here. We don't seem to be any closer to Athens than we were last night.

That changes quickly. Exit seven, the University of Georgia, overlooks a portion of the campus with parking lots overflowing with abandoned cars. A last stop for the doomed, most likely, seeking safe harbor with their last few drops of unaffected gasoline. Next, on our left, sprawls an empty parking lot with solar power poles scattered throughout like solitary trees in a grove.

As we come up along the eastern side of the loop, I am forced to maneuver the HRV around enormous abandoned construction vehicles, strewn across a work site where the county must have been renovating the roads just before the crisis began. Ten years later and still no one has tried to move them out of the way.

The loop is pinched off like a twist tie in the northeast corner, and I have to navigate off the highway for a few minutes before we can continue west along the northern arc. The rest of the loop is just as unpromising, and by the time we have come full circle it is midmorning.

There seems only one route to take. Exit seven, to the university. I take the HRV across the southern part of the loop again and slow down to a crawl as we come to the exit offramp.

"I guess we walk from here," I say, shutting off the engine after pulling the truck onto the grass along the left shoulder, hiding it partially behind the overgrown trees and bushes.

Barkov suggests that we move all of our equipment into the trees themselves, in case someone notices the apparatus and comes to strip it down. We will have to travel lightly. Marilyn takes only her medical bag. Barkov slings the Remington over one shoulder.

We walk down the rest of the way to College Station Road and observe at last the first sign of modern life: a chain link fence spread across the street beneath the loop overpass. There is a second fence a few yards behind it, forming a double gate. I'm confident this is their main entrance, at least for the larger vehicles that come to the Little Five for trade.

We stay hidden behind a few bushes. Two men, ostensibly guards, play a game of cards on a portable table near the inner gate.

"We should just walk up there," Marilyn says.

"We don't know enough about this community," I reply.

"It's Clarke County. They've been trading with us for years." Marilyn lifts a hand to stop my objection. "Yes, I know this is where those two men came from. But that doesn't mean anyone else here knows anything. Or if some do, not everyone, surely. Mikhail, you said the men who took Phoebe were enforcers."

"Yes, that is what the fat man told us."

"Couldn't they have just been along for the ride?" Marilyn asks. When Barkov and I look at her with stupid expressions she adds, "I was just offering a suggestion. Look, we don't even know if they're here. If we go slinking around and sneaking our way in, we could get in trouble that has nothing to do with Phoebe and the enforcers."

I understand the point she is trying to make and part of why she is trying to make it. She's not used to thinking in clandestine terms. For Barkov this must be second nature, and for me—well, I'm getting used to a lot of things I've never done before.

"Like you said, we don't have enough information," she continues. "We don't know where to look. It's not like Athens is a small town. We're going to have to talk to somebody eventually." She throws a sour glance at Barkov. "Sam, don't let Mikhail talk you into doing something extremely stupid twice in one trip. Conyers was more than enough."

For some reason Barkov looks to me to make a decision, though he says nothing, even to object to Marilyn's insult.

I think back to what we know. Randall and Banderas are enforcers for the trafficking network, run by someone named Ravana. They arrived in the Little Five in trucks operated by the Clarke County trading group. Norm Ithering knew them and treated them like members of his operation. He and Mayor Weeks discussed leaving the two men in the Little Five for a few extra days, to help Braithwaite and Vargas. That turned out to be a cover for their real task, but again, Ithering need not have known.

Those details could send us in either direction. Either Randall and Banderas are a central part of Clarke County's operation—in which case the whole of Athens stinks of trafficking—or they are agents hidden in plain sight. Ithering and Clarke County as a whole might not be aware of their true roles.

"But wait—" I begin, talking more to myself than to Marilyn or Barkov. "It was a couple days they were supposed to stay in the Little Five. Randall and Banderas. That's what the mayor said: Ithering was leaving them for a couple of days. How were they going to get back?"

"The trucks took Randall from Inman Park after we evacuated," Barkov says. "That is obvious."

"It's obvious, yes, but at the time, that wasn't necessarily the plan, and it definitely wasn't what we expected. It was an above board, routine sort of thing. So how were they going to get back? Were they going to take one of the Volvos? Did Ithering tell Weeks they were going to pick up the two men later?"

"You talked to him, not me," Marilyn says.

I can't remember, and at the time, it wouldn't have occurred to me to ask. It wasn't important. Now, the information would make my decision for me. Either they had alternative transportation, or Ithering and his trading group know all about the trafficking.

"Marilyn's right," I admit. "We should go in clean." Before Barkov complains I add, "But just the two of you. I'll find another way in."

"Sam," Marilyn says, in the tone she used at the tire store.

"No. Think about it. Mikhail, your enclave never trades directly with Clarke County. You use us as a proxy because we have the better highway access. So they've never met you. And Marilyn, you were visible, but I don't think they ever really noticed you. Not enough to remember your name or what you look like. But everyone on Ithering's crew knows me. If I walk in there clear as day, and they're part of Ravana's organization, they'll know immediately something's wrong. They'll know why I'm here. But you two can be travelers. You'll get in, find out what you can, and we'll meet back here tonight. Midnight. I'll spend the time looking for another way in. If I find one, I'll take a look around, but I'll be careful. No heroics. I promise."

When my speech ends, Marilyn is quiet for a long moment. I can see the conflict in her face. I expect her to tell me again that I don't need to prove anything to her, that I don't have to be the one to save the world. But I've never been the sort to turn away just because something is dangerous.

"Sam," Marilyn says again. "Damn it. You're right. Of course, you're right." Her shoulders drop as she resigns herself to my plan.

I open a side panel on the HRV and retrieve the heavy-duty toolbox, one of the few things we didn't discard when we packed in the diesel. Inside I find what I need: bolt cutters, a spool of wire, and insulated electrical gloves. I add these to my pack and accept the Remington when Barkov offers it.

I take a deep breath, preparing myself. "If there's any chance of you getting caught by Randall, by anyone, get the hell out. And I promise I won't take any pointless risks, either."

Marilyn clutches me in an embrace, her cheek against mine. She brushes her lips across my face, then kisses me firmly and steps back. "Midnight," she says. "We'll be here."

I am momentarily charged by the kiss and the memories that surface from it. I want to linger, to be greedy for what I lost.

"I'll be here," Marilyn says.

I secure my pack and climb the ramp back onto the loop. I glance back briefly to see that Marilyn is watching me leave while Barkov gathers his own things. As I reach the main highway, my friends disappear from view, and I'm alone.

I cross to the opposite lanes and move north along the shoulder, looking through the trees at a meandering fence line that we didn't notice from the truck. It's clearly a new construction, post-collapse, made from scraps and repurposed parts. Some sections are simple plank walls. This suggests to me that the community here may be much larger than the Little Five: we had more than enough chain link fencing and only a few sources to choose from. The Clarke County group may have run out and had to improvise.

I walk until I cross a bridge over a small stream. Listening to the birds in the trees and the animals in the underbrush, I become acutely aware of my solitude. A pack of feral dogs rushes along the other side of the road, chasing a cat, barking loudly and making me worry about hollow-heads.

I see none until I move farther into the trees and approach a section of fence that I can breach with the bolt cutters. A pair of hollow-heads move away from the fence and toward the sound of the dog pack. Both are male and scrawny, faces rotting from some mouth infection that may have taken a decade to get this bad, given the hollow-heads' resistance to disease. Even from a distance, I can see rows of blackened teeth, lips pulled back as if to growl. But there is only silence.

They see me immediately and turn to face me. I stop still and hold my breath, waiting for shrieks, but they don't come. They stumble across the rough ground, one of them reaching out as if to clutch at my face.

They are half a dozen yards off, no farther. At their speed, I might be able to cut my way through the fence, but I wouldn't be able to secure it again quickly enough to prevent them from coming through. So I drop my pack and let the Remington gently down on the ground. I draw my knife and wait for the hollow-heads.

They both look like they've been through fights before. Long cuts and scars dominate the skin of their bare arms. Someone foolish enough to fight unprepared at close quarters must have made those wounds and suffered the consequences.

The first hollow-head comes into range, and I kick it hard in the chest, knocking it off balance and onto its back. As it rolls over to rise up, I take three quick steps forward. A hollow-head's skull is as strong as anyone else's, and a knife isn't usually going to do the job. Even if it does penetrate, there's not much left in there for it to destroy. So I plunge the knife deep into the second hollow-head's neck, then dash back out of reach as it sputters and seizes from the gushing wound. My hand is covered with blood.

The first hollow-head, finally back on its feet, notices its dying companion. I could swear that the change is visible on its skin: muscles tighten, eyes bulge, the rictus of its mouth grows wider. This one is going to be harder to kill.

It lunges at me, bringing its teeth to bear. I swing the knife up to catch it under the jaw, but I only succeed in shearing off its left ear and part of its cheek. It keeps moving, pushing me over before I can get my feet behind me. I land with a heavy thump against my pack, a spasm of pain in my back, and the wind knocked out of me.

The hollow-head snaps at me, tearing part of my shirt. Its blood, pouring from its ear and cheek, spatters my chest. Getting clear with my knife arm, I stab the monster hard in the back of the neck, severing its spinal cord. The body goes limp, though the head continues to gnash away, and I grunt hard as I lift and roll the dying thing off me. I shiver like a child walking through a graveyard. The fetid smell of the hollow-head's mouth nearly makes me retch.

It was a foolish mistake. I should have risked firing two rounds. I could have moved another half mile down the road and tried another entry point, just in case anyone came to investigate the gunshots. Now I'm covered in blood, which will make it difficult for me if I run into anyone on the streets of Athens.

I wait for twenty minutes, making sure that there are no hollow-heads or people nearby, then hide the Remington by the largest tree in the area. Quietly I cut open a small space in the fence and squeeze through. I replace the cut section and tie it back into the fence with the spool of wire.

The ground slopes down to the edge of the stream, which I imagine must have been a river at one time and will be again once the last of us has been scoured off the planet and all the world's dams crumble from disrepair. The water is greenish brown, murky. I consider crossing over, but it will be even harder to explain muddy and drenched pants than hollow-head blood on my shirt.

A dirt road runs parallel between the stream and the fence. I follow it, staying in the trees and hugging the fence line, until it comes out on a major road. There is another gate here, but it appears to be unguarded. The fence line continues to follow the stream, but I've had enough of slinking around in the trees. I turn left onto the sidewalk. I am on the edge of the downtown part of Athens, surely: abandoned cars litter the streets and parking lots.

I check my clothes. The blood is drying, darkening, but it's still obviously the product of misadventure. My boots are muddy but that won't be a problem for long. My pack is clean, except for a few grass stains. I look like a traveler. I don't look like I belong here.

I follow the sidewalk until it ends at the soft corner of Williams and Oconee Streets. Williams Street takes me southwest, past a university parking lot, to the Interim Medical Partnership Building. The grass and trees are as overgrown as any abandoned streets back in Atlanta. I've yet to see a living person. I wonder, almost aloud, why the fence extends this far if there's no one to use the space.

And then I see it: an apartment complex, just south of the university building. The parking spaces out front are empty, completely cleared of unused cars, and for the first time since leaving the Little Five I see a freshly cut lawn.

A man in his late sixties works on a small garden plot in front of the nearest apartment building, turning dirt and moving decorative plants from one hole to another. It's an odd sight: back home, every sizable piece of arable land is used for growing food. The Clarke County community definitely has space to spare.

Although I stay across the narrow street, next to a ramshackle toll booth that must have controlled access to the university's lot, the man notices my observation and thumps his gloved hands against his thighs. He stands and wipes a light sheen of sweat off his forehead.

"We got a breach?" he calls over.

My clothes give away what I've been up to, but it seems that's not necessarily unheard of. "Yeah," I call back, "but I've fixed it." I give my pack a light pat with one hand. The other hand I keep on my holstered P229.

"Must've been a mess of 'em," he says, pulling off his gloves. "Any of that blood yours?"

"No," I reply, surprised at the nonchalant manner of that question.

"Well, I know it's a long trek back to the post. If you want to clean up, I've got fresh water inside." He beckons me over.

Everything about this feels wrong. It would have felt wrong fifteen years ago, unless I'd been living in some whitewashed rural midwestern town where no one locked their doors. And I've never lived in a place like that. Except the Little Five, I suppose. But we know what a stranger looks like.

Yet if I refuse, he might become suspicious. He might raise an alarm, expanding the threat to include the whole community. If I have to, I can manage a single man. I doubt I could take on a whole town. So I shrug and accept the offer as noncommittally as I can, following him into the building. As we go up a flight of stairs, he makes small talk, perhaps to cover the slow, creaking speed with which he climbs. "Haven't seen you out in this quadrant before. You just get rotated in?"

"Yeah," I say, wishing there were more I could offer. I feel like the worst spy in the world.

The old man opens his apartment's front door and ushers me within. The space looks clean, well-cared for, and I see evidence of at least two people living here. Two bookshelves with markedly different contents, a sofa with two collapsible dinner trays in front of it. Through a large sliding glass door, I notice a small generator on the balcony. This is what passes for luxury now, and I'm impressed. As if calling up an old instinct, I remove my mud-caked boots as soon as I step over the threshold.

"Come on through," he says, pointing to a hallway at the back of the main room. "Tyler, my roommate, he's still asleep, so the bathroom's all yours. There's towels, and I'll get you another shirt. Swear to God, that one you've got on is not getting out of here alive." He chuckles and opens the bathroom door.

I step in and shut the door behind me. I take an extra second to work the lock, then test it. The bathroom is as clean as the rest of the place, with an unused toilet and sink. The tub is filled almost to the top with clean water. Hanging on a hook on the tile above is a small plastic bucket shaped like a sandcastle.

I hesitate. It's entirely possible that the old man has now gone to get help from the real guards of Clarke County, and I'm waiting like a moron to be captured. But if that's true, then I'm too obvious as it is. If I leave now, I'll still look like I've been in a hollow-head fight, and I'll stand out too much. I need to get clean, regardless.

I drop my pack to the floor and peel off my coat, shirt, and bra. Soaked-through blood sticks to my skin. I look in the mirror and see a nightmare: my arms and chest are red, my neck and face look like they've been sprayed with paint.

My pants aren't much better. They're covered in mud and grass stains, but I will be able to live with that. I remove them, so I can run a bit of water over them to get the worst of the road off. The gun in my holster clunks on the tile floor. My socks stink like cheese left out on a Louisiana stoop. I peel them off, too, hoping I can impose on the old man's hospitality a little more.

Feeling a bit sheepish about staining one of the sharply creased towels, I draw water out of the tub and start to wash the blood from my body. I pour a little bit of water through my hair as well, using my fingers as a comb.

A knock at the bathroom door causes me to jump.

"Just a minute, I'm not decent." I laugh a little, staring at my haggard face.

I hear a key entering the lock. The door handle moves. My heart pounds twice before I can recover my wits. As I reach down for my holster, the door crashes open and the old man jumps in, wielding a knife. He moves quickly, faster than I would have guessed from the way he climbed the stairs. Before I can retrieve my gun, his free forearm is across my shoulders and he is pushing me back against the bathroom wall.

"Tyler!" he shouts. "We got one!"

Another man enters the cramped space. He is younger than my attacker. Leaner, with a pretty face.

With his knife arm, the older man cracks me across the cheek-bone, using his elbow to deliver most of the hit. I see stars in my left eye, but I don't think my jaw is broken. I curse myself for not keeping my shoes. I try to knee him in the groin, but he seems ready for it and hops out of the way.

He is stronger by half than he has any right to be. I try to wrench myself clear, but it's no use, and Tyler is blocking the door anyway. The old man grabs my wet hair and throws me past him, forcing my head down into the water-filled tub. Before I can adapt, I scream the air out of my lungs, counter to everything I ever learned in the Coast Guard.

As I struggle beneath the water, my chest starting to burn, the old man's rough hand slides across my back. His fingers hook into my underwear, and he pulls them down. I buck once, then come to my resolve.

It's been a while, but I'm trained for this. I go limp. With any luck Tyler and his partner will think I've passed out: most people have no idea just how long it actually takes to drown. And even without air in my lungs, I can hold my breath longer than most.

I can hear them talking. The old man's body is pressed against mine, wanting release, but suddenly timid. They don't want me dead. As soon as I feel the added grip on my hair, I know what's coming. The old man pulls me out of the water and as he does, I rotate my whole body and deliver a solid roundhouse punch. Not to his face, as he did to me. That won't help. His skull is a lot stronger than my knuckles.

I punch him hard in the throat.

I feel his trachea compressing, crunching. He screams rag-gedly, the sound of a dog trying to retch up vomit. He stumbles back, lifting himself up, crashing against the sink and the mirror. He's bent backwards across the sink now, his pants down around his ankles, and his engorged penis quickly losing interest.

I punch him in the balls. He yelps with more pain, losing air he can't replace. Tyler backs away and I lunge at him, my wet, naked body clobbering him against the hallway wall. I slam a clenched fist into his right eye.

As the two men roll around in pain, the old man suffocating on his own cartilage, I scramble to recover my pants and holster. With one eye watching the men, I throw open a hallway closet until I find what must be one of Tyler's shirts. I dress from top to bottom as I move toward the front door, hopping into my pants as if I were in a sack race.

Tyler barrels into me from behind and I nearly lose my own eye on the edge of a TV tray table. My forehead takes most of the hit. There's going to be a nasty bruise later.

I can't care about it. Tyler's knees are on my back. But he's stupid and can't see my gun side. I draw, move my arm around in an arc to get position, and shoot off the right side of his face without looking.

Tyler topples off me and I climb to my feet. The old man, wheezing out the last of his breath, careens from the bathroom and stumbles toward me. But I'm done with this place. I jump down the stairs four at a time and break across the street, toward the university building's parking lot. I crouch down behind the toll booth to catch my breath.

I forgot my boots and coat. I consider going back to get them, but the old man is out in the yard now. He drops face down in the grass. I can't get close: with my luck, someone will see.

I forgot my pack, too. So no bolt cutters, no wire. No flashlight, no food. No ammunition except for the rounds I have in the P229 and the four in the Remington beyond the fence.

I bang the back of my head against the toll booth, humiliated by my gullibility. The old man knew I was a stranger. That was why he took me in.

DAY FIFTEEN, 12:00 P.M.

At least I escaped. But in order to do so, I had to shoot one man in the face and kill another with my bare hands. As I rest against the toll booth in my borrowed clothes and bare feet, I start to shake from adrenaline. Though my fist struck mostly flesh and cartilage, my knuckles still hurt, a reminder of the force of my blow. I search out the sensation of regret and discover that I don't feel it. I am more bothered by its absence than I am by what I've had to do.

I've had friends, at the academy and after, who were raped. Some more than once. It was a hell I never suffered. Even through the worst of my adolescence, that, at least, never came for me. But relief at having escaped, and my near satisfaction at the method, only adds to my frustration. I'm an adult with training and experience. Phoebe is a child.

I stand, check my holster and the gun. It's time to get moving again.

I head west under a dilapidated railroad bridge made of wood and rusted metal. At the sound of a police siren—strange to my ears after a decade without them— I hide behind the bridge's wooden beams, watching as the campus cop car passes, its electric engine running silent. Someone must have seen the dead man and alerted the city's police. There will be a search; I need to be as far away from this area as I can, as soon as humanly possible.

As I hurry to the intersection and hook a left down East Campus Road, I wonder how the police received the message so quickly. Perhaps they're using shortwave radios here for local communication. Or they've found a way to get the telephones working again. Either way, the emergency response speaks to an infrastructure much better established than anything the Little Five has put together, despite the work of Braithwaite, Vargas, and the power company.

Not that we've needed so powerful a framework. It takes me only a few minutes to walk from one end of the Little Five to the other. We are insubstantial. And I thought we were a beacon among the barbarians.

I must take care. I pass old university housing on my right. Then beyond it, what at first looks like a massive parking deck. Closer, I recognize it for what it is: a stadium. One of the entrances lets out onto the street that I'm on, but its original name has been pulled off, leaving only the cleaner surface of the wall behind to tell me that this was once called the Lettermen's Gate. Hanging above the name is a banner made of tablecloth that reads "Defensive Training Field B" in big red letters.

I can't worry about it now. They could be building an army in there for all I know, but I'm here for one purpose only. The Little Five is my post, not the whole former state of Georgia, and I can tackle only one problem at a time. Maybe after all of this is done I can worry about what I'm leaving behind.

I see more people in the streets south of the stadium. The population is growing denser by the block, and it's becoming harder for me to keep my distance. There isn't much cover in this area. My bare feet are sore from the asphalt and concrete. The more I walk, the more exposed I feel. I need to find shoes.

Eventually I come to an intersection beyond which there is nothing but hills and woodland, as far as I can tell. To the right there are more buildings. I debate the question for only a moment: trees and grass aren't going to get me any answers. So I turn again, heading deeper into the town.

A massive building, made of flat red brick and sporting the title "College of Education," rises to my right. In front, on a patio between two sets of stairs leading to the front doors, is a squat guard house that clearly was not part of the original construction. It looks like a transplanted toll booth from one of the parking lots. That alone would have caught my attention, but something more makes me pause: the guard house window is facing the larger building's doors.

I step behind a small enclosed bus stop on the other side of the street to watch and consider. A guard house facing the wrong way isn't protecting the contents of the building from outsiders. It's protecting outsiders from the contents of the building. Or—knowing where I am, and why I'm here—preventing what's inside from leaving.

A building this size could house a thousand people.

I close my eyes and memorize the location, tracing my path back to the fence where I entered. I'm going to have to come back here, I'm sure of it.

Then I move on.

I pass the university's veterinary hospital on the left. The larger buildings mean fewer trees, less cover, and a greater chance that someone will notice I don't belong here. There once was a time when a person could walk into any abandoned house and find clothes, food, tools, books, shoes—anything one might need. But those days are long gone, especially in a town like this. By the time a fence goes up, everything within the perimeter has been scavenged clean.

I keep to the bushes wherever I am able and continue west until I see another large, repurposed building. A large gray G dominates the red brick wall to the left of the entrance, and under it the old name is still attached: "Coliseum Training Facility." That explains the oddly shaped, glass-fronted building just beyond, which looks to me like an eyelid and eyeball: the Coliseum itself. Beneath the original name of the red brick building is a newer banner, less hastily raised than the one at Defensive Training Field B. It reads, in bright blue, "Police & Militia."

The combination sends a shiver down my spine.

I am far too exposed. It feels like there are a hundred eyes on me, even though the parking lot across the street from the training facility—the "police and militia" building—is empty except for a dozen city police and campus cop cars.

And three battery-powered university buses.

And six moving vans.

"Oh, Jesus," I mutter, needing to hear a friendly voice. I recognize one of the U-Hauls: the faded, blood-smeared factoid graphic on the side is identical to the one Norm Ithering drives.

Answers to old questions click into place. So Ithering's trading caravan returned to Athens within the last two or three days. If he picked up Randall and Phoebe along the way, then the two of them may be in town. Further, there must be a dozen or more parking lots throughout the enclosed area that makes up the Clarke County community. Some nearer to the main exit toward the state highway, certainly. But Ithering parked his trucks here, nearer to the heart of the town, and directly across from the police and militia building.

He knows.

The building with the inward-facing guard house isn't some hidden, well-kept secret place that the citizens know nothing about.

I would bet the HRV and my Remington that the guarded building serves as the quarters for the people abducted by Ravana's human trafficking network. A modern longhouse.

Ravana, whoever he is, can't be a shadowy figure on the outskirts of power in Athens.

And yet—something about that thought nags at me. In Conyers, Orwell insisted that no one knew who Ravana was. That the ringleader operated through proxies, thugs like Randall and Banderas. Maybe the same is true here. The sort of network that encrypts its communications is certainly the sort that could hide its leaders—even in plain sight.

If I'm going to get any closer to the truth, I need to get closer to people. I need a solution to my shoe problem. A patch of loose dust underneath a dying bush offers an answer, at least for now. Someone walking through town with clean bare feet might attract attention, but someone with dirty bare feet who looks to be the sort of person who goes everywhere barefoot may not be noticed.

I cover my feet in red-brown dust, smearing it into my skin, doing my best to look like an old-world hippie. My borrowed shirt is too clean; I dirty it, as well. I unhook the holster from my belt and tuck it into the back of my pants. The men's shirt hides the SIG easily. Last, I check my gait, and try to move like a person without a destination. Like I'm taking a midday constitutional, not spying on the heart of a human trafficking empire.

And there it is again: "empire." An empire at our doorstep, for years. How did I not know about it? How did news or rumors never reach the Little Five? Either I'm wrong about the extent of the network in Clarke County, or they do such a good job of controlling information that no one who leaves the town—

I feel a chasm open in my gut as I realize with horror that I may have sent Marilyn and Barkov into a trap. Perhaps no one ever leaves the town.

But no: that would make no sense. Surely people would be missed. Someone would come searching, like we've done. We can't be the first.

There are a hundred reasons why that is a foolish expectation, but I need to ignore them. Worrying about Marilyn will put both of us in greater danger. So I focus my attention ahead of me, on the glass eye building that was once the university's Stegeman Coliseum. Some of the glass panes have shattered in the intervening years, and many more are grime-caked, but the ones within easy reach have been well maintained.

A trio of men guard the front glass doors, which are well-disguised among the massive window panes. The men wear fatigues, civilian knockoffs from a trendy sporting goods store. They look down at me from their perch on the raised platform in front of the building. All three carry assault rifles, the distinctive silhouette of the Heckler & Koch G36 or HK293. German weapons, built also by the Saudis beginning a few years before the collapse, G36s should be rare in the former United States, except maybe in D.C. and Maryland. They would have been illegal for civilian use. So most likely they're HK293s, civilian weapons, incapable of automatic fire out of the box and not easily converted.

Not that this eases my mind at all. I can't think of any above-board reason for fielding the HK293. If you're in the habit of killing large masses of hollow-heads, you'd want an automatic rifle. I'd dismiss it as being a case of using what's available, but all three men have the same weapon. You bring an H&K assault rifle to the fight on purpose. And you use it against people.

"Hey," one of the guards calls out. I've been lingering too long, probably staring as I worry. I look around, hoping he had someone else in mind, but he's looking straight at me.

The men carry their weapons with decent trigger discipline: barrels down, hands loose, fingers off the triggers. And the one calling out to me doesn't use his weapon to gesture, which typically happens when you don't know how to act with a rifle in your hands. But they're too young to be ex-military.

"Yes?" I call back, trying to gauge the level of familiarity I should show. Are these men thugs, or do they think of themselves as protectors?

"Gotta check your arm," he says, taking a step forward.

I cross the street, approaching, watching his eyes to see which side of my body interests him more. His gaze flickers in the direction of my left side, upper arm. I roll up my sleeve and present my side to him, hoping that my expression of mild inconvenience is the correct one.

"You're good," he says after he makes his brief inspection.

I hazard a question. "Why'd you stop me?"

The man raises his eyebrows. "Are you serious? No shoes, a shirt too big? You look like a runner."

One of the men behind him laughs and says loudly enough for all of us to hear, "I told you! Why would a runner be walking back *toward* the fields? That's just stupid."

"Yeah, yeah," my inspector concedes. "But you never know."

"Sure," I say, rolling my sleeve back down. I look down at my feet as if to admit that I look suspicious.

"You need shoes?" the guard asks. "I mean, you're going to central distribution, right? How'd you lose them, anyway?"

"Stupidly," I say, shrugging. "Nothing exciting, though."

That seems to be enough of an answer for him. "So you need shoes or what?"

"I wouldn't say no," I reply.

He turns toward the glass doors, letting his buddies know that they're on their own for the next few minutes. He stows his H&K on a folding chair behind the laughing man, the first sign of incomplete weapon training I've seen.

I follow him into the building, which looks typical for a modern indoor sporting complex. Men and women pass us by, some but not all of them looking at me and my shoeless feet.

"Sorry I thought you could be a runner," the guard says, turning to shake my hand while we walk. "Name's Calvin."

"Sam," I offer back. "No worries."

"It's just, you know, it happens sometimes. Usually they go to the fences from The Box, though." He says "the box" as if it constituted the name of a building. Perhaps he's referring to the college building with the guard house that I passed on the way. "But I figured, maybe you were trying to break someone else out. And they'd be in the fields right now, you know?"

"Yeah," I say, knowing none of that and hating all of it.

"Here," the guard says after a few more paces. He takes me into a locker room bustling with other guards in various stages of undress. They scurry around like rats, and my skin crawls at the sight of them. The guard escorting me stops and points to a rack of mud-covered army surplus boots.

"Take what fits," he says. "They won't be missed." Laughing, he adds, "Maybe they'll assume one of the workers took a pair."

As I sort through the shoes, I race to process what I've seen. After the collapse, many of us stayed awake at night worrying about some nightmare scenario where a band of thugs geared up and rolled over every community in sight. Perhaps an army company with no orders to carry out and no chain of command to obey would decide to claim a pocket of the state as a new dystopian republic. These were familiar fears: Hollywood had taught us they were plausible. Militias were another fear.

But they never came. We rebuilt, survived, slept soundly in our beds after the first few years. And we stopped worrying about preparing for invasions. With the number of soldiers I've seen in the last five minutes, Clarke County could take over most of Georgia in a week. That it hasn't suggests a different agenda or a very long game.

I find a good pair of boots and lace them up. They're rough but familiar. Perhaps a little less comfortable than my Bellevilles.

"Jokes aside, though, you should probably get some proper shoes at distribution, and turn those in so I don't get in trouble."

"Of course," I say, standing up. "Thanks for the help."

The guard shrugs shyly. "Glad to be of service. I'll let you out back, across the fields."

Calvin takes me around the loop of the Coliseum's atrium to heavy wooden doors that groan when they open. From here, I can see the fields that he mentioned, and everything I've pieced together comes into place in a single vista.

The "fields" are four university sports fields, converted for growing crops within the city limits. An arena's land isn't deep, and the drainage is too quick, but there must have been some survivors from the agriculture college to work on a solution. I see rows of potatoes and corn, a cluster of tomato and cucumber plants. And among them all, like out of some antebellum Southern vista, dozens upon dozens of men and women toil under the whips of overseers.

We were right. All roads led to Clarke County. I strain to keep my heart in my chest, to avoid the appearance of scanning the faces for the one I've come here to find. Calvin can't discover that I give a damn about the men and women they're keeping as slaves.

"Lumpkin Street's just across," Calvin says, pointing toward another street and then sweeping his hand across to show me the route. "Don't go down Rutherford, you'll get stopped a hundred times a step." He smiles awkwardly, then adds, "You can bring the boots back to me yourself, maybe."

I thank him again. I want to rush like a bull into the midst of the people in the fields. To retch my disgust for Calvin and the rest like him into the tough soil of a university sporting complex. The antebellum echoes are haunting. They remind me that some things never seem to change, no matter how much the world is wiped clean.

A wall separates the street from the fields, but I pass a heavy iron gate and slow down to look through its slats for the familiar face of

Phoebe Weeks. I can only hope that she's here. It would be better to find her in this place than anywhere else I can too easily imagine.

The captives' faces are red and dirty, sheened with sweat. Their clothes are old, some tattered, all marked with soil and grass. On the nearest captives I can see the tattoo the guard didn't find on my arm: a red letter R inside a black circle. Some of them look at me as I pass by, fatigue barely masking a resentment they have every reason to think I deserve.

The scope of the horror here is beyond my expectations. But I should have known better. This all began in the codes of Braithwaite's numbers station. Complexity and secrecy of that caliber demand a sophisticated organization behind them. And such a thing doesn't exist without need.

I came here focused only on Phoebe, but I knew there had to be more. I knew, and I ignored. Facing the captives now, I feel the accusation in their eyes. They believe I'm complicit. Maybe I am. Maybe when all of this is done, when Phoebe is safe in her mother's arms, I will have to come back.

I'm able to get a better look when I turn left at the intersection and follow the iron fence. Although I can count at least three dozen people toiling on the other side, that can't be close to the total number of people Clarke County has taken as slaves. The Little Five, which is less than half the size of this community, needs a lot more crop space than these fields provide. There must be more—more land, and more people being forced to work it. Most of the workers in these fields are men and teenage boys, and the few women alongside them are adults.

I don't see Phoebe. And I belatedly concede that it's not reasonable for me to think she would be here. She's too small, not strong enough for this kind of work.

An overseer lounging against the fence takes to staring at me as I pass him. He is wearing an H&K P30 semiautomatic pistol on a holster not designed for the best fit. I'm again struck by the odd choice of weapons—but at least it's consistent. The P30 was fielded primarily by European law enforcement.

Hustling past the overseer so that he doesn't get a close look at me, I consider the chances that the Clarke County powers acquired a shipment of Heckler & Koch weapons at the Port of Savannah, either before or after it was shut down when the last of the fuel for the ships ran out. It's an easy explanation, but one too well-fitted to my former life. Of course, that's the possibility I'd consider first: I was involved in a number of anti-smuggling operations in the last two years of my service. Perhaps the truth is as simple as having contacts with people willing to exchange an armory for forced labor.

Once I'm out of view of the fields, I stop in the shade of a tree near a squat Mormon church. The building looks long abandoned, still boarded up as if there were no perimeter fences now to protect it. There is no one nearby to question my presence.

Calvin told me that the distribution center was nearby, and since I have no other particular destination in mind, I decide to press my luck. I wander down a few corners until I come to the front of an elementary school on the block beyond the fields. It's a sprawling complex, as elementary schools go, and nothing like the big lunchbox that was my school up north, thirty years ago.

A covered walkway leads from the street to the front entrance, which is bannered with the word "Distribution" in careful green lettering. Still somewhat hesitant, I walk to the doors and peer in. The interior is soothingly familiar, identical in concept to virtually every other elementary school interior I've seen. Murals still adorn the walls, though their paint is fading and scuffed away in places. Pin boards hang in their designated places, but the signs posted there are not the colorful kind from my youth. They look like pages out of a regulation handbook, cranked from a mimeograph.

A reception desk has been set up in the lobby, and the woman seated there resembles a principal's office secretary about as much as a dog resembles a cat. She is stocky and muscular, and her dark hair is cropped close to her head. With the flick of a hand she gestures for me to enter, her mouth pursed in a display of impatience.

"Local or visiting?" she asks, opening a ring binder in front of her.

"Local," I reply, not sure how safely I could answer otherwise.

"Are you here for supplies or labor?" She looks me over, peering over her ring binder as she flips through laminated pages. "I'm guessing supplies."

"Yes, ma'am," I say, suddenly reminded of my time at the Coast Guard Academy in Connecticut. I feel exposed and unprepared, like a green-faced first year cadet. My oversized shirt and the ill-fitting boots are not helping.

"When did you get here?" she asks, her face the avatar of skepticism. "How long were you on the road?"

"A while," I answer. "I haven't been here long." I take a long shot and go for ignorance. "One of the guards told me to come here. He said I could pick up a few things. I'm not really sure—"

"Oh, honey," she interrupts, and her demeanor changes entirely. "You've come to the right place." She stands, setting down her binder, then comes around to the front of her desk to put a hand lightly on my arm. Her fingers press into my bicep, precisely where a tattoo would be if I were one of the town's slaves. No doubt checking for my reaction. A new tattoo would hurt, and an old one would make me react self-consciously, defensively. "Orientation's always a bit slow. You're probably scheduled for tomorrow, right?" She nods before I get a chance to reply. "Well, I'll get you started at least."

She hustles me into a sturdy chair next to her desk, then takes up her original position again. "They'll find you an apartment and assign you some help to get settled. So don't you worry about that. But it sure looks like you need clothes. I'm sure we can find something in your size. We get enough people with your build through here, we've probably got a surplus."

"So the clothes and supplies—" I start.

"Confiscated," she says without a hint of dissonance or self-reflection. "Workers don't need anything except simple uniforms, after all. And the ones we trade on, they get kitted out by the buyers. You know how it is. We can't know ahead of time what they'll want them for."

Perhaps my true feelings are starting to leak past my controlled expression. The receptionist leans in sympathetically. "You'll get used to it, hon. It's us or them, after all, and the world needs rebuilding. Just be glad you didn't catch someone's eye out there. This is a sanctuary. If you've got what it takes to get here on your own, you're safe as houses. If not, you weren't really fit for it, anyway. Right?"

"Of course," I say.

"You're not too chatty," she says with a satisfied nod. "I like that."

"It isn't what I expected. That's all. I was hoping to meet Ravana. I've heard good things."

"Oh, hon, no one meets Ravana." She chuckles, looking through her binder, glancing at me every few seconds. "Just his staff, you know. People like you and me, we're too far down the line. But everything you hear is true. Trust me. We've got food, warm beds, safe streets. The guardians keep an eye on everything and don't impose too much. You can build a family here." She pops a finger at a page in her binder. "Here we go. Just as I thought. We've got clothes to spare. Come along, hon. We'll get you situated in no time."

I spend the next hour listening to my new friend explain the basic workings of Clarke County, while getting fitted for three changes of clothes and two pairs of boots. I do my best to ignore the fact that these clothes belonged to someone else, not too long ago, and that she may be under the whip a block away, or worse.

According to Eileen, the government of Clarke County works out of the police and militia building. They are in bed with the trafficking network but are not themselves part of it. It's only in the last year that the traffickers have taken a more central role in the town. The citizens reap the bulk of the fruits, and in return give Ravana's people a secure place to operate. Eileen grows wistful for a time, talking about the more innocent early years after the collapse, but she doesn't let the nostalgia compromise her new condition. The facts of the world are what they are, and she is glad to be on the winning side.

Once I have my new clothes and Eileen's trusting ear, I risk asking more important questions. I learn that this "distribution center" is where abducted men and women, some as young as twelve, are traded to outsiders in exchange for whatever Clarke County can't produce itself. It is also the place where all confiscated possessions go before being redistributed throughout the town, to the advantage of anyone lucky enough not to be a captive here.

When I press with additional questions, Eileen backs away from the conversation. "I know my small part," she says. "If you're looking to join up, you should go talk to the drivers. You'll start out doing retrieval runs with the boys. If they trust you enough, and you want to stay planted in town, you might be able to get a job here at the center, wrangling the merchandise. You look like you can take care of yourself, too. You could always go in with the militia. That's a better fit for some people. The ones who don't like getting their hands dirty."

"I'd think they'd get their hands dirty a lot."

Eileen smiles. "They're not an army, hon. They're here to protect us. So far, just their being around is enough."

"And what about you?" I ask as we walk back around to the front of the school. "You get your hands dirty."

Eileen nods as if this were a poignant observation. "You know what I was, before? High school guidance counselor up in the Bronx. Old New York, you know. People there lived worse than half the merchandise that comes through here ever will. See, most of the merchandise goes out. They go to towns that need certain skills. They go to little communities that just need bodies to keep from winking out of existence. They go where they're needed or where they're wanted. Sometimes here, sometimes out there. That's not something everyone gets to do."

I agree amiably and thank her for her help and advice. I leave with a bundle on my back and a deep and abiding urge to scrub my skin raw. Eileen has been forced to justify her life for so long that it's become a natural part of her, and maybe I shouldn't judge her for surviving.

But I can, and I do. The town's acquiescence to the soiling of its collective conscience is surely due to the dark rewards for compliance.

My new clothes and cleanliness, and reasonable confidence that I won't be singled out as a stranger, allow me to spend the next few hours investigating every block of the town. By the time dusk comes, I've scoured most of Athens. I make note of the locations of every significant site on a rudimentary map that Eileen supplied. It appears, however, that most of the university's buildings are unused or at best underutilized. The population of Clarke County is spread out, occupying the space within the perimeter far less efficiently than the Little Five.

I want to be rid of this place, but once the sun sets I am back at the College of Education building, observing from across the street. The guard house is still occupied: the man at the post comes out once to piss in a bush nearby, his HK293 slung over his shoulder. More soldiers come out of the building, locking it up as they depart, and one of them I recognize as an overseer from the fields. A brief, loud argument follows about the guard's habit of leaving his post, then the overseer leaves, no doubt going back to a comfortable home and a warm bed.

The other entrances have been locked and boarded, but are unguarded, and trees give enough cover around the perimeter of the building. The overseers must be confident that the captives inside can't use the side doors, but they wouldn't be terribly concerned about outsiders trying to get in.

Unfortunately, to get in by a side entrance, I'd need Barkov with me—or Luther, who was much better at picking locks than I. So I return to my hiding place across the street and wait for my opportunity. I prepare my bundle of clothes by taking out all of the soft items and leaving only my new spare boots.

My chance comes just over an hour later, well after dark. The guard at the gate leaves his post again, moving toward the bushes and unbuckling his belt. I dash across the street, then wait at the edge of the relocated toll booth, just out of sight of the man as he makes his return trip. He keeps his weapon slung over his shoulder as he buckles his belt again and adjusts himself the way men who think they're not being watched tend to do.

Swinging hard, I connect my boots with the side of the guard's head, and he fumbles off-balance into the toll booth, falling over his chair and crumpling into the back wall. As he struggles to rise to his feet and get his assault rifle out from under him, I step into the cramped space and shut the lower half of the door behind me.

I think of Barkov's work at the police station. He allows his anger to push him to places that I've never wanted to go—until now. I tell myself I'm only slipping into his skin, not finding a new layer of my own, and kick the guard squarely in the face. The strike breaks his nose and dislodges a few of his teeth. He cries out, but with a few more stomps of my boot the noise stops. His arms flail weakly as I relieve him of his weapon. With some mild surprise, I realize that it's not an HK293 at all: it's a proper G36, fully automatic. It lacks a reflex sight, which means it was probably originally intended for export to Spain. Pre-collapse, this would have been a highly illegal weapon to own. I wonder how it got here. Maybe I was right about the Port of Savannah.

I take the knife from the guard's belt and cut the belt loop that holds a sizable ring of keys. I step back out of the toll booth, shut both halves of the door, and lock them from the outside. If I leave him here, he will find his way out eventually or make enough noise to be discovered, but I don't intend to give him the chance.

What I'm doing is a risk. Even if I'm not caught, I've no doubt the police and militia will heighten their attention as a result of the incident, making it more difficult for me to search for Phoebe later, if she's not inside. My best chance for the future is to keep everyone thinking the missing guard deserted rather than got his head kicked in by an outsider. It won't last forever, but it might last long enough.

Watching for people on the road and seeing no one, I move quickly to the front doors and work the lock until I find the right key. Every second is an eternity while my back is exposed to the street, but I don't need as much time as I feared. I'm inside within twenty seconds.

I'm tempted to start searching every room immediately, but I need to dispose of the guard first. The ground floor is a nest of classrooms and offices, plus a utility closet that would have served perfectly had anyone thought to provide the key. I have to settle for one of the front offices: a room set behind another room, both of which can be locked. I hurry back out, retrieve the guard, and haul him into the building as quickly as I can.

Once he is secured behind two locked doors—and bound to a heavy metal desk in the inner office—I lock the entrance again and take a breath. Now to search.

I find nothing on the ground floor. All of the rooms are empty, most of them covered in layers of dust. The second floor is a different matter. Immediately upon coming through the stairwell door, I catch the stench of sweat and shit in the hall. With fewer outward facing windows, the corridors are dark, but I find a small flashlight secured to the wall opposite the stairwell.

As I expected, the rooms are locked. The guard's ring of keys opens the first door I check, but it's another empty office. The next door opens into a classroom, but the keys don't open the padlocked flush bolt that has been attached to it.

There is a small security glass window in the door, and peering in, I can barely make out a few forms on the floor. I chance a flash of my light and see a collection of occupied mats and blankets on the ground, much like what we saw in Conyers.

Some of the captives stir and look toward me. I'm sure they can't see much, since I'm the one with the light; they probably assume I'm one of the overseers. So I sweep the light across as much of the room as I can see through the window, searching in vain for a face I recognize.

The smell that was overpowering when I came onto the floor fades with familiarity. I can breathe more easily, which lets me pick up my pace. I ignore the offices after the second one is also empty and focus on the classrooms. Each one contains between four and eight pitiful people whom I can't reach. None of them is Phoebe.

In frustration I yank hard on the last bolt I come to. None of the keys fit in the padlock. One of the men in the room beyond rises from his makeshift bed and comes to the security glass. He can't be any older than twenty-five, but his gaunt face and sun-darkened skin project a man nearly twice that age. His head is unevenly shaved.

He puts his hand on the glass and looks directly at me. I turn off the light, leaving him only in silhouette but giving him the chance to see my face.

"I'm sorry," I say as loudly as I dare. "I can't help you. I can't unlock the door."

"You shouldn't be here," he says. "They'll catch you."

"Are there more of you on the upper floors?" I ask.

He shakes his head. "I don't think so. Not yet."

"I'm looking for a girl, around sixteen years old, named Phoebe."
My chest aches at having to ignore this man's plight in favor
of another's, but I can only do so much—and not even that,
apparently.

"I don't know that name," he whispers, and the disappointment
in his voice makes me feel even more guilty. Then he adds, "She's
probably not here. The girls, most of them, don't do the heavy
labor. Unless no one wants them. Unless no one bids. Are you her
mother?"

"No," I reply. "But she's my responsibility. I wish I could help you."

He spreads his fingers against the glass, pressing his face close.
"If you find her, save her. And if you can't save her, make it quick.
You should go now. They'll catch you."

When I hesitate, he repeats his last words, and I move away from
the door. I place the flashlight back in its holster and hurry out of
the building, back into fresh air.

I've gambled and lost. I suppose it was always a long shot, but
it was necessary to try. Now the job is going to get a lot harder.
Twice now, once by implication, I've been told that Phoebe is in a
different kind of hell from the one suffered by these workers. And
she's been gone three days.

Three days. How much has she suffered already, and how much
more will she suffer before we find her? If we find her. And even if
we do, and she's not traumatized beyond all recovery, there are still
more like her. Many more. And I can't save any of them.

My eyes burn at my own impotence. I navigate a route directly
back to the breach I made in the perimeter fence. It's time to rejoin
Barkov and Marilyn and to pray that they've had better luck. I find
my Remington where I left it but don't take it with me, since the
G36 is going to serve me a lot better, and I don't need the extra
weight. I trek the dark and muddy distance back to exit seven.

As I make my way down the ramp toward the HRV, I see my
friends standing in the road, facing the street that leads to the

perimeter gate. I stop short, my spine tingling. Something isn't right.

They knew I walked back up the ramp. They shouldn't be expecting me from the other direction. They should be watching the loop, not the surface street.

I crouch down in the deeper shadow of a tall tree and watch with a pounding heart.

Barkov and Marilyn fared worse than I. They've become bait in a trap meant for me.

DAY SIXTEEN, 12:00 A.M.

I check the magazine of my confiscated G36: a full thirty rounds of 5.56 NATO ammunition. Despite being designed in Germany, this weapon takes ammunition readily available throughout the former United States. I'm not too worried about wasting shots, though just to be safe I switch the fire selector to E: semiautomatic fire.

Somewhat awkwardly, I sight through the scope, scanning the trees around the ramp. Marilyn would be easy to control, but Barkov would require at least two people to manage him. Probably more. I'm looking for a team, not a single ambusher.

My friends have given them the impression that I'll be coming from the street, not the highway. I expect Barkov did this, so he and Marilyn could signal to me that something was wrong by keeping their backs turned away from my approach, with the added benefit of focusing the ambushers' attention in the wrong direction.

It also means that the ambushers are probably a lot closer to me than I find comfortable. I'm on the high ground; they wouldn't be stupid enough to take the low, surely. I sweep across to the trees on the other side of the ramp and spot a stray flash of metal in the moonlight, maybe thirty yards down the street.

So I have one of them marked. But there must be more. Unfortunately, a second sweep across my field of vision produces no better result. I'm going to have to draw their fire—force them to reveal their locations.

All of my frustrations, all of my recriminations, wash down the drains of my conscious thought. I no longer taste Conyers in my mouth. I slip back into a memory of my old life, my training. I tell myself that for the next few minutes I can simply get the job done. I can worry about the consequences to my soul later and pray I haven't already traded away my humanity for the tools I need to finish this job.

Carefully I climb back up to the loop, then move across to the center of the overpass. Slowly lifting my head and bringing the rifle into position, I find my original target through the scope. I venture to rise a little higher, just long enough to catch a glimpse of my friends. They don't look like they've been hurt, but it's clear they're not happy with their situation. I see Marilyn whispering to Barkov, no doubt using fierce tones that match her expression.

As soon as I shoot, the rest of the ambush team is going to track the source, and I will lose surprise. I can perhaps rely on Barkov to take the cue and start whatever plan he's surely been cooking up, but I don't want Marilyn caught in the crossfire.

They are only a few yards from the HRV. Marilyn could reach it in a few seconds; she could find cover inside. I'm going to have to take that as a gift and hope that Barkov knows what he's doing. She won't react quickly: he's going to have to shove her to safety.

It'll have to do. I sight the ambusher and take a few long breaths. The scope settles down as my rhythm steadies. I tremble at the awareness that I am about to shoot a rational man, then find a way to quiet that feeling, too. I squeeze the trigger.

The next ten seconds are an eruption of gunfire and motion. Two more men sprint across the ramp from their downed companion's side, heading for my friends. They run with pistols raised, reacting to my shot by expecting a response from Barkov. It comes immediately after he does what I was hoping—pushing Marilyn toward the HRV—when he draws two small knives seemingly out of thin air and throws them full force at his assailants.

At the same time, shots ring out from the tree line, most of the bullets dancing within a few yards of my position. In a crouch I move along the overpass wall toward the top of the exit ramp.

One of the weapons down below is fully automatic. It sounds like another G36. The weapon fires almost thirteen rounds per second, so a count to three tells me definitively that the shooter's weapon is fitted with a C-Mag and is able to fire a hundred rounds before reloading. The idiot below is unloading his entire magazine. I have to wait only five more seconds at most. As soon as the rapid shooting stops, I pop up, aim as quickly as I can, and squeeze off three rounds of my own. At least one of them strikes true.

Shots are still being fired, one at a time, sporadically. I move all the way to the ramp and stick close to the trees as I make my way down toward the HRV. Another shot, from a handgun, is the last of them. Barkov calls out, "That's all five."

His voice is strained. I hurry to the truck and find Marilyn crouched over him, calmly applying pressure to a wound in Barkov's side. He has one of the ambushers' pistols in his hand, but he drops it to the ground when he sees me.

"You have to move," he says as soon as I reach him. Blood is squeezing out from under Marilyn's hand as she reaches into her medical bag with the other.

"We can't," Marilyn says with the stoicism of a modern doctor. "There's a chance I can stop the bleeding or slow it until I can see what I'm dealing with. But not if we're moving."

I clasp Barkov's hand. He shakes his head. "They knew we were coming. They were warned. You, me, Marilyn. They had our names. You have to take the truck and go. Hide. It's too dangerous."

"The bullet went clean through," Marilyn says as she stuffs gauze into the open wound.

"You see?" Barkov says. "You have to move."

I sit in stunned silence for longer than I'd like. A bullet that has passed through front and back leaves two holes, not just one. Everyone always thinks it's better for the bullet to come out clean, but for immediate survival, a bullet trapped inside the body is orders of magnitude better than one that got away. The blood has only one way out.

"Tell me what happened," I say at last. I know my friend: he doesn't want sentimentality to interfere with the mission.

"We were taken almost as soon as we got to the gate," Marilyn answers for him while he coughs up blood. She continues to work, fighting against inevitabilities. "They knew our names and wanted to know where you were. Mikhail told them as soon as they asked. Your whole plan. All of it. I thought he was crazy. But it worked. They already didn't trust him. So they didn't believe a thing he said. He told them you were going to meet us here at midnight, coming down the ramp. So they watched the street instead."

Barkov finishes his coughing fit and wipes the blood from his chin. When he speaks, his voice is much weaker than even a minute ago. He is forced to pause for breath every few words. "They didn't ask us many questions. They didn't care what we knew. I tried to learn what I could. Your friend's daughter is still here. Still in Athens. But the man they call Ravana is not."

Marilyn tells Barkov to stop talking. She has bound the wound as well as she can and rocks back on her heels to inspect her work. She doesn't look happy. "I can't do any more," she says. "I'm sorry."

Barkov smiles. "Amy will be happy to see me. Even though I never caught the man who killed her."

"You didn't see Randall," I say, realizing that neither of my friends has yet mentioned him.

"No," Marilyn says. "He wasn't there. They recognized us from descriptions they were reading off papers at the gate."

"But—" I start. Barkov's new fit of coughing interrupts my thought: no one from Clarke County has ever met Mikhail. How did they know what he looks like? How did they know his name?

"Go," he says through the pain in his lung. "It isn't safe." He reaches for the pistol at his side and waves it weakly at me. "They will be coming."

We debate moving him into the HRV, but there is no place to put him where he won't bleed out in less than a minute. Already his skin is pale, and his breathing is labored. He has accepted what is coming. I need to do the same or at least pretend long enough to leave him here to die alone. But I'm already so tired.

"I'll—" Marilyn says.

"No," I interrupt. "You're not staying with him. I should never have—"

"Sam." She clutches my arm. "It's not your fault. We're not here because of you."

"Okay," I reply. "But we can't stay. Mikhail's right."

Controlling the ache in my chest by grinding my teeth hard enough to shoot pain along my jaw, I start the HRV's engine and put it in gear. Mechanically, refusing emotion, I turn it around on the ramp and head back onto the loop. I don't look back. Marilyn doesn't look back.

I drive three exits down and park the HRV on the nearest ramp, hiding it again. I just need a minute to plan. To think. To make all of this make sense again. I stare out the front window for a long while, and Marilyn does the same. There should be words for this, but I don't know which of us needs the greater comfort.

Marilyn's hand clasps mine. "I love you," she says.

Those are the words.

"I'm sorry," I reply. "For before. For this. I'm not—whatever I thought I was. Whatever I thought I had to be. First Luther, then Kloves, now Barkov. All on my watch."

"I love you," she says again, "and I needed you to know that."

There is no pity in her voice. There never was. She never asked me to seek comfort in her. It was simply there. She doesn't want me to drown in self-recrimination any more now than she did when I lost Jeannie.

I blamed myself then, too. And then, too, she simply said, "Don't."

I look away from the window. I look at her. I see her again, and the rising pang of missed opportunity is obliterated by the smile that tells me nothing ever changed. She was always there. But we could only be together when I accepted myself to be as strong and as weak as I truly am. The day I lost sight of the truth was the day she walked away.

So I push aside the anguish. I let go of the self-pity. I find in Marilyn's declaration the capacity to continue. I will mourn later. Right now, I will do my job.

"Clarke County is run by traffickers," I begin. "They're all over the place, like an infection. But Phoebe isn't with the primary population of captives. If she's still in the city, she's either in private hands or being prepared for sale elsewhere."

Marilyn lets go of my hand and leans forward in her seat, propping her elbows on her knees. "What can we do?"

"There's an old elementary school that's being used as a kind of clearinghouse. I'm hoping they have records. I might be able to find her through them."

She glances at me briefly, about to speak, then looks away. She clenches her fists, one over the other. The dried blood on her palms spreads over her knuckles like soft clay. "Of course, you have to go back. And I want to be angry at you for being stupid like always, but I'm not. And I know—" She spreads her hands wide, then rubs some of the blood between her fingers. "We've lost so many friends. Of course, you remember. You lost Jeannie. And I'm going to lose you."

"Lyn—" I interrupt. I haven't spoken that name in years.

"No," she says, clutching my wrist. "I'm not being maudlin. Maybe I was, before, a long time ago. Though I wouldn't have admitted it. But I am going to lose you. Someday you're going to go do something stupid, something ridiculous and heroic like you've always wanted. To make up for everything you lost. And then you'll be gone. I know I'm going to lose you." She pulls away, opens her door. "I just don't want it to be today."

Marilyn drops to the pavement. "So I'm coming with you," she says. "Let's go."

◆

The first changes I notice on our way back in are the perimeter patrols, sweeping the fence with flashlights and lanterns, passing by my breach every five minutes. I uncover the Remington from its hiding place and sling it across my shoulder, handing the G36 to Marilyn.

"Just to carry," I say. "So they don't rattle together."

She puts the assault rifle on its side and looks at the switches. "Tell me what these do."

"We're not going to need them. If we need them, we're already screwed."

But the intensity of her stare disarms me. So I show her how to operate the safety, how to set the fire selector, how to aim, how to shoot. We can only afford a few minutes, but she feels more confident about my chances after the instruction.

I time the next passing of the patrol, then untie the wire from the cut section of fence. We slip through and head down the path

I took before. Once we reach the streets, however, I turn to take ones with more trees, fewer big buildings, using Eileen's map. The darkness is overwhelming, and we can hear voices in the distance. They shout orders and updates to each other, making it easy enough to avoid them, but with each voice I grow more anxious. My heart begins to race. My ears strain for the slightest sound.

We approach the elementary school from the north, through the remains of a Mexican restaurant that once must have looked like something out of a beach resort. I can't see the school entrance around one of the spurs of the building, so I tell Marilyn to hang back around the corner while I check. She wants to hand me the G36, but I refuse it. I've started to feel safer knowing she has the weapon, even though she's as likely to shoot the branches off a tree as she is to hit a real target.

Coming around the front of the annex, I notice immediately that we've been anticipated. Three guards are planted in front of the door, with a fourth on the sidewalk at the end of the covered walkway. Although their presence does create a problem, it's also a relief to know we're on the right track. People tend to make plans based on their own knowledge. They know we're here for Phoebe, so it makes sense for them to guard the place where her location can be found, even though there's no good reason for them to assume I would know to look here. Eileen had no idea who I was.

Perhaps I have another advantage here as well. I didn't see any guards on the other entrances as we approached, and if my experience at the slave camp building is typical, there won't be anyone watching the other sides of the complex. For all their preparation as a militia and fledgling army, they don't have any experience defending against incursions.

I slink back to Marilyn and tell her my plan. We move clockwise around the building until we come to a section directly opposite the guards on the other side. As expected, there is an unguarded door and a number of ground level windows, none of them boarded up.

Unfortunately, the door is locked securely. I doubt even Luther could have gained access. So we will have to use a window—but they, too, are locked down.

"We'll have to break in," Marilyn says. "But that's going to make a hell of a lot of noise."

I look behind me, through the trees. Across the street is the edge of the coliseum field complex, where I saw the workers yesterday. An open space like that won't contain sound well: any loud noise would echo around the buildings beyond it.

"When you hear the gunshot," I say, "break this window with the rifle stock." I demonstrate what I mean, showing her exactly where to hit. Most of the windows are made of wire-threaded security glass, but one of them must have been replaced on a budget. The pane is thick but made of simple glass. A well-placed strike will crack it like an egg.

I leave Marilyn with questions but an agreement to do as I've asked. Crossing the street, I come up to the low iron fence that separates the complex from the road. In the moonlight I can tell that the field directly across is ringed by an outdoor track. I allow myself a smile at my own cleverness. The rifle is going to make one hell of a racket against that surface.

I aim for the opposite side of the track and fire off a single round. The echo is like rolling thunder, and while I can hear Marilyn breaking the glass behind me, I'm sure it's only because I knew it was coming. I dash back across the street and find Marilyn in the shadow of the building.

"I made enough noise to wake the dead," Marilyn says. "You're sure they won't find us?"

Already I can hear calls and responses from the guards and from the roving search teams. I see shadows running across the streets a block away, heading in the wrong direction.

"We're good," I assure her and hoist myself into the classroom on the other side of the window. After helping Marilyn through, I take stock of where I am and realize that this space is just as much a holding area as every classroom in the College of Education building. Mats and blankets litter the floor, though none of them are occupied. Another reminder of the scope of Ravana's network. I lead Marilyn out into the hall and do my best to navigate to the front offices where I first encountered Eileen. Each step adds to my anger, my desire to wash this town clean, or burn it to cinders.

I'm thankful that I can't see anything out the front windows. The guards may still be standing a few yards away, but I can see only vague, diffuse shadows on the glass.

The principal's office is unlocked. I make sure to lock it once we're inside. "I can't see anything," Marilyn whispers, staying close to the door. I wait a moment for my eyes to adjust. Even if I had a flashlight or lantern, I wouldn't use it. The risk would be too great.

The furnishings of the space very much resemble the administrative desk of an elementary school principal's office, but the walls seem to reject the very thought of it. Maps are tacked to every surface, looming over me like taunts. One of them must be like the one that Owen had, that Phoebe saw—the one that I never found.

I allow myself a few minutes of searching the maps, even though they're not likely to show me what I need to see. The first map I come to has been divided with permanent marker into sections like counties, though the boundaries don't match old Georgia's political segmentation. There are nine sections in all, covering just over half of the state. Most are labeled functionally by cardinal location: northwest, north, northeast, and so on. A central section covers most of what used to constitute the greater metro Atlanta area. The whole display resembles a child's drawing of a flower.

Other maps don't seem to have been modified at all, serving only as close views of different sections from the first map. The last map I come to, however, haunts me with the ghosts of Owen and Abigail.

Dozens of pins are pressed into a map of Georgia, and beside each one is written a set of numbers that appear to represent short-wave radio frequencies. There are two pins close together inside the boundary of Clarke County. Another in Dahlonega. Griffin. There is a hole where a pin once sat squarely in Conyers. Another one in Marietta. Roswell. And many more.

But something about the map isn't quite right. I run my fingers over the section bounded by the I-285 perimeter loop around Atlanta and don't feel anything. There is no pinhole and certainly no pin.

I glance at the flower map. Then look again at the radio map.

There is not, and never has been, a numbers station anywhere within the perimeter of metro Atlanta. At least not according to this map. The human trafficking network appears to operate only in the petals of the flower, not in its center.

Now I understand why Owen and Abigail sought sanctuary in the Little Five, despite him having a map that presumably showed where the network held influence. For whatever reason, our community's participation has been kept hidden.

They knew we were coming. They knew our names, our faces. They knew Barkov and Marilyn, even though Randall and Banderas had never met either of them, and the men of Conyers never got our names.

Someone must have warned them. Someone I didn't uncover before I left. Or one of the conspirators was released from the Little Five jail and permitted, intentionally or accidentally, to contact Clarke County.

Or—

"Oh, hell."

"What is it?"

"We have to get back. We have to find Phoebe, and we have to get back. Right away." I turn away from the maps and start hunting for papers, files, anything that will lead me to the girl. "This whole thing was a setup. It bothered me from the beginning. Why take

Phoebe at all? To punish Braithwaite? That made no sense. She was already trying to comply. To send a warning? But why? I was running down everyone who was part of the conspiracy."

I open a metal filing cabinet and rifle through folder after folder of notes and forms spat out by mimeograph. "Phoebe was taken to get us—to get me—out of the Little Five. Because I didn't have everyone. They were afraid I was going to track down whoever was really running that numbers station. So they needed me out of the way. Out of the way and hopefully never coming back."

"How can you be sure you didn't get everyone?" Marilyn asks, matching my frenzy at an adjacent cabinet.

"Because there's no pin for the Little Five in that radio map. It's a secret location. Secret even to the traffickers themselves."

Marilyn stops rifling the folders. "I don't understand. Why would they have a location they don't know about?"

"Ravana," I say. "Because Ravana is there. No one's ever seen him." I move across to the map and stab my finger into the center of Atlanta. "Because he lives here. With us. Ravana is one of ours."

"It could be Braithwaite," Marilyn says, continuing to look through the folders, now with greater urgency.

"Possibly. But I don't think so." I find a batch of records that are organized by the locations on the map. There is no folder for the Little Five. "She seemed genuinely upset. Genuinely trapped. And I don't think she knows who Ravana is, either. I think she was getting her orders by proxy. Maybe through the shortwave. That could even be how it started for her."

"Look at this," Marilyn says, handing me a thick pile of papers. The front of the folder is marked "Import/Export." Detailed reports and lists comprise most of its contents, and a cursory glance doesn't reveal any names I know, but at the end of the pile is a schedule that catches my eye. It lists transactions over the last two years between a cell of the trafficking network based in Savannah and a fleet of transatlantic sailing ships.

"It's a new Middle Passage," I whisper in horrified awe. The darkness curls in around me, and my skin grows cold. "They're trading slaves to Europe and northern Africa." Now I know how the large collection of H&K weapons got here: they were delivered in exchange for captives taken from communities throughout Georgia and beyond.

Marilyn, looking over my shoulder, points to the last, incomplete entries in the list. "This shipment is scheduled for the morning. Leaving from here, going to Savannah. Boarding a ship bound for Portugal."

Every entry in the list indicates the name of the transporter. The last one is a name I recognize: Ithering.

"We—" I start. I put down the file.

"We don't have time," Marilyn agrees. "We can't save all of them. I know."

I push aside junk on one of the desks and dump out a mountain of files. But nothing here is useful. I yank open a desk drawer and stop short.

A portable shortwave radio is nestled in the drawer, underneath a small stack of handwritten pages. And under the radio is a half inch thick set of sheets torn out of a pre-collapse book, bound with a heavy paperclip.

I remember what Furness told me about the one-time pad encryption being used by the numbers stations. The stations depended on a companion text that was shared by the sender and receiver. This must be it. It looks to be a dry, academic work, full of footnotes and dense type. Along the top of each page is the title of the original book: *The Many Heads of Ravana*.

I set it aside. It's not going to help me find Phoebe. The handwritten notes are more promising, as they are clearly the transcriptions of messages sent to and from this office. Each is dated; the most recent is from today. Buried in the lower half of the stack is a message that anguishes me when I read it. I show it to Marilyn: we've found Phoebe.

Marilyn reads it aloud. "New order. Weeks to Savannah. Allow no contact." The message is dated three days ago, on the day the four of us left the Little Five. The next handwritten transcription is longer, naming and describing Kloves, Barkov, Marilyn, and myself in sufficient detail to identify us with a cursory inspection and a few seconds of conversation.

"Ithering is taking Phoebe to Savannah today," Marilyn says.

"Most likely," I agree, looking through the transportation list again. "This doesn't show any shipments to Savannah for another three weeks, and none for three weeks before today."

I shove everything back into the drawer and take up my Remington. "We should go. We need to find Ithering, and I think I know where to start."

We leave the way we came. Calvin, the guard who gave me boots, warned me that there would be guards on the street leading directly behind the coliseum. I don't want to risk being caught by a patrol on the north route back to the parking lot where I saw Ithering's trucks, so I lead Marilyn south past a baseball field and into a tree-lined residential area.

It must be close to three or four o'clock in the morning, so I'm not surprised to see the streets empty. Still, I make sure we steer clear of any large windows and move quickly across the intersections. I take us on a long counterclockwise loop around the former sports complex, now the central hub of a militarized slave-trading outpost, until I am once again on the street that runs between the militia building and the captives' quarters in the College of Education.

Using the scope on the G36, I scan for Ithering's caravan trucks. I don't see the university bus or one of the U-Hauls, but the truck I recognized yesterday is still parked in its spot.

"That's a problem," I mutter, pointing this out to Marilyn. "I was hoping they'd all be here, so we could catch Ithering before he's set to leave. But it looks like he's taken them already. Probably to a staging area. We can look for a parking lot near the gate, but I'd be afraid to run into patrols there."

"Wait," Marilyn says, tapping my shoulder. "Look there." She gestures toward a pair of men crossing the lot, past university police cars, toward the remaining truck.

"Stay here," I say, trying to sound insistent. Marilyn ignores me, and together we cross the street and hurry toward the men, weapons raised.

We catch them just as they reach the truck. One of them almost screams in surprise before I crack him across the side of the face with the stock of the Remington. Marilyn, having moved past her personal distaste of violence, covers the other man with a reasonable approximation of good rifle form.

I recognize both men as part of Ithering's crew. I've seen them before, many times.

"Wait! Wait!" the uninjured one shouts. I threaten him with the stock to make him quiet down. He says, "You're looking for Norm. Right? You're looking for Norm?" I barely get an answer out before he says, "I'll drive! I'll drive. No tricks, I swear."

We leave the man with the cracked face in the parking lot. Marilyn rides in the back while I crouch down in the foot well of the cabin, the G36 aimed up at the driver as he makes his way to the perimeter gate.

I'm not an idiot. I know this is a setup. It has to be. It's been much too easy. I could excuse the sloppiness of keeping Phoebe alive, available to be rescued, by supposing Ravana doesn't have absolute control over this cell. They wouldn't waste a perfectly good sixteen-year-old girl for any reason. But leaving the notes in the desk—and now that I think of it, guarding that building from only one side—were stupid mistakes. Intentional errors.

If the driver had been a better actor, it might have taken us a whole two extra minutes to get him to agree to take us to Ithering.

Why the charade? I can't see the advantage in it, unless they are expecting to parlay and don't want someone else to know. Perhaps there is more than one interested party in Clarke County: one that wants us dead, one that wants us—why?

We pass through the perimeter gate without incident. I can't detect any kind of hidden signal in the way the driver speaks to the guard; perhaps they just don't check very thoroughly when these trucks are leaving Clarke County.

Once we're back on the loop, I rise up into the passenger seat. But we're not on the loop for long: the driver turns off onto Milledge Avenue, exit six.

It's later than I thought and nearly dawn. As we travel down Old Macon Highway, the driver slows the truck. His hands tense on the wheel, and I tell him to stop as we cross a bridge and approach an overpass with another gate, unguarded.

"It's just past there," the driver says. "There's a house up on a hill, on the right."

"Get out. Start walking."

I open the truck gate and help Marilyn down. I consider giving her back the G36 and taking my Remington, but I don't plan to let her anywhere near what's coming.

"You need to stay safe," I insist. "We're out in the open. Outside the perimeter. There's bound to be hollow-heads around here."

"I'm coming—"

"No, you're not."

"Sam."

"No. Stop thinking like that. I can't do what needs to be done and be worrying about you at the same time."

"I'm not some—"

"No. You're a doctor. That's why you're here." I gently clasp her face in my hands. "She was taken on my watch. From my post. This isn't me being a hero. This is me doing my job. And when it's done, I'm going to need you around to do yours." I kiss her, like old times. Like no time has passed at all. "It's not going to be today," I tell her. "I promise you."

Beyond the bridge and the unmanned gate is a dead-end road with two buildings on an abutting hillside. The first is a church, set far back with a long, sloping yard in front of it. To its right is the house that the driver described: a single-story home with its own sloping yard and a raised front porch. Down on the street are the other two vehicles in Ithering's caravan, facing the main road. Surrounding everything on three sides are bushes and trees that delay the coming of dawn.

The place is a kill box. If I get any closer, the militia members I am sure are hiding in the trees and around the house will be able to pick me off in an instant. I could try to go around and approach from the rear, but I would make so much noise in those trees that they'd be able to find me just by standing still for a few seconds.

I choose to assume that they don't plan to kill me immediately. I have to believe that they want information. The gunfight on the ramp was a result of panic on their part: they hadn't intended to shoot every square inch of the place.

So I approach. I go first to the U-Haul and the bus, but both are empty, with their doors and gate open. I wait, listening for any change in the subtle sway of the trees, in the chirps of the birds that are getting ready for morning.

There are two paths to the house: a slightly curved walkway and a pothole-ridden driveway. I take the walk, climbing a short set of stairs, then following the brick to the porch. My heart races from the expectation of ambush, but nothing comes. I look down the slope of the yard and see the beginnings of a morning mist obscuring the road beyond. This house is outside the primary perimeter, tucked away on a dead-end street. To all appearances, it is completely abandoned, except for the fences that protect it.

The door opens, and I turn. Norm Ithering is standing on the other side of the screen, faded tattoos visible on his arms below his tee shirt.

"It's just us," he says, pushing open the screen. "You can leave the rifle on the porch if you like. But I'll understand if you'd prefer to keep it."

I do prefer to keep it. I step inside, rifle loose but ready, into a candlelit space that has the feel of a ghost house. Ithering has collected countless useless trinkets and tchotchkes, letting them fill up every surface and parts of the floor. There is no rhyme or reason to any of it: it's not a collection of any discernible kind. I see a small pile of rings on a lamp table. Toy soldiers lined up on the mantle. Watches hanging from nails on the wall. I wonder how much of this décor used to belong to people who are now slaves. A heavily compressed sofa in the center of the room, facing a dead fireplace, is the only clutter-free area that I can see.

"I'm surprised you made it this far," Ithering says. "You have a habit of stumbling around like a bull. The Conyers node going silent. That was you, wasn't it? And then you killed two of Ravana's best trappers. That's no easy feat." When I stare at him, uncomprehending, he adds, "I was sure it was you. Old man? Pretty boy? Yes, it was you. They like to play rough with their food." He shrugs. "He always let them, since they were so good at their jobs. So you've done me a favor. Customers don't take kindly to damaged merchandise." Ithering rests on the edge of the ancient sofa. "You shouldn't have come," he says, almost pitying.

"You know why I'm here," I counter. "Did you think I wouldn't?"

"You should have known it was a trap from the beginning. I thought you were smarter. And now all the others are dead, aren't they?"

I let him believe it. "You set the trap," I point out. "If you didn't expect me to come—"

"I didn't set the trap," he says, almost smiling. "I had nothing to do with it. Do you think I have any say in how this operation's run? Do you think I would have let Melton and Tyler off their leashes if I did?"

223

"You can't convince me you're just a cog. You're a transporter. Your name is all over those papers in that school you call a distribution center. And you were with Randall and Banderas. I know they're enforcers for Ravana."

The almost smile disappears. "Yes. Ravana. He sent the girl here, figuring you'd go after her. And our job was to eliminate you when you did. He got Clarke's entire police force out looking for you. Just getting you here to my house put me in danger. Made me as much of a target."

My finger slips along the trigger guard. I feel the pressure to act, to find vengeance. But that's too sloppy, and I'm still not ready. "You can't claim innocence in this," I say, raising my voice, projecting as much contempt as I can. There is a lot of it. "You can't play the victim. So Clarke County's in bed with Ravana. You get all these shiny toys and as many slaves as you can feed. Maybe more. In exchange, you do a little dirty work from time to time. Don't try to sell me a line about how you wish your hands were clean."

Ithering laughs and crosses the room, exposing his back to me. From the top of a precarious pile of junk, he takes an old, scuffed two-way radio and holds it up. "One word from me and the house will be swarming with police."

"Police," I spit. "You don't have police. You have soldiers."

"Of course," he says, nodding. "You take pride in your title, Chief Edison. So let's call them soldiers. The point remains. I can bring them here with a word. And if you kill me, which I don't think you'll do, they'll come when they don't hear from me in twenty minutes."

"Tell me what you want," I say, ignoring the threats. They're obvious and expected.

"You're proud. So am I. So is my city. And we are a city. We're the second largest community in Georgia now, thanks in part to Ravana. I won't deny that. None of us would. But we are an independent city. Do you understand me?" When I don't answer, he continues, "This isn't Ravana's home. He lives with you. In the Little Five. And from the absence of shock on your face, I know I was right. You already know this. You take pride in your title and your position. You're a good cop. So be a good cop, and tell me who he is."

"What?" I ask, feeling suddenly stupid.

"Tell me who Ravana is. Surely you know. And then we will take our soldiers, as you call them, down to the Little Five and arrest him for you. Put him on trial for his abuses. And after, once he's executed, Clarke County will be truly independent, and the Little Five will be free to operate without interference. Without threat. We will leave you alone."

"And in the bargain, I will leave you alone to carry on with the network." I make sure my voice contains no hint of agreement.

Ithering points at the rifle in my arms. "That weapon. Do you know where it came from? No. A better example. The chemicals Belinda Braithwaite needs to make her biodiesel. Do you think it just grows on trees, ready to be plucked? No. It has to be discovered. We have to scour all of old Georgia. We don't have the manpower for that on our own. We need workers. Like it or not, Edison, you benefit from this arrangement."

"From the slaves you keep," I say, insisting on the truth, even though it sheds light in places I wish it didn't.

Ithering's face reddens in the dawning glow from the windows behind me, and he shakes his radio in my direction. "This isn't the United States of fucking America anymore. I don't like it any more than you do, but it's the way things have to be for now."

My hands tense on the G36.

"If you really want it to be different," he continues, dialing back his intensity, "then tell me who Ravana is. Let us bring him back for trial. The prodigal son returns home for judgment."

And then I know. In an instant, I know, and it fills me with anger and sorrow in equal measure. And above it all, betrayal. The answer was always in front of me, waiting to be seen, but I've been blind and stupid and too willing to trust. In spite of everything that's happened.

"Tell me who—"

Ithering doesn't finish his demand. His head snaps back, blood and brain splashing out behind him, and he crumples to the floor in a heap of dead weight. The crack of the sniper rifle follows, and I dive to the floor, away from the shattered window.

The radio crackles, and I hear a man's voice frantically calling for Ithering, asking about the gunshot. I crawl toward the window and quickly peek over the lip of the frame. There is no one in view, which means the shooter is probably in the trees across the street.

Ithering was the target. The shot was too centered, too perfect. But that doesn't mean I'm not a target also. The shooter is probably one of Ravana's men, perhaps Randall, or someone who caught wind of Ithering's betrayal and wanted to keep things as they are.

It isn't safe to stay in the front room, so I crawl backwards past Ithering's body and slip into the kitchen, which isn't visible from the front windows. There is a back door here, leading out onto a gravel yard behind the house. In the corner of the yard is a one car garage and what looks to be an apartment above it, with an external staircase. A small window faces the driveway: a perfect perch for watching the approach. I hurry across the gravel and pound up the stairs.

I hear tires on pavement. Multiple vehicles climb the long driveway. Doors open, and people flood out: militia soldiers responding to the shot and to Ithering's failure to respond. And somewhere out there still, the shooter. Ithering's people, maybe a dozen of them, rush the house.

I try the door to the apartment, but it's locked. A quick strike from the stock of the G36 to the foggy glass panes on the upper half lets me reach in to unlock the dead bolt. But the knob isn't there: it's been removed. I can feel the gap where it should be. Risking more noise, I smash the inner window frames and hoist myself through the space, into darkness.

The one room apartment is carpeted with hotel-grade pile. Along the back wall is a double mattress and a curled form resting on it.

The girl is naked. Her hair is tangled, dirty. Her skin is scraped, cut, bruised. Bloody in sorrowful places. She skitters back against the wall when I enter, but her eyes are better adjusted than mine, and she recognizes me first. She climbs to her feet and stumbles toward me, collapsing against me, against the rifle in my arms. Her soft, warm skin like counterpoint. Phoebe sobs.

I want to ask her if she's hurt, but the question would be a horror. I need to know if she can walk, if she can run, but any answer she could give wouldn't change what I have to do.

"Get back against the wall," I tell her, gently extracting myself from her arms. "Stay down. There are people coming."

I go to the front window and unlatch it. I swing it wide open and feel the breeze of a misty morning. The air outside is clean. I brace the gun.

I've never been in a war. Some of my friends went to Iraq, Afghanistan, elsewhere. They knew what it was like to be holed up against an enemy on his own ground. Even as the collapse was happening around me, I never got caught in a situation like this. So I forgive myself for my shaking hands and set the selector to automatic fire. I'm going to have many sleepless nights, if I make it out of this.

But not as many as Phoebe will.

So I ready myself, because Marilyn was never wrong about me.

"Cover your ears, Phoebe. This is going to get loud."

The shriek catches me entirely off guard. The three that follow it are even more surprising. But I recognize them. I've heard them up close. Micah's recording, blasting loud through the speakers of the HRV. And when the HRV comes, bright red and growling, crashing onto the driveway and slamming hard into the last police car in the line, I almost shout with relief.

The door opens, and Marilyn falls out, stumbling from the height of the runner. She carries the Remington like she owns it, firing a shot and pulling the bolt, then firing another shot. She is shooting back onto the street, at something I can't see with the house in the way. And I love her.

Because she came dragging Hell in her wake.

The horde isn't the largest I've ever seen, but it's at least five times bigger than the team of men inside the house. Marilyn jumps onto the hood of a police vehicle and moves with surprising speed across the tops of the other cars in the driveway, staying just in front of the hollow-heads. But they aren't following her: they're attacking the house, from which gunfire has just erupted as Ithering's men begin to panic. I can't see them, but I can hear the way they're shooting, and I don't think they have a chance. Fancy German guns and smart uniforms don't make up for training and practice. Clarke County's fences are just a little too secure.

"We need to go," I say, turning back into the dark room. I sling the rifle onto my back and hurry to Phoebe, who shrinks away from me for a moment. But she knows me. She should be able to trust me.

She does. She reaches up to clutch my neck as I lift her into my arms. I kick the door until the lock breaks, then sprint down the stairs and across the gravel. My back aches from the strain of carrying Phoebe's weight.

Marilyn sees us coming and turns back, heading for the HRV. I reach it only a few seconds after she does, and I help Phoebe in through the passenger side.

"You drive. You're better." Marilyn climbs in beside Phoebe, and I go around to the other door as the horde's attention turns to us. Many of them are inside the house already, and many more have been reduced to bodies littering the sloped yard, but they refuse to give up. The hollow-heads have been worked into a frenzy, and they're not going to leave until they have their meat or the last of them is dead on the grass. They sweep in our direction like a squirming pile of rats.

228

In moments, they're blocking the driveway down to the street. I slam the door shut and check the windows, then put the HRV into reverse. The rear of the vehicle barrels into the hollow-heads behind us and I feel the shudder of the back tires climbing over the bodies. I turn the wheel hard, almost too far, and the HRV lifts off the ground on the right side. Bushes crack against the passenger window.

A trio of hollow-heads slams against the front windshield, streaking blood and bile on my field of view. They grasp at the glass. Then it breaks with hardly a sound: a spiderweb of cracks spun out from a small hole made by a stray bullet from the house. The shot has penetrated the cabin, passing through the top of the driver's seat behind me.

The windshield holds, but now it shudders with every strike. I wrench the HRV into gear. If it were a sports car, the tires would be squealing for all the pressure I've put down on the accelerator. Phoebe is tossed around the cabin between us as I center the wheel and plow through the horde for the street, knocking over the mailbox and nearly tipping the truck into a ditch before we reach the road.

In the flesh-streaked side mirrors I see the horde turning away from us, making for the house again. I hear cries for help from inside, and then the slaughter is no longer in view or earshot. When I finally get a moment to think, I slow down and take the road more cautiously.

Marilyn breathes hard on the other side of Phoebe. The girl is leaning against her, holding on. Marilyn removes her shirt to give it to her and I see blood spilling from a wound in her side, just below the ribs.

Teeth marks.

"Lyn," I say, looking forward again.

"Don't," she says.

"Just tell me what happened."

"You made a promise, Sam." Marilyn presses a hand to her side to staunch the bleeding. "I made sure you kept it."

DAY SEVENTEEN, 10:00 A.M.

The HRV ran out of diesel just past Monroe, heading southwest to Conyers. We took it off the highway and parked it deep in a suburban subdivision, so that anyone tracking us wouldn't have a bright red sign to follow. We slept in a garage, Marilyn and I taking turns to watch over Phoebe.

Marilyn tended to Phoebe's wounds, to her anguish, while I kept my eyes open for hollow-heads and pursuers. The girl could walk, but not quickly, even after we found her some clothes and shoes that fit. And Marilyn was beginning to feel the fever of infection from the bite. We took our steps slowly, down Highway 138, and stopped outside of Conyers near midnight.

Now it is midmorning and we are coming to the interstate that will take us west back to the Little Five. We are in no condition for a fight, and if the Conyers men are still here and looking to get even, we'll be in trouble—so I decide to leave Marilyn and Phoebe together in a gutted gas station north of the overpass while I scout ahead.

"I'd object," Marilyn says when I tell her my decision, "but I don't think I have the energy for it." Her face is ashen, and she breathes with some labor. The last few hours of walking have been torturous for her: every step an ordeal, the fever and exertion making her face slick with sweat.

Phoebe is marginally better. She hasn't spoken, and her focus is on the far horizon most of the time, but there are moments when she seems to have clarity. At those times, she clings to Marilyn or to me, suddenly afraid of the nameless horrors that she must have endured before I found her.

The door to the gas station's convenience store is broken open. Inside, most of the aisles are empty, having been picked clean years ago. A spin rack of cell phone chargers lies dead on the floor in front of the counter. Magazines in their racks are wet and limp. At some point someone smashed through the cashier's window. Probably the same someone who took most of the cigarettes. There are signs of old blood here, too, partially washed away by rain coming through the broken windows. The place smells of mold, rat droppings, and oil.

I find a clean space behind the register, hidden from the windows and door. The floor is hard, but there aren't any other options. Anything soft rotted away long ago or was taken for the same reason we need it now.

I help Marilyn settle down against the wall as Phoebe huddles under the front of the cashier's alcove. I want to fuss over Marilyn for a while longer, but she resists my concern. "Go on," she says. "Do your job. I'll be all right."

"You won't," I tell her. "If I knew it was safe—"

"I'll watch over her," Phoebe says. She says it softly, with nothing like her old confidence and teenage bluster, but they are heartbreaking and wonderful words.

I stand up from a crouch and turn to her. "I will be back in an hour. If anything happens—"

"I'll find you," she says. When I hesitate, she repeats: "I'll find you."

I hand Marilyn the Remington, though she isn't in any shape to use it. I close the door behind me and continue south to the bridge, focusing forward instead of behind.

I arrive at the ramp to Interstate 20 without incident and discover incontrovertible proof that the Conyers men are not going to be a threat to us. Their machine gun technical, which they'd kept inside their tchotchke store home as a defense against hollow-heads, is positioned halfway across the bridge. The weapon is still strapped to the back of the truck. On the side nearer to me is a pile of hollow-head bodies, identifiable by their worn clothing and gaunt features—or what is left of those features.

I step past the rotting corpses and the swarms of flies and find the remains of the Conyers men in a similar pile on the other side of the technical. They are in worse shape than their enemies, with body parts ripped off and most of their faces missing. Buzzards feast on their flesh.

I might have told them it was a bad idea to rely on a machine gun for defense, especially in a bridge corridor like this. What happened here is easy to see. They must have been caught between two hordes and were unable to sweep their gun fast enough between the groups. Eventually they were overrun on one side. Since their personal weapons were in disrepair, they didn't have the firepower for close combat.

Satisfied, I turn back, only to see Phoebe running down the center divide of the highway, throwing her arms in the air to get my attention.

"What happened?" I call to her as quietly as I can, rushing to meet her. "Where's Marilyn?"

"We heard a truck. And then we saw it. It's him."

"Shit," I mutter. Ithering is dead. Phoebe can mean only one other man: Randall.

Seconds pass before I can wrap my thoughts around the problem. Too long.

"Did he see you?"

She indicates to me that she doesn't know by shaking her head— her words are gone again. "Stay here," I say. I look behind me, at the technical. I waste more seconds while I consider trying to start it. But even if I could, I wouldn't get very far with it. I can't drive and shoot at the same time. I wouldn't get close enough. If it was Randall who took out Ithering back in Athens, then he has a long-range weapon.

I sprint north, my finger on the G36's selector switch. I should have kept the Remington. Given Marilyn the assault rifle. Randall will have an enormous advantage. I could try to find cover, but the gas station is too good a defensive position.

All of the decisions are made for me, anyway. Randall is standing among the gas pumps with a handgun against the back of Marilyn's head. She is between us, shivering with the chills of her infection, her eyes closed. The U-Haul, ever the same one, is parked only a few yards away with the driver's door open.

I lift the rifle when I'm fifty yards out.

"Where is she?" he calls over.

"Safe," I answer. "Far from here." I take a few steps forward. Randall, to his credit, doesn't react by threatening me further. I would have to be within a dozen yards to have any chance of shooting without killing Marilyn.

"What is she to you?" Randall asks. "Just a girl. Not even yours. I don't want to kill her. You know that."

"Death would be a mercy over what you have planned."

"Not me. I have nothing to do with that."

"Whatever helps you sleep," I say, taking another step. It makes me feel better, even though it doesn't do me any good. "Why didn't you kill me, before? You shot Ithering first and let me get away."

He laughs. It sounds like amusement, not contempt. "Where were you going to go? You came for the girl. I could afford to wait and have you all in the same place."

One more step. I still don't know what I'm trying to accomplish. I'm not going to be able to distract him or make him angry. That was Barkov's skill.

I think I just want Marilyn to look at me. Her eyes are still closed.

She's trying to tell me something.

Always so goddamn slow.

I push the selector to full automatic fire with a grandiose motion, letting Randall see.

"You're not going to shoot," he says, still confident. "Don't insult me."

Stupid heroics. But this time, they're not mine.

"Look at her, Randall. She's shivering. You can see the sweat on her face." I take another step. "Death would be a mercy."

The click in Randall's brain is as palpable as a thundercrack. The smug satisfaction radiating from his body is replaced with tension and surprise. Not surprise that Marilyn is sick; that's obvious enough. Surprise that I would take such advantage. But this was Marilyn's idea. I know because her eyes have opened. She is not afraid.

Barkov would have been impressed.

Moving toward the truck, Randall fires two shots in my direction, missing both times. He throws himself into the U-Haul and slams the door behind him. I fire at the windshield, shattering it, but hesitate to shoot at the engine or the tires. If I can stop Randall without damaging the truck, we can use it to get home.

It's a mistake. The biodiesel engine roars and the truck heaves forward, with Randall still hiding below the wheel. At the last moment I realize the error and walk the fire downward, into the driver's door and across the side of the truck as it swerves past me. I pivot as the U-Haul hops a curb and makes a wide right turn onto the northbound lanes. I shoot at the back tires, but they're hidden under a few feet of metal. I'm too close; the angle is too steep. I throw myself to the pavement and shoot again, until I've emptied the magazine.

At least one bullet found its mark. The U-Haul sags to one side. It lists toward the sidewalk, but Randall is able to keep it in the road. It travels a quarter mile before slowing to a stop. I watch with steady eyes as I draw my SIG, waiting for Randall to emerge from the cab.

I keep waiting. I count two minutes. I itch to give chase, to seize the advantage, but despite my instructions, Phoebe has rejoined us. Marilyn is crouched against a gas pump. I have obligations that won't let me risk another shootout.

I tell Marilyn and Phoebe to gather their belongings and go south while I count another two minutes. I stand by the pumps, watching, letting my hands go slick with sweat.

The truck lurches again, grinding one rim, then limps away, back toward Clarke County.

A quarter mile, and an infinite distance.

DAY EIGHTEEN, 7:00 A.M.

At least we were safe. As safe as we could be, as Marilyn's health began to worsen. Many times, I considered running ahead, making it to the Little Five to retrieve one of the remaining Volvos, but I knew it was a fool's errand. By the time I got back, the woman I loved could be gone. Or Randall might return. From time to time I regretted not going after him.

So I walked with them. I watched as Phoebe's strength improved with each step away from Clarke County, and I watched as the fever began to take its final toll on Marilyn. Her body was tense with aches, and she moved with a slow shuffle.

We didn't talk about what was happening. Sepsis, I knew, could be fatal on its own. But that wasn't the worst possibility. With no way to control the fever, at some point along the way, Marilyn might suddenly feel better. We know very little about the virus that turns people into hollow-heads, but we know this: if a fever breaks early, and the patient feels better than she has in years, her friends and loved ones have six hours to say goodbye.

It is early morning, the seventeenth day after Abigail and Owen arrived at the gates of the Little Five, and I have only three hours left.

While Phoebe sleeps, Marilyn and I sit on a low wall by the side of the road and watch the sun rising on our right, shining through the trees, Marilyn's last morning.

"I can feel it starting," she says, almost absently. Then she turns to me and continues, "It's like an itch in the back of my brain. And I'm losing track of certain memories."

I don't know how she can be so calm. Though I try to put on a brave face for her, inside I am screaming and crying and cursing the world. Cursing myself most of all, for having put her in the position that brought us to this. I should never have persuaded her to come with me. Because she was always right about me, but in the end, it wasn't my life that was lost.

Marilyn Trainor is too serene for my pain. And it's selfish of me to be worried about my own guilt when a woman I love is all but dying.

"Things were good, weren't they?" she asks. "Between us, I mean. I never really let you go. I tried. I think I tried. But you were always there. Strong and stoic and alive. Anyone else might've been crushed, but you kept on."

"That was your doing," I tell her. "You know that."

She shakes her head gently, smiling with the slightest condescension. "No, Sam, I don't think that's true. I hope it's not. You'll do all right, even without me. You'll take Phoebe home, and you'll get a hero's welcome. And you'll tell the story of what we did. And you'll remember me. And then you'll move on, just like before. You'll go on. You're a survivor. We all are, now. But you always were. This world didn't make you. So I know you'll be all right."

I have nothing to say. Six hours is not enough time and far too long. It's made harder by Marilyn's readiness. It's not defeat, or resignation, that I see in her eyes. It's completeness. I've never been as strong as that.

But she's always been right about me, so I must trust her.

"You should do it now." She smiles at me again, this time with nothing but genuine affection and regret. "Before it starts to get difficult for me."

"I don't think I can."

"You—had a daughter, right?" She struggles for a moment to remember. "You've had to do this before."

"I had you then. To help me back from the ledge when it got too hard to bear."

She kisses me softly on the lips, her hand on my cheek. "You were never going to fall, Sam. I knew that when we met. That's why you had me."

◇

Phoebe stands on the road alone while I bury Marilyn in soft ground beneath a sycamore tree. By the time I return to her, my tears are mixed with sweat, and I have regained myself enough to take the girl's hand for the last miles of our journey home. I let Phoebe see my grief. Marilyn deserved as much. To be remembered in the open, with all the pain on the surface for the world to see. I never gave that to Jeannie.

But Marilyn was right again. I am going to survive this. I have to: there is work to finish. Phoebe's ordeal must be avenged. Owen and Abigail deserve justice. And after, when the walls have been knocked down on the Little Five's house of cards, I will have to find a new way forward. There is too much filth in the fields for me to stay. And even if I cut off the head of Ravana, there will be others, and many more. An end to the horror won't come with an end to its architect.

As we come into view of the wall under the bridge, a shout goes up from the top of it, and more shouts beyond, relaying the news of our return. After a few minutes of scrambling on the other side, the door is opened, and men and women of the sweep team tumble out, rushing to us, cheering. The exuberance becomes muted when they realize that I am alone with Phoebe.

Regina hugs her daughter, and Phoebe cries. I linger for a moment. I need to see one last time that there is still love and hope in the Little Five.

The crowd that forms around us wants to know what happened, how my friends met their fates, and where I found Phoebe. They believe they do, anyway. I don't answer because they will know soon enough, and their lives, too, will change. Without the materials Ravana's network provided, the Little Five will go back to being a small speck on a much bigger map, with powers and principalities surrounding it, never to be the center of attention again.

But that's as it should be. Without knowing, we made too many compromises. Compromises that allowed all of this to happen and gave us the luxury of turning away from questions we should have asked. We were better than Clarke County, but not enough.

Pritchard finds me in the crowd. He looks tired and relieved to be able to hand the reins back over to me. I don't have the heart to tell him the truth of things, so I let him brief me on what has been happening in the Little Five since I left. Braithwaite and Abraham are gone: they were given a choice between imprisonment and exile, and they both chose exile.

"The mayor authorized that?" I ask as we maneuver through the throng toward the station. "Whose idea was it?"

"It came from the rest of the power company, I think. You know how they are. They look after their own. It's going to be rough without those two. Vargas is taking it hard. There's been talk that he might leave us, too."

I let Pritchard go on into gossip, but I'm not listening. I don't care about Vargas and what the power company feels or wants. My thoughts are moving forward, toward a future different from the one the Little Five deserves.

Even so, there are still a few loose ends I need to address. "Where are the women Marilyn brought here?" I ask as we reach the station, interrupting Pritchard's rambled updates.

"Oh boy," he replies, one hand on the door, lingering. "Echevarria looked them over. Some of them were—well. You know, Chief. And we did the best we could. But all the refugees from Inman Park were here, and we were trying to clean that area out for them, so some things slipped through the cracks. A couple of the girls got out past the fences, and we have to assume they didn't make it. One of them killed herself. The others are still here, but I don't know, Chief. It doesn't look good for them. It's like they're broken."

I take a moment to accept what he's telling me. I didn't have reason to think there would be happy endings for anyone in this mess, but I wanted to hope.

"Where's the mayor?"

Pritchard wants to follow me into the station, but I stay on the street. "I don't know," he says with a furrowed brow. "Probably gone to see Phoebe. You all right, Chief?"

"I'm fine," I say with a manufactured smile. "Find him for me. Let him know I'll meet him at his office. There's something he and I need to discuss privately. Then come find me in an hour."

"Sure," Pritch agrees, hesitant. Then, as if realizing it only now, he adds, "I'm sorry about Augustus. And Dr. Trainor. I know you two—well. I know it's a hard thing."

"Phoebe's safe," I tell him. "That's what matters."

I cross the street and make my way north, avoiding the eyes of those few who haven't yet heard the news of our return. The mayor's office is open when I arrive but empty. I enter without hesitation, as I've done so many times before. I know this place well. The oak desk. The bookshelf stuffed with the academic works Weeks used in his former life as a professor. I remember looking at them with envious curiosity many times over the years.

And I remember the pages of the book I saw in Athens.

Norm Ithering called Ravana the "prodigal son." That phrase, that name, broke open a floodgate that filled in all of the empty spaces in my sluggish brain. Ithering knew almost nothing about the one they call Ravana, but he knew that the man once had lived in Athens. It's only possible to be a prodigal son if you're returning to a place you've already been.

The book pages that serve as the key for the numbers station codes should have been a stronger clue, but I wasn't thinking along the proper lines. It was important, of course, that the name of the book was *The Many Heads of Ravana*. That must be how the traffickers came up with the name of their elusive, invisible leader: they took it from the title of the code book. They had no other choice because they had only part of the text.

They didn't have the title page or the cover. So they didn't know the name of the man who wrote it. Under most circumstances there would be no reason to keep only a few pages of a book like that. The code didn't require a specific kind of writing; it could have used key text from anywhere in that book. Tearing pages out of a whole text would be unnecessary work.

But Ravana needed to remain hidden. Revealing the author's name would have told too much.

I find it on the shelf among the other treasures, unremarkable except for a painting of an Indian god on the cover. And the author's name in bold yellow lettering below: Aloysius Hanover Weeks.

The professor of Southeast Asian religions at the University of Georgia in Athens, turned mayor, and stepfather to Phoebe. I had been right about the reason Phoebe was abducted—to force me out of the Little Five, so that I could be killed in private to keep the secret he was afraid I would learn—but it hadn't occurred to me to consider why it was Phoebe, specifically. It hadn't occurred to me that she was not selected at random. She isn't the only child in the Little Five.

But she had seen Owen's map. The same map that Marilyn and I found in the elementary school distribution center. And Phoebe is a trusting girl, and though she has only known her stepfather for a few years, I've no doubt that she would share her experiences with the man. She must have told him what she saw, just as she told me.

So she, too, had to be removed.

I was played for a fool from the beginning. For years. Everything that the mayor helped to build has been on the backs of slaves. The edifice of his particular greed, with its deep basements hiding chained souls. Hiding its very architect. I doubt Braithwaite and Abraham and Luther ever learned the identity of the person who pulled their strings, taking orders by proxy. But I was kept in the dark entirely. Weeks, like Marilyn, knew that I would not have sacrificed others' lives for my own comfort.

When Mayor Weeks finally enters his office, finding me here by the wall of books with my P229 level with his chest, he already knows why I've come. I can see it on his face: it twists through a series of expressions ranging from dismay to fear to preparation.

Not for death, surely. For persuasion. He must be very good at it, to have built an empire in the crevices of the world. Even his reputation as a man of few words is probably a construction, a lie that holds a secret in its quiet fingers.

"You don't have to do this," he says, taking a step toward me. His voice is the same velvet it always has been. What once soothed now only disgusts me.

"I do," I reply.

"Think of Phoebe," he says.

"You forget, Weeks, I was a mother once. And like Phoebe is to you, Jeannie was not blood of my blood, but blood of my heart." If I had any second thoughts before, they are certainly gone now. This is for the women I have lost and the ones that he has destroyed. "I would have died in her place, if there had been a way. I would have gone to my grave with gladness knowing that I had kept that pain from her. I never got the chance, and I have to live with that. But you! You chose this. I did not give birth, but I was a mother just the same. And you should have been a father."

"Sometimes we have to make hard choices," Weeks says.

I steady my weapon with both hands. To make sure I don't miss. "You never even tried. And the thing is, I don't care why. I'm not interested in what made you the bastard you are or how you've hidden it for so long under the noses of people who loved you."

"You don't know what's at stake. This is bigger than one little girl."

"You don't get to tell me what the stakes are. I remember them every day. I put the last ounce of myself into this job because I know what I've lost. There is nothing bigger than one little girl!"

I squeeze the trigger, and blood blooms on Weeks's shirt. He staggers back into his doorway, grasping at it for balance. But he can't breathe, and that brings panic and vertigo. He stumbles to his knees.

"Think of Phoebe," I tell him and put the next bullet in his head.

Holstering the gun, I step over the body, leaving through the bright glass doors of the Carter Center.

I cross the farmland, pass the chicken coops, and open the front door to my home, marveling for maybe the first time that I've never locked it and never had the need. The Little Five was safe.

I retrieve my Coast Guard Foul Weather Parka from the closet. I open my pack and sort through the contents, replacing and refilling it with what I will need for a longer journey. I fill another backpack as well, with the books I've worn out most. At first the selection is difficult, but once I accept the process and acknowledge that even my library was always, inevitably, transient, it becomes a mere calculation. I strap the G36 to the heavier pack and hoist them both onto my back.

And then I sit down.

Still on the bedside table is a framed Polaroid of Jeannie, almost identical to the one that I keep in my pocket. Her third birthday, one of many good days that I was able to give her. But not enough of them. Not nearly enough. In the end, I failed at the one thing that mattered more than all the others.

Marilyn tried—she tried so very hard—to show me a way to live beyond the pain of Jeannie's passing. But she had never been a mother. She knew loss. She knew the frustration and anguish of a patient dying on her table. But she had never lost a daughter. She never had to make the most painful decision a mother can make.

And yet she was there, with me. And I was there, with her, when it was time for her to go. And I was there with Phoebe in that dark room as the hounds bayed at the door.

Jeannie died in my arms. Marilyn, too.

But Phoebe made it home.

I didn't understand why until now. But of course, Marilyn did. She must have. She wouldn't have striven so hard and so long if she hadn't. She didn't want me to stop caring about the Little Five just to be with her. She wanted me to understand why I cared. She wanted me to remember what it was like to be Jeannie's mother. She wanted me to be that, again.

For the Little Five.

Not blood of my blood, but blood of my heart.

Coming into this room I believed I was finally moving on, leaving behind a place where I never should have stayed. I was ready to cut the strings of my life here and forget all about the Little Five. But I can't do that. I can't forget her any more than I can forget Jeannie. I won't betray these people just so I can stop hurting.

I would have died in her place, if there had been a way.

I leave Jeannie's photograph on the table. She will be waiting for me when I return.

I lock the front door just as Pritch arrives. I hand him the key. "Keep this safe."

"You're not staying," he says.

"I can't. Not yet."

"Because of what I found at the mayor's office," he says as we walk south.

"Yes."

"Was it for the reason I think it was?"

"It was."

"You don't have to leave, Chief. They'll understand. The Little Five is your home."

"You'll take good care of her while I'm gone," I tell him.

Pritch stops me before I step through the tunnel door. "Thank you," he says. "For staying. All those years ago. You're the reason the Little Five's been safe."

"Not yet," I tell him. "But soon."

For Ravana is a god of many heads, and the beast is not yet ended. Randall is still out there, itching for a rematch, still following his master's last order. Slave ships still sail from the Port of Savannah. And I'm sure at least some of Ithering's people still live. They will be wanting their piece of the empire when the network learns that Ravana is gone.

So there is still much left to be done. More stupid heroics.

But I think that's how Marilyn wanted it, after all.

ACKNOWLEDGMENTS

This book would not have come about without Shannon T. Stewart. His multi-faceted support and trust made the writing process possible. Bernadette Baker-Baughman at Victoria Sanders and Associates has been an unflagging and zealous shepherd of *The Post* from the beginning. By her excellent analysis and advice, Gretchen Stelter at Cogitate Studios illuminated the right roads to take. Lia Ottaviano and Jaime Levine at Diversion Books discovered solutions to difficult problems and shined my work far brighter than I could have done on my own. My partner, Rebekah Turk, has been a wonder of support and confidence in all the dark places along the way. I am grateful to be able to thank each and every person for their crucial roles in getting *The Post* in front of you.

But most of all I wish to thank Reader One, Nancy K. Muñoz, who has a closet full of everything I've written since I was a child. She has been a constant and indispensable advisor for over forty years.

ABOUT THE AUTHOR

Kevin A. Muñoz earned his Ph.D. in New Testament studies at Emory University in Atlanta, Georgia. He has been a game designer, language instructor, and adjunct professor, and now is following the path of his father as a published novelist. *The Post* is the first of many.